The Rake's Mistake

One Night in Blackhaven
Book 6

MARY LANCASTER

© Copyright 2024 by Mary Lancaster
Text by Mary Lancaster
Cover by Dar Albert

Dragonblade Publishing, Inc. is an imprint of Kathryn Le Veque Novels, Inc.
P.O. Box 23
Moreno Valley, CA 92556
ceo@dragonbladepublishing.com

Produced in the United States of America

First Edition September 2024
Print Edition

Reproduction of any kind except where it pertains to short quotes in relation to advertising or promotion is strictly prohibited.

All Rights Reserved.

The characters and events portrayed in this book are fictitious. Any similarity to real persons, living or dead, is purely coincidental and not intended by the author.

ARE YOU SIGNED UP FOR DRAGONBLADE'S BLOG?

You'll get the latest news and information on exclusive giveaways, exclusive excerpts, coming releases, sales, free books, cover reveals and more.

Check out our complete list of authors, too!

No spam, no junk. That's a promise!

Sign Up Here

www.dragonbladepublishing.com

Dearest Reader;

Thank you for your support of a small press. At Dragonblade Publishing, we strive to bring you the highest quality Historical Romance from some of the best authors in the business. Without your support, there is no 'us', so we sincerely hope you adore these stories and find some new favorite authors along the way.

Happy Reading!

CEO, Dragonblade Publishing

Additional Dragonblade books by Author Mary Lancaster

One Night in Blackhaven Series
The Captain's Old Love (Book 1)
The Earl's Promised Bride (Book 2)
The Soldier's Impossible Love (Book 3)
The Gambler's Last Chance (Book 4)
The Poet's Stern Critic (Book 5)
The Rake's Mistake (Book 6)

The Duel Series
Entangled (Book 1)
Captured (Book 2)
Deserted (Book 3)
Beloved (Book 4)

Last Flame of Alba Series
Rebellion's Fire (Book 1)
A Constant Blaze (Book 2)
Burning Embers (Book 3)

Gentlemen of Pleasure Series
The Devil and the Viscount (Book 1)
Temptation and the Artist (Book 2)
Sin and the Soldier (Book 3)
Debauchery and the Earl (Book 4)
Blue Skies (Novella)

Pleasure Garden Series
Unmasking the Hero (Book 1)
Unmasking Deception (Book 2)

Unmasking Sin (Book 3)
Unmasking the Duke (Book 4)
Unmasking the Thief (Book 5)

Crime & Passion Series
Mysterious Lover (Book 1)
Letters to a Lover (Book 2)
Dangerous Lover (Book 3)
Lost Lover (Book 4)
Merry Lover (Novella)
Ghostly Lover (Novella)

The Husband Dilemma Series
How to Fool a Duke (Book 1)

Season of Scandal Series
Pursued by the Rake (Book 1)
Abandoned to the Prodigal (Book 2)
Married to the Rogue (Book 3)
Unmasked by her Lover (Book 4)
Her Star from the East (Novella)

Imperial Season Series
Vienna Waltz (Book 1)
Vienna Woods (Book 2)
Vienna Dawn (Book 3)

Blackhaven Brides Series
The Wicked Baron (Book 1)
The Wicked Lady (Book 2)
The Wicked Rebel (Book 3)
The Wicked Husband (Book 4)
The Wicked Marquis (Book 5)
The Wicked Governess (Book 6)
The Wicked Spy (Book 7)
The Wicked Gypsy (Book 8)

The Wicked Wife (Book 9)
Wicked Christmas (Book 10)
The Wicked Waif (Book 11)
The Wicked Heir (Book 12)
The Wicked Captain (Book 13)
The Wicked Sister (Book 14)

Unmarriageable Series
The Deserted Heart (Book 1)
The Sinister Heart (Book 2)
The Vulgar Heart (Book 3)
The Broken Heart (Book 4)
The Weary Heart (Book 5)
The Secret Heart (Book 6)
Christmas Heart (Novella)

The Lyon's Den Series
Fed to the Lyon

De Wolfe Pack: The Series
The Wicked Wolfe
Vienna Wolfe

Also from Mary Lancaster
Madeleine (Novella)
The Others of Ochil (Novella)

Prologue

THE VALE TWINS had just sat down on the stairs to begin their post-family-meeting discussion when their brother Aubrey jumped over their heads with a flying leap that took him to the bottom.

"Goodnight, twins!" He grinned over his shoulder as he strode across the hall and left the house in a blast of cold, salty, wet wind.

"He has a woman in Blackhaven," Leona said wisely.

Lawrence, who rather suspected Aubrey had several, replied, "At least we don't have to worry about *him* not meeting people."

"But are they the right people?" Leona wondered.

"That is rather up to Aubrey."

"If he's happy," Leona said, with just enough doubt to focus her twin's attention.

"You think he is not?"

Leona considered. "He's behaving a bit like Papa. And Papa was only happy *at times*."

"Well, Aubrey's a lot happier being a rakehell than an invalid," Lawrence said. "Julius and Rod aren't worried. Under normal circumstances, he'd have sown his wild oats at Oxford, but since he was too sick to go, he's doing it now instead. And he is only four and twenty."

"So long as he doesn't beggar us like Felicia's Nick," Leona said, scowling.

This, Lawrence allowed, was a more serious possibility. "We'll keep an eye on him, but frankly, Aubrey is the least of our worries. He doesn't need to settle down for years yet."

"No," Leona agreed, "but he doesn't have any purpose in life, does he? Beyond wine and women, I mean. I know he's having a wonderful time, but there is much *more* to Aubrey. I expect he will work things out for himself. And if he doesn't, we shall give him a push."

"Agreed," Lawrence said. "In the meantime, since he knows lots of people, he might actually be good for the rest of them."

"That is true. Especially in the first instance of making everyone go to the assembly room ball. Now, about Julius…"

Chapter One

PREPARING TO ENJOY his evening to the full, Aubrey Vale swallowed the last of his champagne and reached for the flask in his pocket. Seated among his family, he admired the glittering ballroom of the Blackhaven assembly rooms and let his predatory gaze wander among the many beautiful women present.

Some of them he recognized already. There was the gentle Lady Sylvester Gaunt, the alluring Miss de Corentin, and the passionate widow Mrs. Rhett, who had granted him a recent, highly memorable night.

Aubrey raised his flask to his lips just as his questing gaze landed on a girl so lovely that the blood seemed to halt in his veins.

In those first, dazzled moments, he could not tell exactly what made her stand out from all the other beauties in the ballroom. After all, he found most women pretty in some way—but this girl was positively stunning in *every* way.

Having just entered the ballroom, she stood for a moment in the warm glow of a wall sconce with another young lady. Though he thought at first that her luxurious, shining hair was dark, it seemed also to spark with auburn fire. Her bone structure was exquisite, from her perfect forehead to her delicate clavicles, so sweetly displayed by the neckline of her gown—a gown so ordinary by the opulent standards of other women present that he would have barely noticed it if it didn't contain her charming person. Her eyes were large and she was laughing at something the other lady said to her, her lips soft and achingly kissable.

Just gazing at her—no doubt with his mouth open like a moonling—was a pleasure. To hold such beauty in his arms, to make love to her... Arousal growled deep in his body.

Without conscious thought, he had abandoned his flask on the table and risen to his feet, eager for the hunt, and yet uniquely dazzled.

The sensation was heady, but at least he remembered to shut his mouth. As he prowled inexorably closer to her, he registered that she now sat at a table with the same lady, both being presented with a glass of wine by a fun-loving man whom Aubrey already knew.

He was Lord Launceton, in Blackhaven so that his wife—who was *enceinte* and frequently unwell—could take the famous healing waters, which certainly seemed to be healing Aubrey. Launceton was half Russian and mad as a sack of frogs, with just enough edge of danger to appeal to Aubrey.

They had met during a tavern fight from which they had escaped together when the watch approached. After a most convivial few hours, Launceton had gone home to his wife and Aubrey to the bed of an actress whose name he had temporarily forgotten.

With a twinge of unease, Aubrey hoped the beautiful girl was not Launceton's wife. At the same time, he noticed that, inevitably, he was far from the only man ogling her. Pulling himself together, he remembered to approach Launceton first.

"Good evening, my lord," he said cheerfully. "I trust I find you well?"

Launceton, dark and recklessly handsome in an exotic blue and gold uniform, a saber dangling at his side, glanced up, blinked as though retrieving the memory, and then grinned and lazily held up one hand. "Vale, my lunatic young friend!"

Launceton was, surely, only a few years older than Aubrey—

certainly not yet thirty—but he seemed enviably more experienced in life in general and sin in particular.

"Allow me to present you to my ladies. My dears, meet Mr. Aubrey Vale, who lives with a hundred siblings outside the town. Vale, my wife, Lady Launceton, and her sister, Miss Gaunt."

Aubrey bowed to the baroness, thrilled she was not the stunning girl but a lively, chestnut-haired lady with bright, quizzical eyes. "How do you do, my lady? Miss Gaunt."

He turned at last to the beauty.

This close, she deprived him of breath, and not just because of her lovely face, but because of the sweetness of her expression, which was both friendly and almost…hopeful. Which delighted him. In the last two or three years, since his health had begun to improve, he had discovered he was handsome and that women tended to like him. It was a matter of particular pride that this young lady appeared to.

He couldn't help smiling and was delighted to see a faint blush stain her creamy skin.

"Join us," Launceton invited him, and, as Aubrey pulled up a chair, added to his wife, "Vale and I met in the tavern. He has a lightning right hook."

"Ah," Lady Launceton said with unexpected interest. "Then it was you who gave him the cut jaw?"

"Acquit me," Aubrey said. "I wouldn't get near enough."

Launceton grinned. "We were on the same side. I think."

"Which side was that?" Lady Launceton asked.

"Discretion," Aubrey said.

Launceton, having snatched a glass of wine from the tray of a passing footman, pushed it in front of Aubrey.

"Then you were happily bruised too?" asked the unexpected baroness.

"Actually, no. I'm very good at ducking," Aubrey said, rather amused by the idea of discussing tavern brawls with one's wife.

"Having three older brothers and a younger."

"Are they with you tonight?" Lady Launceton asked.

"Well, the older ones are. Unless Julius has legged it—no, there he is."

His eldest brother, looking both imposing and dashing in his Royal Navy captain's uniform and a black patch over his missing eye, sat beside Roderick, who passed him Aubrey's brandy flask.

"Do you all live here, then?" Lady Launceton asked. "Or are you just visiting, like us?"

"No, we were born here, or most of us were, at Black Hill, a few miles beyond the town. We have just recently come home after several years scattered across the globe. My father was a diplomat, so we traveled a good deal."

"Lizzie's uncle probably knew him, then," Launceton remarked. "In fact, *we* might, though I don't recall his name. Was he in Vienna for the Congress?"

"No, he was taken ill." Aubrey quickly changed the subject to include Miss Gaunt. "Were you all in Vienna, then?"

"We were," Launceton said, his eyes alight with lazy amusement. "And thereby hangs a tale for another day."

"I remember being there several years ago. Did you enjoy Vienna, Miss Gaunt?"

Her face lit up. "Oh yes, we had such adventures, and the Viennese are so kind and friendly. Even to Dog."

God, she was lovely, and so young and untouched. She couldn't have been more than seventeen or eighteen years old. Since Lord and Lady Launceton had turned to greet another lady, Aubrey let his intense, admiring gaze dwell on Miss Gaunt.

"Dog? I like dogs," he murmured, subjecting her to the full force of his considerable charm. "Though right now I can't remember why. Do you know, Miss Gaunt, you are the most beautiful creature I have ever seen?"

This heartfelt compliment did not quite have the effect he intended. Something dulled in her eyes, her amiable expression overlaid with something that was almost…disappointment.

"Do you have a dog?" she asked politely.

"Well, there's a few on the estate, working dogs, but not pets. Would you do me the honor of dancing with me? The next dance, if your sister permits you to waltz?"

"Thank you, you are very kind."

"Utterly selfish," Aubrey assured her, holding her gaze, "since the pleasure will be all mine. I shall be the envy of every man in the room."

"Elephant sausages," Miss Gaunt said vaguely, drawing her gaze free and inclining her head to a passing elderly lady. "With flimsy farradiddles."

Aubrey blinked, feeling he must have misheard. "Might I fetch you some refreshment?"

"Hubble bubble," Miss Gaunt murmured, "toil and trouble." She met Aubrey's gaze and smiled. "Buttered swamp parsnips."

Chilled with the sudden fear of her insanity—which seemed ridiculously cruel to so lovely a creature—Aubrey said, "Are you quite well, Miss Gaunt?"

The music stopped. Her eyes changed again. "You heard me. Oh dear."

"Didn't you know you spoke aloud?" he asked uneasily.

She flushed. "Of course I did, but men like you don't normally listen."

Men like you was insulting, yet somehow pushed into secondary importance beside *don't normally listen*. No one knew better than he how it felt to be labeled by appearance—*invalid* had been the world's only judgment of him for most of his life.

"You mean they are too busy gazing at your beautiful face to hear anything you say? Seriously?"

"Seriously," she replied. "I was in London for the Season when I first noticed, and my brother Michael said I should just laugh and see how long it took such men to notice I was spouting gibberish."

Aubrey began to laugh. "And even if they noticed, the brainless would be repelled by your apparent insanity."

A fugitive smile flickered across her lips. "They never did notice. Until you."

"Didn't it bore you after a while?"

"No, it was quite entertaining, actually, though I merely amused myself. And Michael and Georgi when I told them. Um, I owe you an apology."

"Not sure you do," Aubrey said. "My admiration is sincere, though I have clearly been crass in expressing it."

"No, no, it is only that I have grown to hate the way some men stare. Which is odd when I was once so proud of my face that we hoped it would save the family fortunes."

"The face that launched a thousand eligible marriage offers?"

She laughed, depriving him of breath. "Ridiculous, isn't it? We were very naïve. But truly, I am very sorry to have been so rude, and you need not dance with me after all. No one heard you ask."

"You did, and I distinctly heard you accept before your flimsy farradiddles."

"I have not put you off?" she asked in surprise.

"Actually, I find you much more interesting," he said frankly, "if somewhat bruising to my self-esteem." He rose, offering his hand while he turned to Lady Launceton. "With your ladyship's permission?"

"Of course," came the gracious reply, although Launceton gave him a look with a very definite edge. There had been no real anger in their tavern brawl, which had been merely a somewhat un-sober release of high spirits on all sides, but for the first time he recognized the hardness in Launceton's eyes. And the warning.

Even so, nothing in the world had ever felt quite like taking this exquisite creature in his arms. She was all graceful curves and softness, and when she moved with him, desire surged.

"You waltzed in Vienna," he accused.

"Only with my family. I was only just sixteen when we left Vienna in 1815. Did you waltz there?"

"As far as I can recall, I did not even walk in Vienna. I saw most of it from a bath chair." The words spilled out without permission, appalling him. He hated even to think of his invalid past. It certainly was not conversation with which to impress. He smiled at her shock. "I exaggerate, of course. I was a sickly child and full of self-pity. Tell me how you came to be in Vienna."

"Oh, my father died and the whole estate is entailed, so we had to leave home and go to my uncle, the diplomat, who took us to the Congress with him. That was where Lizzie met Vanya."

There was, he suspected from the fascinating array of vital expressions flitting across her face, a lot more to this story. He almost saw her reminding herself that she didn't know him well enough to tell. There was something endearingly natural about her, including the unconscious sensuality with which she waltzed. Which made it all the sadder that she believed no one saw beyond her physical beauty.

"And what adventures did you have? Did you meet many famous and fascinating people?"

"Not as many as Lizzie—who actually refused to dance with the Tsar of Russia!—but yes..." For a little, she chattered on about amusing encounters with kings and princesses and Metternich's feared secret police, all with quite unselfconscious humor. She was utterly charming, and he found himself laughing with her and interrupting with frequent questions.

Aubrey was enchanted.

HENRIETTA GAUNT WAS unaccountably flustered by her companion. She was too aware of his arm at her back, his light clasp of her gloved hand, and the confident way he guided the dance with his tall, lean body.

She was also secretly embarrassed to have misjudged him.

As soon as he had approached Vanya, she had liked his laughing eyes and his easy smile, for he was disturbingly handsome in a uniquely delicate way for a man.

She thought he must be that rare specimen, a sensitive male—until he had opened his mouth and spouted the usual dull fustian about her beauty, the tired words that made her feel so worthless.

Disappointment had been unusually sharp, but she was so used to men ignoring what she said that she lapsed immediately into drivel for her own entertainment. Normally, it helped. But not only had Mr. Vale noticed—in an admittedly appalled sort of way that inclined her to hysterical laughter—he was not even immediately repulsed.

No doubt he was being heroically polite in persevering with his invitation. Which was mortifying in itself. She knew she was chattering too much as they danced, but she became fascinated by the way his eyes creased with amusement. Perhaps—just perhaps—he really did like her. She found herself wondering how the sickly child in the bath chair had grown into a man who could keep up with Vanya's propensity for trouble, but it seemed rude to ask.

Eventually, when she forced herself to stop talking, he said, "You do have fun, don't you? Do people *really* not notice when you talk nonsense to them?"

Despite the heat seeping into her face, she felt comfortable enough with him to answer honestly. "They don't *seem* to, but then, I usually only do it to a certain type of man whose greatest ambition seems to be to be noticed speaking to me. Not because I have ever done anything remotely important, you understand, or even because I am witty or kind, just because of the way I look, which, really, I have no hand in."

"What's the worst thing you've said?"

She thought about it. "I told one young man to shab off."

Mr. Vale grinned with delight. "Did he?"

"No, he said, *How delightful,* and carried on staring at me and wittering about my eyes. It makes one feel small to be so reduced. Do you not find that?"

Mr. Vale blinked. "I suspect I'm not beautiful enough. Please don't tell me to shab off."

She laughed. "I am not normally so rude. But admit it, you must be used to admiration."

"When I find it, I rather like it," he replied. "It's good to be appreciated for whatever reason."

She frowned. "I think it's different for men. The whole idea of the Marriage Mart is repellent to me. And to some other young ladies I met in London. One acquaintance knew she was courted only for her wealth and her brother's political influence. She felt like a side of beef waiting to be bought by the highest bidder."

"And you feel invisible. It hurts you."

She blushed again. "It is a little pathetic, I know. But, well, Vanya loves Lizzie because she is fun, because she is Lizzie."

"I expect he likes the way she looks, too. She is beautiful."

"She is, but she makes him laugh. He listens to her."

"And goes carousing and gets into tavern brawls," he pointed out.

"Yes, but that's just Vanya," she said impatiently. "He is faithful, and she loves him as he is."

"The whole man. Like it or not, your beauty is part of you."

She held his gaze. "Is that why you approached Vanya? Because you think I am beautiful?"

"Yes. But actually, you're much more interesting than that."

"Oh, well recovered," she said cynically. "And do you still think you deserve to be the envy of every man in the room?"

A faint hint of color might have touched his cheekbones, but he merely twirled her around with rather too much exuberance and said, "Indubitably."

And for some reason, she didn't want to shrink under the floor.

"What do you do, Mr. Vale?" she asked.

"I am a gentleman of leisure and entirely useless to Society."

"I expect most people here tonight are a bit like that. Very well, if you could choose, what *would* you do with your life?"

"Dance with beautiful girls who make me laugh. What would you do?"

She fixed her gaze somewhere beyond his left shoulder. "I don't think I'm going to tell you that."

"Spoilsport."

She laughed, and the rest of the waltz passed in light and amusing banter. When it came to a close, he conducted her very properly back to Lizzie and Vanya, who were now with Miss Talbot and Lord Linfield, old acquaintances from Vienna whom they had just discovered. Aubrey sauntered off again with a smile and a bow.

Which was when she saw Lord Maynard two tables away, watching her.

Chapter Two

Lord Maynard, widowed barely a month, would not have felt it right to attend a ball in London. But up here in rural Cumberland, he fully expected even a public ball to be a much quieter affair than it turned out.

For one thing, the Earl and Countess of Braithwaite were present, along with several other faces he recognized—not least of them Lord and Lady Launceton, news of whose presence here had encouraged him to follow.

He sat quietly in the shadows near the door with a glass of wine and looked around the ballroom for *her*.

There she was, waltzing with a lean young man of annoyingly good looks. Even so, Maynard dismissed him as a lightweight country bumpkin and waited for her to notice *him*. He anticipated her reaction with excitement, for there was always a reaction—it was how he knew he affected her—which turned her beauty into a living work of art.

Maynard, the owner of fine collections of paintings, porcelain, and antique jewelry, loved beauty. And Henrietta Gaunt was the most beautiful of all. At some point during the Season, he had realized that gazing at her was not enough.

He wanted to possess her.

He did not even mind that she was as cold as the exquisite porcelain figurines gracing his drawing room. It was part of her charm. And those rare moments of emotion were all the more precious.

She did not look cold as she danced with the handsome bumpkin. In fact, her smile lit her with such loveliness it could make one weep. She liked her partner. She was comfortable with him, as she was with her brother or her brother-in-law. Maynard still had nothing to fear from that quarter.

He sipped his wine. It was not the stuff they gave away free but a rather decent bottle he had been surprised to discover in such a place. For now, he was content to watch his quarry and admire her grace as she curtseyed and walked on the bumpkin's arm back to her family.

Her family were hoydens, of course. Lady Launceton was informal to a fault and said whatever came into her head. Her husband, barely an Englishman at all, was a man of violence and scandal by all accounts. Certainly, he had little idea of how to behave in Society. He even wore his sword to a country ball! And as for the younger siblings—the boy was a bastard actually living with the legitimate family, and the younger girl...

Maynard shuddered. His Henrietta was like a different species from the others, and he would feel no regret in removing her from their contaminating presence. She should live only among beauty and order, not the chaos of her dreadful family.

As her waltz partner sauntered off, Henrietta's face returned to its calm repose. He could watch her thus for hours. And had done. This time, as though she sensed his gaze, she turned her head, looking about her, and even in the shadows of his corner, she saw him.

Oh yes, there was her reaction. The widening of her eyes, the discomfort... Oh yes, she noticed him. Exultant, he smiled and inclined his head. She returned the gesture as minutely as possible, then turned away.

An instant later, she rose. For a wild moment, he thought she might actually come and speak to him—a lapse in propriety he could treat with lenience—but she walked in the other direction, her grace more alluring than ever. A moment later, she was with Lord Braithwaite's sister, Lady Alice, who had been her friend in London.

Maynard took his chance and emerged from the shadows to set his new plan in motion. Launceton was dancing with Lady Braithwaite, exhibiting a very foreign exuberance. The two women with Lady Launceton were temporarily distracted, so he paused beside her and bowed.

"My lady. What a pleasant surprise. I trust I find you well?"

She glanced up and smiled in her friendly way. "Lord Maynard! How do you do? Have you come to Blackhaven for the waters?" As he had hoped, she indicated the seat beside her, so he sat down.

"Actually, no. To be frank, I find both my houses too large and empty. Widowerhood is not a pleasant state."

Her rather brilliant eyes showed what seemed to be genuine sympathy. "I can only imagine. I was so sorry to hear about Lady Maynard. I liked her."

"Did you?" For a moment, he was surprised. And then the unexpected grief hit him. He had liked his wife, too. She was not beautiful, of course—he had married her to oblige his family—but she had been amiable and worthy and kept his homes just as he liked them. She had given him a beautiful daughter and a fine son… "Forgive me," he said hastily. "She was a most likeable lady, and I miss her. Which is why you find me here, roaming the country with very little purpose but to wait for time to heal."

"Are your children with you?"

"Alas, no. They are better with their aunt and their nurse, just for the next few weeks."

Lady Launceton nodded understandingly.

"You are in Blackhaven with all your family?" he said. "I trust no one is ill?"

"No, no. We are all here, of course. It was Vanya's idea. He insists I take a course of the waters, but I am not ill, just a little exhausted…"

From which Maynard understood she was expecting a child.

"But it is so pleasant here," she enthused. "Such beautiful countryside, and everyone is so welcoming. We have taken a house in Graham Gardens—I hope you will call on us when you feel like company."

This, of course, was the invitation he wanted, and he responded graciously. He stayed only to exchange another few words, then rose and bowed and strolled on around the rest of the ballroom. He saw Henrietta, though he did not yet approach her. Instead, he returned to his lonely table in the shadows.

※

WHY WAS MAYNARD here?

Through her amusing reunion with Lady Alice and her dance with a pleasant young man of her acquaintance, the question bothered Henrietta. Of all the men who looked at her too long without actually seeing her in London, Lord Maynard was the most disturbing. Not just because he was married but because there was an intensity in his eyes that frightened her. As though he were devouring her.

She shivered. She had never talked gibberish to him, for he was older than Vanya and it seemed presumptuous. Besides, he answered what she said. He never tried to dance too close to her or to catch her alone. And yet he was the one who made her most uncomfortable.

Had he followed her to Blackhaven? She thrust the suspicion aside. Why should he? The poor man had just lost his wife. He was probably lonely, a theory Lizzie confirmed when she asked about him.

"I think he doesn't quite know what to do with himself," she said. "So he is here, surrounded by company, but not *of* it, if you know what I mean. Perhaps it is a comfort of some kind. I asked him to call if he wished to."

Of course she had. Henrietta hid her dismay. She had no real reason to dislike Lord Maynard and resolved to treat him with kindness if they happened to meet. She just hoped they wouldn't.

In this, she was doomed to disappointment. She had just danced with Lord Linfield, whom she recognized from Vienna and rather liked, when, on their way back to Lizzie, they passed Maynard's table.

Remembering her vow to be kind, she made the mistake of glancing at him and saw that he was indeed looking at her. He rose, forcing her to pause. Linfield paused with her.

"Good evening, Miss Gaunt," Maynard said, bowing.

She curtseyed. "My lord. Allow me to express my condolences upon your loss."

"Thank you. You are very kind."

"You are acquainted with Lord Linfield?"

"Of course." Maynard inclined his head. So did Linfield. Maynard's attention returned to Henrietta. "On this occasion, I would not ask you to dance, but perhaps you would take a turn with me around the room?"

Dismayed, for this was exactly what she did *not* want, Henrietta cast around for an excuse and found none that would hold water if no one else asked her to dance. Even if she wanted to, she could not humiliate him in front of Lord Linfield.

"Of course," she said politely. "I would enjoy that."

She cast Linfield a quick smile and transferred her hand from his sleeve to Lord Maynard's. Linfield, the perfect gentleman, bowed and withdrew.

Henrietta tried not to hold herself rigid as they strolled. There was a great deal of movement in the room as gentlemen sought their partners for the next dance, which made their progress agonizingly slow. *Half an hour,* she told herself. *I can give a grieving widower half an hour of my time.*

"I hope you find Blackhaven a soothing place," she said nervously.

"I find it somewhat busier than I expected. I imagined an isolated village, which would really have been much more suitable."

"I believe the town has grown enormously in the last ten years—since they discovered the benefits of the spring water. More and more people brave the weather and the appalling roads to get here. In fact, I am told the main roads have improved wonderfully recently." She was babbling again from nerves, only a different kind from those Aubrey Vale inspired in her.

Involuntarily, she glanced about the room and found him, flirting outrageously with a vivacious lady in lavender lace. She looked away, strangely disappointed in him, even though she'd made it plain she was not interested in silly games of flirtation and meaningless compliments. And the man was a born flirt. She imagined he was very successful, with attentive, laughing eyes, his quick wit, and his rather appealing hint of self-deprecation.

"Lady Launceton tells me she is taking the waters," Maynard said. "I trust she is well?"

"Oh yes, I believe she will be right as rain in no time. Vanya is just very protective."

"Is he?" Maynard sounded surprised.

Henrietta smiled. "You think because he never seems serious that he does not notice? In fact, very little escapes him. And he is a good man."

He looked at her in surprise. "You admire your brother-in-law?"

"I do."

"Perhaps I should get to know him better. Your sister, Lady Launceton, invited me to call."

"I hope you will," she managed. "Although our house is the usual chaos. Georgi and Michael are always quarreling, and, of course, there is Dog."

"How many dogs?" Maynard asked uneasily.

"Just the one. Though he seems like several. He is very large and poorly trained." That, she thought, was a fine touch. Maynard did not like disorder, and he would hate Dog.

After some thought, he said, "Perhaps we could take a walk one afternoon."

"Dog loves to walk," she said at once.

"I was not inviting your dog," he said distastefully.

She glanced at him to find his gaze unblinkingly on her face. Her stomach tightened. "He is not everyone's taste," she allowed.

"I shall call for you tomorrow at two of the clock," he said.

Foolishly, she had to squash panic. "I will speak to Lizzie. I don't know what she has planned..."

"Allow me to speak to Lady Launceton," he said. "I assure you, there will be no difficulty."

He patted her hand on his arm, his fingers lingering so that, despite their gloves, her flesh crawled. Worse than that, she hated the avid certainty in his intense eyes, like possession. She wanted away from him so badly it felt like pain. And yet politeness chained her to him, as it would tomorrow afternoon, unless she could contrive somehow to be elsewhere, or at least to bring along Georgi and Michael. Better still, Lizzie and Vanya.

She could think of nothing to say, so she gazed straight ahead, trying to concentrate on the music and the enjoyment of the dancers, trying not to shiver under the gaze burning into her skin. *Twenty more minutes to bear...*

Then, quite unexpectedly, Aubrey Vale sauntered across their path, a fresh glass in his hand, and appeared pleasantly surprised to see her. He halted, forcing Maynard to stop too.

"Miss Gaunt, well met!"

She was so relieved to dilute the company that she bestowed a delighted smile upon him. "Ah, this is Mr. Aubrey Vale," she told Maynard. "He belongs to a Blackhaven family. Sir, Lord Maynard, whom we met in London."

The two men bowed, very distantly in Maynard's case.

"Come to take the waters?" Mr. Vale inquired.

"No," Maynard said discouragingly.

"No? You should try them. Did me no harm at all."

"You have a physician's word for that?" Maynard said with polite derision in his voice.

"Yes. Actually, the local physician doesn't believe in the waters any more than you do, but he agrees with me that they do no harm. Thinks everyone should drink more clean, fresh water."

"Indeed?" Maynard said, clearly bored by the opinion of a rural doctor.

"We can buy some here," Mr. Vale said. "Allow me to—"

"That won't be necessary," Maynard interrupted. "Though your kindness is appreciated."

"Actually, I would love a glass of water," Henrietta said. It would take Mr. Vale away, but at least he would come back.

Mr. Vale offered her his glass. "Have mine. It's quite untouched, I assure you."

Maynard bristled and was clearly about to issue a blistering rejection.

Irritated, Henrietta all but snatched the glass. "Thank you."

"Shall we sit?" Mr. Vale suggested brightly. "Your sister seems to be looking for you."

Unexpectedly, Maynard retired from the lists, though with one clear advantage. "Thank you for your pleasant company, Miss Gaunt. Until tomorrow at two."

And somehow, she was strolling along with her hand on Mr. Vale's arm, feeling a bit like a parcel passed from person to person. And yet she no longer minded.

"You're shaking," he murmured, frowning. "What did he say to you?"

"Nothing," Henrietta said. "Nothing exceptionable. It's just that he *looks*, and I cannot stop him. Oh, I am so foolish—you must ignore me!"

"Come, I'll take you back to your sister."

A breath of laughter trembled on her lips. "She's dancing with Vanya. I hope Lord Maynard doesn't notice."

Absently, she raised the glass to her lips, and instantly, Mr. Vale's hand free hand shot out to cover it.

"I wouldn't," he said apologetically. "It's gin."

This time she laughed aloud, even as the unpleasant fumes flared her nostrils. "You are outrageous! And most inventive. Where on earth did you find gin?"

"One of the footmen. My brothers beasted my brandy supply, and it's dashed expensive here. Do you want a breath of air? There's a balcony just here, if you won't be cold."

Since fresh air was exactly what she needed, she allowed him to guide her through a French door and inhaled the damp, salty breeze from the sea. She took her hand from his arm and held on to the balustrade. "That is better."

He lounged against the rail, facing her. For a moment, she was afraid he would ask questions about Maynard that she could not answer even to herself.

"Shall I fetch you that glass of water?" he asked.

She shook her head. "No, thank you, I don't really want one." With returning amusement, she passed him back his glass. "Please, enjoy your gin."

He took a sip. "Ah, blue ruin! I quite like it, actually, though it's terribly common."

"Oh, all the sporting gentlemen drink it at places like Cribb's Parlor. They just pretend to be above it elsewhere."

"What a surprising source of information you are."

"Not really. I'm observant, and Vanya is hardly discreet." She met his gaze with genuine curiosity. "Why do you drink so much?"

His eyebrows flew up. "I enjoy it. I enjoy all the glories of life."

And that, she thought, was the truth. It made her smile. "I believe you do. Like a child in a shop full of sweetmeats. Is that because of your past illness?"

He remained still, but something changed in his eyes. "No. I am merely a shocking hedonist, making the most of every pleasure."

"Now you sound like Vanya in one of his moods."

Deliberately, he set down the glass on the balustrade. "I am nothing like Vanya. Vanya is your brother. In law."

He leaned toward her, his smiling eyes curiously fascinating. So were the fine bones of his face, lean and sharp in the glimpse of moonlight, and the warm texture of his sensual lips. He paused, much too close, as though expecting her to run. But she was not afraid, though her stomach seemed to be behaving most oddly.

His sculpted mouth quirked once and then covered hers in a quick, soft kiss that made her gasp, because her stomach dived so hard. Flustered, she swallowed and opened her mouth, but before she could tell him off, his parted lips took hers again in a much more shocking manner.

Just for an instant, she melted in novel, delicious weakness, and then anger saved her. She pushed him away with unexpected ease and stalked from the balcony back inside. Furious disappointment flooded her so that for several moments she didn't realize he was walking beside her. Being gentlemanly? Preventing scandal? Or sheer opportunism? Whichever, she refused to look at him, let alone speak. In the absence of Lizzie, she sat down abruptly beside Lord Linfield's sister, Miss Talbot, who looked delighted, if surprised.

When she glanced up, he was still there.

"Mr. Aubrey Vale," she said tonelessly, because she could do nothing else without creating a fuss. "Miss Talbot, a great family friend from Vienna."

Chapter Three

Aubrey knew he had made a serious mistake. He just wasn't quite sure what it was. He should not have kissed her, of course, but the temptation had been too great, especially when he had given her the chance to stop him and she hadn't. He had seen in her eyes that she would welcome it, and known it with the first touch of his lips to hers. And in the second, for in that instant, she had melted so sweetly.

She smelled of flowers and sunshine. Her taste was fresh and uniquely, utterly alluring. He had the sense of something tender and joyous and exciting—just before she thumped him in the chest with surprising strength and stormed off.

From sheer instinct he had followed her, walked beside her without touching or speaking, waiting to catch her eye, to somehow assure her of his respect and that a kiss was not necessarily inspired only by its recipient's physical beauty. Whatever annoyed her, whatever mistake he had made, he wanted to right it.

That in itself was odd. If a lady dismissed him—and it *had* happened, though not often—he merely shrugged and moved on. But with this girl, he had the odd feeling he had somehow hurt her.

So he found himself bowing to her friend, Miss Talbot, who said unexpectedly, "Vale? I don't suppose you are a connection of Sir George Vale?"

"He was my father."

The lady smiled upon him. "How wonderful! I was so sorry to hear of his passing. My brother Linfield and I are staying at the hotel. You must come to our at-home on Wednesday afternoon. But you have many siblings, do you not? Are any of them staying with you?"

"All of them, ma'am."

"Excellent. I shall send you all a card."

It sounded like a dismissal, and judging from Miss Gaunt's closed face, he would be granted no immediate opportunity to make this right. So he bowed and would have turned away, except that a hand fell on his shoulder.

"Ah, young Mr. Aubrey. I thought I saw you earlier on."

Amaury de Corentin was an elderly émigré in ill health who had come to Blackhaven with his daughter for the waters. In fact, Aubrey only knew him because of his daughter, with whom he had conducted a most enjoyable flirtation at a concert in the hotel. And a couple of days later at a dinner party in town.

Politely, he introduced the old gentleman, who seemed charmed to meet both Miss Talbot and Miss Gaunt.

"Gaunt?" he said, apparently intrigued. "But someone pointed out your brother-in-law to me as Colonel Savarin."

"Oh, Vanya was brought up in Russia," Henrietta said vaguely. "His father changed his name to his Russian wife's, so Vanya *was* known by that name. Now, he is actually Lord Launceton."

Corentin smiled. "Then he is not quite an émigré like myself. I am very charmed to meet you, Miss Gaunt. I am sure you and my daughter would be great friends. Young Mr. Aubrey here will surely introduce you."

"I hope she is here this evening?" Aubrey said politely, knowing perfectly well that she was.

"Dancing, of course," Corentin said, smiling. He bowed. "I hope to meet you both again."

The old gentleman walked slowly on, leaving Aubrey with the idea he was up to something. Such as punishing Aubrey for neglecting his daughter. Though, dash it, he had only flirted, not offered the girl marriage. He hadn't even kissed her, merely responded to her overtures.

With that in mind, he parted with as little awkwardness as he could from Miss Talbot and Miss Gaunt, and resolved to go in search of Diane de Corentin when the dance ended. He swerved casually toward the card room to avoid Mrs. Rhett, and there encountered several congenial acquaintances with whom to pass the time.

He was not surprised to see his sister Felicia there either. She loved cards and could beat everyone to flinders with alarming ease. She claimed it was all to do with mathematics, and certainly it happened too frequently for luck.

After an entertaining half-hour, as he was about to leave again, he ran into Lord Launceton, who clapped him on the back with a little too much enthusiasm.

"Vale, my friend. You are joining the waltz crush?"

"I thought about it. Are you?"

"Guard duty," Launceton said, drawing him out of the stream of men jostling their way into the main ballroom in search of partners or promised partners.

"Guard duty?" Aubrey repeated, inclined to amusement.

"Yes, it's funny, is it not? When I first met Lizzie's family, Henrietta was only fifteen years old, but already so beautiful that we used to joke that by the time she reached seventeen, we would need my entire regiment of Cossacks to protect her from men."

"She is extraordinarily lovely," Aubrey agreed. *And sweet, and so intriguing...*

"The thing is, I don't need my Cossacks," Launceton said, so significantly that Aubrey glanced at him. The older man's eyes were like flint. "Don't be one of those men, Aubrey."

Before Aubrey had properly understood the words, he was alone, and Launceton strode toward his womenfolk.

He just warned me off, Aubrey thought, stunned. *The bastard warned me off.*

Anger surged at the total unfairness. Where had Launceton been when the very presence of that fellow Maynard had upset her? How dare the man treat him like some encroaching commoner? Did he imagine Aubrey was afraid of him and his theatrical threats?

Fuming, Aubrey fixed his gaze on his original quarry, Diane de Corentin, and strode across the room to her. If part of his anger was a twinge of guilt because he had taken the opportunity to kiss Henrietta, then he ignored it in righteous indignation.

No doubt his siblings would recognize the signs that Aubrey was ripe for trouble. He knew it himself, but he was damned if he'd let anyone scare him off, let alone Launceton.

Diane de Corentin was right in front of him, sitting alone against the wall and pretending not to see him or to care about her wallflower status.

Aubrey pulled himself together.

"Mademoiselle!" he greeted her with a smile and a bow.

"Miss will do. I remember nothing about France and don't want to, either."

"You are in an ill temper."

"I am not. I am merely bored with Blackhaven, and Papa insists on staying."

Aubrey held out his hand to her. "Come and dance, then. It passes the time until you can leave."

Something leapt in her eyes, though she said at once, "So does sitting with my own thoughts."

"You can't dance with thoughts," he pointed out, and she smiled reluctantly before placing her hand in his and rising to her feet, just as the waltz began. "What is your father up to?" Aubrey asked, swinging her into the dance.

Her eyes changed again, just for a moment revealing worry. "I am afraid he is more ill than he pretends. I don't want to think about it."

"Not tonight," Aubrey agreed, and, recognizing her need for distraction, set out to entertain her. If he beguiled her on the way, he didn't mind that either.

HENRIETTA, WALTZING WITH the handsome Earl of Braithwaite, was glad to find him less stiff and formal than he had first appeared. In fact, he was quite funny, with a pleasant smile and a friendly manner. They had met in London, during the Season, when his sister Lady Alice had become one of her very few female friends, but she had never danced with him before.

He did not stare or prattle about beauty, so she could relax and enjoy the dance. Or at least she would have done had she not caught sight of Aubrey Vale twirling by with a highly attractive young lady in his arms. She was laughing, gazing up into his face, and he was definitely flirting with her.

There was no reason for that to hurt. Henrietta barely knew him. She had dismissed him for being overfamiliar, and he knew it. The memory knotted her up with confused emotions—anger, disappointment in the man who could have been a friend, and if, somewhere, there had been an insidious pleasure, it was swallowed in her unreasonable sense of betrayal.

She hadn't wanted him to be like everyone else.

The knowledge made her spirits droop. She wanted to go home to Launceton and be with her own family and the friends she had known since childhood. She wanted to hide.

Why should I? she thought indignantly. *I will not let him spoil this evening, or any other. I am here for Lizzie's sake, not his. Most certainly not his.*

And yet every time she glimpsed him with the other girl, her stomach tightened in anger at herself as much as at him. With an effort, she concentrated on her own partner, and liked him for himself, not just for being Alice's brother.

Afterward, his wife, the young countess, came to join them for a moment, and invited Henrietta and her family to her garden party at Braithwaite Castle the following Saturday.

"You mean the children too?" Lizzie asked in surprise.

"Of course! It is an informal party. We hold one every year and the children always enjoy it, whatever their age. Our staff will be there to help look after younger children and organize games. For the adults, there will be an exhibition of paintings, musical recitals, poetry readings—we are expecting Simon Sacheverill himself. So even if it rains—and judging by the summer so far, it *will* rain!—we should still be entertained."

"It sounds wonderful," Lizzie said. "Micheal and Georgi will love it. Oh, please just assure me that we cannot bring the dog."

"You are welcome to bring the dog," the countess said good-naturedly. She paused, catching Henrietta's eye, and began to smile. "I mean, of course, that the dog is *not* included in the invitation."

"Then the matter is comfortably settled," Lizzie said, grinning. "Truly, Dog is chaos in a fur coat."

The countess leaned closer. "Might I come and meet him one day?"

"I hope you will, but don't wear anything you particularly like!"

The supper dance was next, and Henrietta had promised it to the local squire's son, Geoffrey Winslow. Although he had a tendency to stare and make fulsome compliments, he was an unthreatening youth who blossomed most when he spoke of his family. They sat down to supper, cordially comparing the antics of younger siblings.

It crossed Henrietta's mind that a husband like young Mr. Winslow might be comfortable. Living outside Blackhaven would be a little like living in Launceton. And Geoffrey himself was very amiable. He could be a friend, she thought, gazing at him over her pastry. Although her mind balked at imagining the intimacy of marriage with him. She did not want to kiss him as Lizzie kissed Vanya when she thought no one was looking. And she couldn't really envision Geoffrey kissing her like—

She blinked away the vision with annoyance, for in her perverse mind, it was Aubrey Vale's face she saw capturing her lips.

Actually, although lots of men had looked and stared, he was the only one who had ever dared to kiss her.

She refused to think about him anymore. That he was in the supper room with yet another beautiful and sophisticated woman did not interest her in the slightest. Not even when his laughter rang out, a sound of pure enjoyment that only twisted her stomach because of her distaste for vulgar loudness. Truly.

When Lizzie and Vanya—supping with Lord Linfield, Miss Talbot, and her companion, Mrs. Macy—stood up, Henrietta rose too, and young Mr. Winslow escorted her back to the ballroom. He was clearly working up the courage to ask for another dance—it was a waltz next—so Henrietta was not displeased to hear herself greeted by an elderly, French-accented voice.

"Ah, Miss Gaunt, an unexpectedly good supper, was it not?" said the frail émigré, Monsieur de Corentin, smiling gently down at her.

"It was indeed, sir. Are you acquainted with Mr. Winslow?"

"How do you do, sir?"

"Monsieur de Corentin," Henrietta murmured, before she saw at his side the girl Aubrey had flirted with during the previous waltz. She was dark haired, confident, with intelligent, sparkling eyes.

"And my daughter, of whom I spoke to you," Monsieur de Corentin said. "Diane, my dear, this is Miss Gaunt."

They curtseyed to each other and made the usual civil remarks before parting. Diane had an interesting face. Under other circumstances, Henrietta would have liked to know her better—as her father clearly wanted—but she did not wish to run the risk of running into Aubrey through her.

In fact, she had barely sat down beside Lizzie once more before Aubrey appeared anyway. "Will you dance, Miss Gaunt?"

She almost jumped at the sound of his voice, which was deep and oddly beautiful, despite the challenge in his words. He was daring her to waltz again, or to deny him and be thought rude. When she glanced up at him, his smiling eyes held an odd glitter that was strangely familiar. And yet they were also beguiling, those eyes... The knot in her stomach unraveled into a hundred butterflies. It infuriated her that she *wanted* to dance with him.

Only to clear the air, she told herself. Perhaps he saw her answer in her eyes, for a hint of triumph showed in his before he deliberately shifted his gaze beyond her—to Lizzie, for permission? But no, it was a very masculine challenge she glimpsed before his eyes returned to hers, charming once more.

Lizzie nudged her. It was rude to say no.

He stretched out his hand. Slowly, Henrietta took it and rose to her feet.

"Good girl," he breathed as she walked with him to the dance floor, her fingers barely touching his sleeve.

"Good? I have little choice. I suppose you consider it a challenge to yourself to force women to dance with you when they have no wish to?"

"Oh, the challenge is not to me," he said sardonically, and swung her into his arms with a flourish.

"You are challenging *me*?"

"Lord, no. I *like* you, and I think you like me more than you let on. I want to know you better."

"Well, there's the rub, Mr. Vale," she said distantly. "I do not like gentlemen who take liberties. It is discourteous and crass."

She thought he didn't quite like that, for his eyes flickered, even if the smile remained. "Oh, not crass, surely. Kissing is very pleasant, kissing you even more so, but I shan't do it again without permission."

"You won't do it again at all!"

His eyes laughed. She narrowed her own.

"You know, you are *very* like Vanya," she blurted.

"I am not remotely like Vanya."

"He used to look like that quite often, in the days before Lizzie. He got drunk to stop himself thinking."

"About what?"

"I don't know. Blood and guilt and shame, and unrequited love, probably."

He carried both their hands to his heart. "Dare I hope mine is requited?"

"Not even if you felt any," she said dryly. "Mr. Vale, you are a flim-flam man."

He grinned, quite unashamed. "Hardly. If I fell in love with your pretty face, you would despise me."

"What makes you think I don't?"

"You kissed me."

She narrowed her eyes, even as the heat surged through her body. "I did not."

"Well, maybe you will one day."

She played her trump card. "If you think that will make Miss de Corentin jealous, you mistake your mark."

It didn't have quite the effect she had imagined. Certainly, he blinked with surprise, but then he laughed with quite genuine amusement. "Oh, my sweet, you have that upside down!"

"What do you mean?"

"I mean I didn't ask you to dance to make anyone jealous. Or even to be seen with the most beautiful girl in Blackhaven. I simply enjoy dancing with you. You waltz divinely. Tell me about the dog."

Almost ready to pull free and leave him standing alone on the dance floor, she paused, frowning with distraction. "Dog?"

"Don't you have one?"

"Well, yes. He's large and silly and ridiculously friendly. Lizzie rescued him because he was deemed untrainable, but he's much better than he was."

"I look forward to meeting him. What's his name?"

Her lips twitched, in spite of herself. "Dog. I know, a sad lack of imagination, but we couldn't agree on a name for ages, and by the time we did he'd got used to just being Dog. So he is."

His eyes crinkled. "Do you have a cat? Let me guess its name."

"It's not Cat. It's Kitchen."

He laughed again with delight. They were slipping into another of these easy nonsense conversations that had appealed to her so much during their first dance. More aware of his danger now, she kept her wits about her. If he was drunk, he gave no sign of it beyond the glittering eyes. He did not stumble or slur his words or lose the conversation. In fact, he was grace personified. But still, she could not lose the idea that he had an ulterior motive in dancing with her. He was angry, although not obviously with her.

"Who has annoyed you?" she asked.

"In my life? How long do you have?"

"I mean tonight. You are angry about something."

"I am never angry. Everyone tells me I am the best of good fellows."

"You don't believe them, do you?" she replied.

He acknowledged the hit with a grin. "Ouch. Seriously, I don't like to be angry. Such a waste of time and life. Madam, will you walk and talk with me, soon?"

She recognized the song. *"No, I will not walk or talk with thee."*

And yet, as their dance came to an end, she could not help remembering his own words: *"Such a waste of time and life."*

Chapter Four

Diane de Corentin was afraid for her father. They had left the ball almost immediately after supper last night, because he was exhausted, even though he had wanted to stay for her sake.

She was afraid he was dying.

Worse, she suspected he was afraid of the same thing and was desperate to see her settled—by which he meant married to a gentleman who could support her—before he departed this world for the next. He was such an odd mix of worldly and unworldly, she thought with a rush of affection as she opened his study door the next morning.

She found him in his chair, fully dressed and deep in thought.

His face lit up. "Diane."

She set his coffee and his favorite breakfast of bread, thinly sliced cheese, and an apple beside him. It had been a long time since they had been able to afford a maid. Truth be told, they could not really have afforded this cottage, unless he had given up their rooms in London.

"You are a wonderful daughter."

"You are a wonderful father," she said lightly. "I think last night was too much for you."

"Not at all. It does me good to see you enjoying yourself. We should not have left before the end. You could have danced again with Aubrey Vale."

Her father was matchmaking. And it was true that Aubrey was the only man who had moved her for years. But then, not so long ago, her father would have rejected him as a penniless younger son, telling her she could do better. Now, he was desperate enough to encourage the match, assuming, rightly or wrongly, that Aubrey's brother would take care of them. That frightened Diane more than anything.

"I can run into him whenever I like. There is no rush."

"The little Gaunt girl is very lovely."

"She would bore him in a week."

He nodded thoughtfully. "Perhaps so. All the same, you should make a friend of her. We will call on her family."

Diane frowned. "Why?"

"Oh, they are an interesting family," Papa said vaguely. "He fought in the Russian army, you know, Lord Launceton did."

Diane eyed him uneasily. They had been down such routes before. "That is no reason you should imagine he knew Gaspard." Or that he'd killed Gaspard.

"The man who ambushed and killed your brother in the winter of 1812 was called Savarin. Count Savarin. Colonel Savarin. Always Savarin."

"Launceton's name is Gaunt," Diane said impatiently. "It must be."

"In Russia," Papa said stubbornly, "he was known as Savarin. We shall call upon them tomorrow."

"Why?" Diane asked, frowning. "You are not to pick a fight with Lord Launceton, Papa. No one will marry me then."

"Don't be foolish, child. I am too old to fight. And Aubrey Vale will marry you. I know you like him. And he likes you."

"Aubrey likes women, Papa," she said brutally.

He raised his eyebrows, smiling a little. "Are you saying you cannot hold him?"

"No, I am not saying that at all. Eat your breakfast."

HENRIETTA WOKE WITH a jumble of emotions churning inside her, mostly to do with Aubrey Vale.

She didn't know if they were friends or not. She didn't know if she ever wanted to see him again. Or not. She didn't even know if she liked him, but he certainly affected her. He intrigued her. Something new she wasn't sure she wanted had come into her life because of him. He did not repel her as Lord Maynard did—quite the contrary, in fact—but he was not quite comfortable to be around.

It would be best, perhaps, if the feeling went away altogether.

Having decided that, she closed her eyes again. And wondered if he would call.

A thud against the door gave her a moment's warning before the full weight of Dog landed on her, and she was subjected to a thorough face wash.

"Amazing!" Michael exclaimed from the direction of the door. "Did you see that, Henri? He jumped all the way from the door straight on to your bed!"

Henrietta threw her arms around the dog and turned her face into the pillow in the faint hope of restraining his attentions. She managed to yank his head away enough to say, through her laughter, "He shouldn't even *be* on the bed."

"Rats, I missed it," came Georgiana's voice. "Get him down, Michael, and see if he'll do it again."

"Don't," begged Henrietta, struggling to sit up. "Dog, *down!*"

Dog, obliging but misunderstanding as usual, flopped down across her legs, still dementedly wagging his tail.

"Well, it's an improvement," Henrietta allowed.

"I've brought you coffee," Georgiana said, setting a cup and saucer on the bedside table.

"*That's* a big improvement," Henrietta said. "Thanks, Georgi. Hold on to him while I reach for the cup..."

Her little sister sat on the bed and stroked the dog to encourage him to keep still. At the age of twelve, perhaps she was growing up. "How was the ball?"

"Very well attended. We met Lord Linfield there, and Miss Talbot and Mrs. Macy. Lady Alice Conway and her family were there, too. They live in the castle."

"We know that," Georgiana said.

"Of course you do. Did Lizzie tell you the Countess of Braithwaite has invited us to her garden party next Saturday?"

"Lizzie isn't up yet. Do you mean you and Lizzie and Vanya?"

"No, all of us—you two as well."

"Really?"

"And Dog?" asked Michael hopefully, his eyes gleaming with mischief at the thought of the carnage the animal could wreak at such an event. He was fourteen now, his penchant for devilment kept in check only by his inherent good nature.

Henrietta eyed him over her coffee cup. "Sadly not. I expect Lady Braithwaite would like to keep her friends."

"Do they have children?" Georgiana asked. "The earl and countess?"

"Only very small ones, I think. Like Jack."

Jack was their nephew, Lizzie and Vanya's little boy, a happy but peremptory child of ten months, adored by all.

"But there will be children nearer your own age," Henrietta assured them, "for it sounds as if most of the county and all the genteel visitors to the town have been invited."

Georgiana laughed. "Are we genteel, then?"

"Not very, by nature, but we are a baron's children, and Vanya *is* a baron."

"Who did you dance with, Henri?" Michael asked.

Aubrey. I danced with Aubrey Vale. "Do you know, I can hardly recall. But it was all very jolly and fun. I suppose we should take the dog out before breakfast."

"We took him already," Michael scoffed. "It's after midday, you know."

Henrietta shooed them all out of the room, Dog and all, so that she could wash and dress in peace. She refused to think about why she chose the most becoming of her morning dresses. It had nothing to do with the possibility of Mr. Vale calling, because truly, it would be better if he did not.

By the time she went downstairs, Lizzie and Vanya were up too and partaking of a late breakfast. The narrow hall was full of flowers, bouquets sent by various gentlemen she and Lizzie had met last night. Lord Linfield had left them one each. Geoffrey Winslow had addressed one to Henrietta, with a card claiming to be at her feet. There were other, even more fulsome messages, some in verse, acclaiming her beauty. At least none were from Lord Maynard, although neither was the name she couldn't help looking for.

Well, Vanya had told her last night that Aubrey Vale was something of a charming rake, cutting a swath through the female population of Blackhaven and its surrounds.

She was about to go into the dining room—the house was too small to boast a separate breakfast parlor—when a small, neglected posy of pretty red rosebuds caught her attention. The maid had forgotten to put them in water, or perhaps they had run out of vases. There was no card with them, though.

Aubrey Vale was not the man to send flowers anonymously, she assured herself. He would not see the point.

She took them into the dining room, where she poured some water from the jug into a glass and plonked the rosebuds into it.

"Good morning, Henri," Lizzie said. "Did you sleep well?"

"I certainly slept for a long time! Did you? How are you feeling after your arduous evening?"

"Actually, I feel fine. No more tired than you, I suspect. I really think I am over the worst of the sickness."

"But you will keep taking the waters," Vanya told her. He was dandling Jack on his knee while eating toast and jam that his son made occasional lunges for.

"Hello, little man," Henrietta greeted her nephew with a smile, since he was grinning at her, and ruffled his soft baby hair.

"Have you seen all the flowers?" Lizzie asked. "You have certainly conquered Blackhaven."

Henrietta should, of course, have been gratified. And grateful. But it all seemed so meaningless, a tribute from people who would never look further than her face or the fashion of the week.

Or did she malign them, as they misjudged her?

"They are very kind," she said contritely. "I met some very pleasant new people as well as old friends."

"Then I'm doubly glad we came," Lizzie said.

Guilt washed over Henrietta, for Lizzie was wonderful. For as long as she could remember, Lizzie had held the family together, and then, after their father's death, when they had been forced to leave their home, she had managed everything, including the aunt and uncle who had swept them off to Vienna for the Congress.

They had had such unrealistic plans then, in which Henrietta had pride of place. A stolen necklace had been meant to keep the siblings in a cottage for two years until Henrietta could make her come-out and catch a rich and generous husband. No one, least of all Henrietta, had doubted that she could. Indeed, Henrietta had been proud to be able to do such a thing for her siblings.

But somewhere in the last two years, everything had changed. Perhaps because they no longer needed money. Vanya, a distant cousin, had been their father's heir, the new baron, and when he married Lizzie, they had all simply gone home. Only, Lizzie had insisted on keeping to the plan of giving her sister the promised Season anyway. And all of Henrietta's gradually accumulating feelings of suspicion and unease had come together.

The long, admiring looks, the ardent pursuits, and the declarations of love meant nothing. No one was interested in anything but her face. Few even imagined there *was* anything else. Lizzie and Vanya had protected her from the advances of rakes, though she had seen the mindless lust in their eyes. The less threatening, eligible young men who flocked to her, begging for notice, could be forgiven because of their youth. But it all contributed to Henrietta's feelings of inner worthlessness.

Sometimes, she even dreamed of slashing her face, to spoil her vaunted beauty, and then watching everyone run from her. A dubious satisfaction. And she would never carry it out because it would so distress Lizzie and Michael and Georgi and the few other people who genuinely loved her.

She blinked and found a smile for her sister. "So am I. And the children like it here. So does Dog."

Later, Vanya and her younger siblings took Dog for a long walk.

"Shall we go to the pump room?" Henrietta suggested to Lizzie, who wrinkled her nose.

"Do you know, I think I would prefer a quiet day at home," she said, and so they repaired to the pleasant little drawing room and Henrietta distributed some of the flowers there while Lizzie gave Jack up to Lottie, his nursemaid, for a nap. Lizzie folded herself into her favorite comfortable chair.

Henrietta had only just sat down beside her when a knock sounded at the front door.

Stupidly, her heart lurched. *Aubrey.*

Robert the footman entered and presented a card to Lizzie, who raised her eyebrows.

"Amaury de Corentin?" she said to Henrietta.

"Oh. Yes, I met him at the ball last night. An émigré gentleman, with a daughter..."

"Then you had better show them in, Robert," Lizzie said. "And bring tea, if you please."

"Yes, my lady."

A moment later, Monsieur de Corentin and his daughter came in. He presented Lizzie with a posy of fresh flowers. "For your sister's kindness to us last night," he said with his sweet smile and a glance at Henrietta. "I hope you will forgive our barging in, but we were walking this way and realized this must be where Miss Gaunt resides."

"You are very welcome," Lizzie assured him.

"Allow me to present my daughter, Diane."

"How do you do, Miss de Corentin? Won't you both sit down? Robert is bringing tea. Did you enjoy the ball?"

"Very much," Monsieur de Corentin said. "It is so good for my daughter to go out and about. She is stuck too much indoors with her dull old papa. Alas, she is my only child."

"But you must be so proud of her," Lizzie said kindly.

"Indeed, she is my world." He gestured with one long, elegant hand. "I suppose we are like that with family. Do you have other family, Lady Launceton?"

"I am so blessed," Lizzie said humorously. "With Henrietta and two other siblings, and a scattering of aunts, uncles, and cousins. Oh, and a husband and one small son whose name I dare not speak in case he hears and wakes from his nap."

The Frenchman's eyes changed, only Henrietta could not quite read his expression. A trace of envy, certainly, grief, almost anger, and something else that might have been regret. Yet still he smiled.

"You are blessed indeed. Alas, I lost most of my family in the revolution and its aftermath." A gentle smile banished the sadness from his face. "I believe I know your noble husband, madame, though only by repute. I believe in Blackhaven they call him the Mad Russian."

Lizzie laughed. "Well, he isn't mad, just a little...reckless! And he is only half Russian."

"I hope he avoided the terrible war of 1812," Diane said with a clarity Henrietta thought was aimed at her father, for some reason. She looked as if she expected Lizzie to agree that he had indeed avoided Bonaparte's invasion of Russia.

"Actually, no. He fought from Smolensk and Borodino until the last French soldier left Russia. He also fought at Leipzig and at Waterloo."

Corentin was gazing down at his hands.

It was his daughter who said uneasily, "Surely not all with the Russians?"

"Well, yes, apart from Waterloo, where he was more of a free spirit. He only left the tsar's army formally in the autumn of 1815, before we came home."

"He must have many tales to tell," Corentin said.

"My brother was killed during the war," Diane said quickly, as though explaining her father's interest. "Will you stay long in Blackhaven, my lady?"

"Certainly until the end of June, possibly longer," Lizzie replied.

"You have a pleasant house here."

Diane was interesting, Henrietta decided, feeling that the woman was trying to change the subject and cover for her father, although he was hardly an embarrassment. Henrietta turned to Diane, but before she could speak, Robert materialized at Lizzie's side bearing another card.

Again, Henrietta's heart beat faster.

"Show Lord Maynard in, Robert," Lizzie said.

Oh, no… He had said he would come at two and she had forgotten, but at least he could not ask her to walk with him while they had other guests. Catching Diane's curious gaze, Henrietta pulled herself together, hoping she had not betrayed too much.

At least Maynard could not sit beside her. He seemed surprised to find other guests already ensconced, although he remained his usual coolly civil self. Robert provided more distraction by bringing in the tea, which Lizzie poured and Henrietta distributed to their guests.

Polite small talk followed, about the various visitors to the town and the more eccentric Blackhaven residents.

"What of the Vale family?" Lizzie asked, finishing her tea. "Are they considered eccentric?"

"Only in so far as the legitimate and illegitimate siblings all live together," Diane said.

"Good," Henrietta and Lizzie said together, for Michael was illegitimate, too, and no less their brother.

Diane looked slightly taken aback. A hint of color even stained her cheeks. She probably thought she had been indelicate by mentioning illegitimacy. She had, of course, but not for the reasons she imagined.

"Mostly, I believe, the Vales are considered heroes," Monsieur de Corentin said. "Captain Sir Julius is a veteran of Trafalgar and many other battles. Another brother fought on the Peninsula and at Waterloo."

"I believe Vanya knows Roderick," Lizzie said.

"Lady Alice is acquainted with some of the sisters," Henrietta said quickly before Lizzie started talking about Aubrey, who, she suspected, was the true reason for her inquiry. How indiscreet had Henrietta been?

Probably not very. Lizzie just knew her very well... Meaning what?

"We are acquainted with Aubrey," Corentin said. "A charming young man."

"Somewhat wild, I believe," Maynard said with distaste.

Glancing rather desperately toward the window for inspiration, Henrietta saw that the rain had come on. Relief flooded her. At least there would be no walk with Maynard today.

Chapter Five

For Aubrey, waking up with a plan was a novelty.

During much of his childhood, breathing had been his one aim each day. If he managed to fit anything else in—reading, studying, a gentle walk, games with his siblings, a few jokes with his father—they were bonuses, though he threw himself into them with enthusiasm while he could.

Only in the last couple of years, and especially since coming home to Black Hill, had his health improved enough for him to go out and make friends, to build up his strength, kick up a few larks and discover the joys of wine and women. And so his one aim, in celebration of his new health, had become fun.

Now he had two aims that were intertwined. Fun, and the winning of Henrietta Gaunt. Exactly what to do with her once she was won remained hazy, but he definitely looked forward to sticking his tongue out—metaphorically, of course—at her arrogant brother-in-law. That would definitely be a great pleasure. Winning Henrietta would be a thrill of its own that he would enjoy to the fullest.

Smiling, he put his hands behind his head and decided how best to begin.

She expected him to call, despite rebuffing him so haughtily. But he was experienced enough to see that she was torn between what she thought was right and what she actually wanted.

Aren't we all?

So, he would wait a few days, increasing her anticipation so that she would actually be quite charmed when he deigned to show up. There was nothing like unattainability to pique interest, as he knew from his own experience. He suspected it was the reason he wanted her so much. At the very least, she was a worthy challenge.

He rose, stretched luxuriously, then washed and dressed and sauntered downstairs in search of breakfast. He found all his siblings at the table, apart from Cornelius, who was most conscientious about turning around their ailing estate. Well, *Julius's* ailing estate, which was to keep them all.

Lost in his own thoughts, he was only vaguely aware of the surrounding conversation—whom Julius danced with at the ball, Lucy's mischief, the sighting by the twins of a herd of wild horses two nights in a row. The company had broken up and left the room before he actually noticed he was alone.

He suspected they were all focused on their own thoughts. Which was just as it should be. The twins were right—not just that Julius needed waking up but that they all needed a shake and a push toward amusement. They had all worked hard on the house and the land, but one needed a little fun. No one knew that better than Aubrey.

And he had a plan.

To begin with, he sought out his widowed sister, Felicia, whom he found emerging from the kitchen with the housekeeper. As they parted without noticing him, Aubrey called, "Fliss? When you rattled about London, did you ever come across a fellow called Maynard?"

Felicia stopped and thought about it. "Lord Maynard?"

"Yes, that's him."

"Not your sort of crony, Aubrey," she said wryly. "A quiet man, the father of young children, a collector of art and antiques about whom I know no scandal whatsoever."

"Is he married?"

"Yes." She frowned. "That is, I think I heard recently that he was widowed."

"He was at the ball last night."

"Was he?" Felicia didn't seem very interested. "Perhaps she died longer ago than I thought. Oh, Julius is going into Blackhaven, if you want to go with him to the pump room."

Aubrey had no objection. He even thought he might see Henrietta there, since her sister was taking the waters, too. Not that he would do more than smile and bow if she was there.

He wandered outside, inspecting the once-formal garden that he took his turn in taming. About half of it was looking quite good now. All the restless energy pouring through him urged him to get to work on it immediately, only then he would be covered in mud and sweat and unfit for the gentility of the pump room. He strode around the paths instead.

Maynard sounded thoroughly respectable, even eligible if he was rich enough to be a serious collector. So why was Henrietta afraid of him? There had been nothing threatening in the man's manner, but even from across the ballroom, Aubrey had seen the change in her posture. It was a mixture of concern and jealousy that had propelled him to intervene, and she had grasped his presence like a lifeline.

Perhaps Maynard had taken liberties in the past—in which case, Aubrey had been quite as crass as she had accused him of being when he kissed her. Yet, according to Felicia, Maynard was no rake, and Felicia knew all about those, since her husband had been one. Even from his sickbed, Aubrey had wanted to kick Nick Maitland down his own stairs.

Whatever the offense, deliberate or merely perceived, it made Aubrey curious. Another mystery about Henrietta to solve. Just remembering her smile, her humor, her softness in his arms, aroused him. And yet there was pleasure too in restraining himself, to plan a greater, more certain win.

"Aubrey!" yelled Julius. "I'm off to Blackhaven, if you're coming."

THAT NIGHT, FOR the first time ever, Aubrey joined in an adventure with all his brothers. Well, all of them except Lawrence, who, at fifteen, was considered too young and kept inside with the assurance that they needed his hawk-eyed vision from the top of the house. Their sisters were deputized to prevent both twins leaving the house and to shine the light at the given time.

The aim of all of this was to find out about the herd of horses that kept crossing Black Hill land and, if possible, to capture the human Julius was convinced must be guiding them. Aubrey, not greatly interested in the reason, was entirely committed to the adventure and didn't even mind waiting in the cold damp of the not very summery night.

Inevitably it was Julius who hurled himself with reckless bravery at the rider he spotted. But Aubrey only discovered this later, for he and Cornelius were further along the horses' route as described by the twins.

A doctor had once told Aubrey's parents to keep him away from horses as much as possible, but since it was impossible to travel without such animals, they had quickly discovered they made no difference to his health. In fact, Aubrey liked horses and rode whenever his strength permitted. By the time they'd returned to Black Hill, he was a decent rider and improving all the time.

Therefore, when he saw his chance, he took it, rushing at the nearest horse and throwing himself on its bare back.

Not unnaturally, the horse was both annoyed and frightened, doing its best to dislodge him. But Aubrey hung on to its mane and squeezed with his thighs until it slowed, accepting his command to turn and trot then canter back to the stable yard, where he was greeted like a hero with thumps on the back from his brothers and hugs from his sisters.

Grinning from ear to ear, Aubrey said modestly, "Actually, it was easy. He's not wild at all. He'd be happier with a saddle and bridle than wrenched about by his mane, poor beast, but he's quite biddable."

Delilah smiled proudly at him and slipped a halter over the horse's neck to lead him to the stables. "Go and see Julius. He's hurt himself trying to capture a rider."

"He got away," Roderick said, slapping Aubrey's back again. "Unlike your horse."

All the same, Julius had enough injuries, and the wound in his leg had clearly been affected by his fight. It clearly irked him that this had prevented his capturing the man, for he scowled at Aubrey while he repeated his story. Then his face relaxed and he grinned.

"Well done, young man!"

Aubrey fell into bed that night deliriously happy with the praise of the brothers he had always hero-worshipped. Perhaps there was hope for him to make something of his life after all.

He fell asleep at once. But it was Henrietta who haunted his dreams with sweet, sensual fantasies about their making love. His blissful groan woke him up, much to his amusement, and he was still smiling when he drifted back into slumber.

AS THE DAYS passed, Aubrey began to wonder which of them was being teased. He did not see Henrietta or her sister at the pump room. Nor were they at church on Sunday.

At least he could laugh at himself.

He certainly didn't mope. He kept up with his convivial friends and went with them to the kind of relaxed, raucous party he liked best. There, he was almost tempted back into the arms of a rather delightful actress he knew. Her name, he finally recalled, was Violet, and she had long, slender legs that seemed to go on forever.

Except, for some reason, he did not stay at the party but went home to Black Hill.

On another evening, he sauntered into the more dangerous environs of the Black Tavern, frequented by much rougher elements of society—common sailors and soldiers, the unemployed and the criminal, all of them close-mouthed and unimpressed by gentility, some of them downright terrifying. You had to keep your wits about you not to be robbed or poisoned by the disgusting ale. On the other hand, the brandy was excellent—no doubt it came via "the gentlemen"—which occasionally attracted a few of the more reckless scions of the upper orders.

It was where Aubrey had first encountered Lord Launceton. He hated the hypocrisy of the man going to a place like that—half brothel, after all!—and then warning Aubrey off his sister-in-law.

Aubrey half hoped he was there tonight, that there would be another fight. However, the only friend he recognized was Bernard Muir, an amiable native of the town whom Aubrey rather liked. And Bernard, inevitably, was playing cards with three excessively bosky young gentlemen.

"Join the game, Aubrey?" Bernard invited. "Nately's out of it!"

So Aubrey fetched himself a glass of brandy and joined the party.

"Here for your health, gentlemen?" Aubrey inquired, noticing several flinty eyes observing them.

"Lord, no," Nately slurred, slumping back on his stool, which was, fortunately, placed against the greasy wall. "Tranmere's on a repairing lease. Came along to keep him company."

Tranmere grinned. "M'grandfather sent me to some inn in the middle of nowhere—thought I couldn't get into trouble there. Proving him wrong and saving money at the same time."

Young Lord Tranmere took a wallet of cards from his pocket and shoved one at Bernard and one at Aubrey. "Having a bit of bit of a party on Friday. Cards and girls and wine. Very welcome to join us."

It sounded exactly like Aubrey's kind of party, until the stakes of their current card game began to rise and Aubrey eased himself out of it. He didn't really mind. Cards bored him after a while, and huge wagers that he couldn't afford to lose gave him no thrill. Amiably, Tranmere poured him some brandy from his own bottle and settled back into his battle with Bernard.

Aubrey peered into the fug of tobacco smoke, which seemed to grab at his breath. The tavern never smelled very nice, and tonight it was particularly foul. He knew he should take it as a warning, and was about to make his excuses when an unlikely figure caught his eye.

An elderly man in plain trousers and an old coat, a simple kerchief tied around his throat. He wore a workingman's cap, pulled low over his face, and looked much like many other denizens of the tavern. Except that he was Amaury de Corentin.

What the devil was the old gentleman doing in this place? Concerned for his safety, Aubrey was about to go to him and try to escort him home—or at least take him somewhere else—when he realized Corentin was not alone.

He was with another man who somehow didn't quite fit here either, though he was better than Corentin at hiding his face. He was speaking quietly. Corentin nodded once and began to talk in reply. At the same time, he passed a small packet to his companion. It vanished so quickly that Aubrey wasn't even sure he had seen it.

Curiosity now thoroughly aroused, Aubrey rose and weaved his circuitous way to the counter. Although he kept his back to Corentin, he made sure to pass his table and heard the low, familiar murmur of his voice. Yes, it was definitely Corentin.

Recklessly, Aubrey bought a bottle of brandy.

Eavesdropping was not in his nature, but he couldn't help wondering what subject so engrossed the old émigré in a place like this. From the corner of his eye, he saw Corentin rise and leave.

Aubrey was relieved, though he watched the door quite carefully to be sure no one followed the old man to rob him of what little he had. Only as he swiped up his bottle from the counter did he realize that while he hadn't been able to make out the individual words of Corentin's conversation, the murmured rhythm of the language was undoubtedly French.

Rather thoughtfully, Aubrey plonked the bottle in the middle of his friends' table. "Thanks for the company, gentlemen. Going to get some air."

"Good man and good idea," Tranmere said, grinning. He stood up and grabbed the bottle. "Let's fetch some girls and go and drink it on the beach."

Bernard laughed. "In this weather? You're mad. I'll bid you goodnight."

Aubrey, however, was quite happy to join the young revelers in the fresh, damp air. But as he drank and laughed and embraced the pretty girl sitting in his lap, his thoughts turned once more to Henrietta.

He had intended to make no effort to approach her before Miss Talbot's "at-home" on Wednesday. But even in this company, his desire to see her grew. Perhaps it was the brandy.

He reached again for the bottle.

***

HE DIDN'T QUITE have a headache the following morning, but he did feel a trifle wooly. Taking a leaf out of Roderick's book—Rod vanished for hours every day, tramping all over the countryside—he decided to walk into Blackhaven and take his daily dose of the waters. He would still have plenty of time to work on the garden when he returned. God knew it was little enough to contribute.

Occasionally, despite his new love of life, Aubrey was dissatisfied with himself. Although he liked living here with his siblings, he was aware that Julius and Cornelius between them looked after the estate. Delilah and Felicia looked after the house and the twins. It struck Aubrey as he strode along the beach toward the town that his years as an invalid had made him too used to being looked after. Was it not time, given his improved health, that he began to take a more active role in the family?

Perhaps the twins were right to interfere as they did. It had certainly done no harm so far. Already, since the ball, they were being invited to local events, and their first dinner party at Black Hill was tonight. That had been arranged by Felicia and Lucy, largely because Julius had danced with someone at the ball, someone Delilah seemed to know about from his past.

From his own observations, he knew interfering in people's relationships rarely worked out well. But that was not the same as contributing.

What could I do? He had a head full of knowledge from books, none from life. He was trained for nothing and had no talents that he had ever discovered. He could no longer blame that on his health.

As if the very thought of his old difficulties revived them, he had to catch his breath. Forcing himself to slow, he breathed in the fresh, salty air and relaxed into a slightly slower rhythm while he let his mind appreciate the beauty surrounding him—the vastness of the restless sea, with its scattering of vessels in the distance, the castle rising on the cliffs ahead of him, and beyond that, the harbor and town of Blackhaven.

He had tried to describe it once in written words, as he used to do when abroad, though the results had been dissatisfying. Still, perhaps he could train himself to write a book. If he could persuade anyone to publish it. Even then, he doubted it would make him, let alone his family, rich.

Julius would and should marry one day. His wife would not necessarily want a huge gaggle of siblings in her house, especially not useless ones.

I could do better, Aubrey thought vaguely, before he realized he was not alone on this stretch of sand. In the distance, bounding toward him, was a large white dog, galloping like a horse, then swerving back in a huge circle to herd his people and rushing forward again.

A dog. His heart began to beat faster. The dog's people appeared to be three in number, two females and a male. As he grew closer, he was almost disappointed to see that the male did not stride and swagger like Launceton. In fact, his movements were much more boyish. The females were young, too, one in the shorter skirts of a young girl, the other…

The other moved with grace and laughter in a way that was suddenly entirely familiar. He knew that here at last was Henrietta, presumably with her younger siblings and their famous pet.

Excitement soared. He could not help grinning as he strode toward them and the huge, hairy dog galumphed across the sand, tongue lolling out the side of its mouth, spraying sand in all directions from its feet and fur.

His heart seemed to surge with happiness, just because it was so funny, and because he was so aware of Henrietta scampering after the dog with her brother and sister, her face alight with laughter and a carefree, youthful, yet ageless beauty that felt like her essence. She would not look at him as she ran, though, only at the dog.

Aubrey halted and spread his arms wide. "Dog!" he cried, as though welcoming an old friend.

And Dog, clearly encouraged by the strange human's friendliness, launched himself through the air.

"Watch yourself!" warned the boy.

"Oh no!" cried the girl, clearly torn between dismay and delight.

"Dog!" shouted Henrietta. "Down!"

It was much too late for such an order. In fact, down was the only way Dog *could* go, and Aubrey knew he was going with him. More than seventy pounds of canine landed full on his chest, knocking him backward onto the sand. Gasping with laughter, Aubrey closed his arms around the animal, who was damp from the sea, salty, muddy, and sandy, though it was Aubrey he seemed determined to clean up with his enthusiastic tongue.

"He likes you, sir, honestly," said the boy reaching for the dog's collar.

Henrietta grabbed the other side, and Aubrey, still laughing, pushed the dog off himself. While he did, Dog shook, and hair and sand caught in Aubrey's throat. His chest felt as if the dog still sat on it. He wheezed horribly and couldn't reach the next breath.

Oh, no, not now, not now…

Chapter Six

Henrietta let go of Dog's collar, staring at Aubrey in alarm. Dog sat back with a whine, making no effort now to get back to the fun human. He didn't like people to be hurt.

"What is it?" Georgiana said, frightened. "What's wrong with him?"

Henrietta dropped onto her knees beside the gasping, suffocating Aubrey. "He is ill," she said with a calmness she was very far from feeling. "Michael, run and fetch Dr. Lampton. Tell him it's an emergency."

A vague memory of a similar emergency jumped into her mind. A new stable lad at Launceton when she was a child, who had gasped for breath whenever the cat came near him.

"Georgi, clip the leash back on and haul Dog back to the rocks if you can. See if you can find a way to tie him there."

Michael had taken off like a hare, but until he brought the doctor, Henrietta had no idea what to do. Aubrey's suffering seemed terrible. She wanted to fall on him, hold him, will her strength into him, but he needed *air*, not more suffocation.

With trembling hands, she loosened his cravat, then the buttons of his coat and waistcoat, and hauled him into more of an upright position, cradling him loosely against her shoulder.

"There," she said, "you will be fine directly. The doctor is coming." She took his cold, agitated hand. *Don't die. Oh, please don't die...* "Breathe out and in, slowly, slowly, and when you can, tell me what I should do."

His fingers grasped hers convulsively while his throat rattled and his terrifyingly white face began to look blue.

"Breathe with me," she pleaded, blindly dropping her cheek briefly onto his hair to get his attention.

Slowly, deliberately, she breathed in and out, over and over, as if she could thus share her breath with him. His gaze met hers, the emotion in his eyes a tangle of pain and shame.

His fingers released hers, but she kept hold of his hand anyway until, gradually, he began to breathe properly. The blue tinge faded from his face and lips, and she allowed herself to hope that he wouldn't die.

"There," she said shakily. "I told you that you'd be fine."

His eyes had locked with hers. But she could no longer read what was there. She released his hand with some embarrassment, and he reached up to her face with something very like wonder. Only when he touched her cheek did she realize it was wet with tears. Tears of terror that he was dying.

She dashed her sleeve across her face, and his hand fell back. When she realized he was trying to sit up, she helped him rest his back against the nearby rock. His shoulders were surprisingly broad for such a lean man.

"Shouldn't you lie down until the doctor comes?" she asked.

He shook his head. "I breathe better...when I'm upright."

"I'm so sorry," she whispered. "It was Dog. Although his hair is so long, he casts it all the time..."

"No, I like dogs."

He seemed about to struggle to his feet, so she pressed his shoulder. "No, sit there for a little. No one else is here. My brother's fetching Dr. Lampton, so we shall wait with you."

His gaze flickered beyond her.

"My sister, Georgiana."

He lifted one hand in her direction, and Georgiana grinned with relief and waved enthusiastically.

"It's I who am…sorry," he said, sounding mortified in his weakness. "Sorry you had to see that."

"Foolish male pride," she said dismissively, and sat back on the sand with her legs drawn up under her skirts before she met his gaze once more. "Was it such attacks that kept you in a bath chair?"

He looked away, and she thought he would not answer. Then his gaze came back to her with a hint of defiance that was oddly endearing. "Yes, sometimes. Other times…I walked around, ran and…played like everyone else. Then I would have an attack…and I was confined to bed again for days. No one thought I would live beyond childhood."

Despite his still-labored breathing, he grinned, as though to show he had proved everyone wrong for mere devilment.

"And now?" she asked.

For an instant, he looked so bleak that it chilled her. "I thought I was…better."

She had no idea what to say. Her heart ached for him. Distractedly, she began to draw patterns in the sand between them with one finger. Then she raised her eyes to his. "Longer between attacks is surely better."

His gaze dropped. She knew he didn't want to talk about it, and she gathered talking of any kind was still difficult, so she tried to distract him with prattle about her family's doings since the ball, including Georgiana's feud with the boy who lived next door, and Dog's antics trying to befriend the local cat. She had been reduced to telling him that she and Diane de Corentin had enjoyed an ice together the previous day when he actually glanced up at her again.

Her heart sank. *If he likes either of us, it is Diane.* "You think it an odd friendship?" she said cheerfully. "She is much cleverer than I am, of course, but often we laugh at the same things. And her father is so agreeable."

He seemed about to speak, and this gaze shifted beyond her. Turning, she saw with relief that Dr. Lampton was striding across the sand toward them, his bag swinging at his side. Michael, at his heels, veered off to help Georgiana struggle with Dog, who was inevitably keen to get at his friend the doctor, whom he had met precisely once before.

Henrietta jumped up and went to meet Dr. Lampton. "The dog jumped on him and he fell back and suddenly seemed unable to breathe properly. I believe it is an illness of long—"

"It is," Dr. Lampton said briskly. "Don't worry, I have seen him before." He spared her a reassuring smile before he walked past her to his patient.

Aubrey tried to rise, but much as Henrietta had done before, the doctor held him down with a hand on his shoulder, and knelt casually in the sand before him, asking questions, focusing his attention on Aubrey's face.

Henrietta, allowing them privacy, walked slowly toward her siblings and Dog.

"I HAVEN'T HAD an attack since before we left London," Aubrey told the doctor. "I thought—" He broke off, afraid he was actually going to weep.

"You thought you were better," Lampton finished for him, "that you were finally strong enough to beat it." He took an ear trumpet from his bag and listened to Aubrey's chest, from the front and then from the back. "Well, the good news is, you are better than you were. You are certainly recovering quickly from this attack."

He put the ear trumpet away and closed the bag. "But we are not talking about influenza or measles here. You don't suffer, recover, and then leave it behind forever. Look on it more as a *condition* than an illness. Like a bad temper, you live with this. It is part of you. You limit its opportunities, which you have done by coming here to the country, close by the sea, and by living much more healthily. Er…you *are* living healthily?"

"I believe so. I suppose I drink too much spirit."

"Have you taken to smoking tobacco? Do your brothers indulge?"

Aubrey shook his head.

"And you had no prior warning of this attack until you hit the sand with the dog on top of you?"

Aubrey threw back his head. "I felt a twinge last night. In the tavern. I left almost at once and it went away. Today, walking too quickly along the beach, I felt another and slowed down a little."

Lampton nodded. "The air in the tavern is toxic. Avoid it."

Aubrey straightened his head and frowned. "You mean that was when the damage was done? Why did I not collapse on the tavern floor?"

"Who knows?" Lampton said unhelpfully. "It was your body warning you. The good thing is, you listened and acted accordingly. Anxiety is not good either. Are you worrying about anything in particular?"

Involuntarily, Aubrey glanced over the doctor's shoulder to where Henrietta waited with her siblings. Perhaps he needed to win her to remove the anxiety, he thought sardonically. At the same time, he felt a fresh rush of shame that she had seen his weakness. Not manly. Appalling, in fact.

"Breathe," Lampton said dryly. "You are not the only man to lose air and wit at the sight of a woman. Particularly that young woman. It's not what we are talking about."

"And the dog?"

Lampton shrugged. "Maybe some combination of sand, dog fur, and the wind being knocked out of you. You could try, in a limited kind of way, meeting the dog again in a different environment. My money is on the tavern and tobacco smoke. Avoid those like the plague and I suspect you will be, if not completely free of the attacks, then mostly free."

The doctor hesitated a moment. "Don't despair, Aubrey. From your description, and the sound of your chest now, this attack was much less severe than those you suffered in childhood and as a very young man. Some people grow out of them almost entirely, but you must remain aware of it."

"Are you going to tell me to go home to bed?"

Lampton considered. "Were you going anywhere else in particular?"

"To the pump room."

"Unexceptionable. You may go with your escort." The doctor flicked a glance toward the waiting Gaunts.

"God, no."

Lampton shot him another perceptive glance that he didn't like. "Don't make an issue out of it. She doesn't."

She hadn't humiliated herself. Aubrey swallowed. "Is she very upset by the experience?"

"Concerned for you. She is not the type for vapors and smelling salts. But if you wish, you may walk with me into town and I shall deposit you at the pump room. Send for me if you feel unwell, but I don't anticipate it."

The doctor rose to his feet, stretching down one hand to Aubrey, who took it, rising somewhat gingerly. His breath came evenly, which gave him the courage to throw his shoulders back and stroll toward the Gaunts.

Henrietta started forward to meet him.

He summoned a smile. "So sorry for the dramatics," he said carelessly. "I hope it hasn't upset you all. My thanks for sending for the doctor." He threw a quick grin at the boy. "And apologies for disturbing your walk. Goodbye, Gaunts. Goodbye, Dog."

Before he swung away again, he caught the flash of hurt in Henrietta's eyes and hated himself afresh. But right now, she was unbearable. He could not endure pity or concern, not when he had imagined himself the great charmer who would win her. So he did not give her a last smile, or indeed show any further interest at all, merely sauntered off with Lampton, heading for the path off the beach to the road and the town.

IN MOST CIRCUMSTANCES, Henrietta saw the silver linings rather than the clouds, the good in people rather than the bad. But after Aubrey Vale's collapse on the beach, something in her drooped.

When she had first realized it was Aubrey striding along the sand toward them, she had felt elated, especially when he had greeted Dog so exuberantly, throwing out his arms with such uninhibited laughter that happiness had surged through her.

Terrified he was dying, she had suffered with him and sympathized so deeply that it hurt. And yet she had been secretly proud of his grip on her hand, clinging to her strength until the storm had passed, and then responding to her calm and her distraction. She had imagined a certain new closeness, almost a conspiracy between them.

And then everything had changed.

She had been dismissed with distant gratitude, like a stranger. Only Michael had received anything like an Aubrey-type smile before the man had gone off with Dr. Lampton and forgotten about them.

Or, at least, that was how it seemed. Of course, she understood he might well have wanted or even needed Dr. Lampton then, and the presence of herself and her siblings—to say nothing of Dog—might well have been unwelcome. Still, the manner of his going hurt her. And she remembered that he had not been near her since the ball five days before.

He was erratic, unreliable, perhaps as Vanya had been before he met Lizzie. Only Vanya *had* always been reliable in the things that mattered, his friendship and loyalty unswerving. Had she, Henrietta, committed the sin she found so unforgivable in others? Been attracted by a handsome face and outward charm, and failed to see the shallowness beneath? Or was it just that she was no Lizzie? Clearly, she had nothing in her to keep Aubrey's friendship.

For a few moments after the rest of her family had left the breakfast table, she sat alone in the dining room, gazing at the posy of rosebuds that had opened so gloriously and which she had foolishly imagined might have come from Aubrey.

She had no reason to want his friendship or his admiration. He had taken liberties that she had certainly not granted. Or at least she hadn't meant to. Vanya said he was a womanizer and a rake. And Vanya was his friend. Or at least they knew each other.

"Henri?" Lizzie said from the doorway. "Do you want to come with me to the pump room? You don't need to."

Henrietta rose quickly. "Of course. Sorry, I was woolgathering."

"Are you worrying still about Aubrey Vale?" Lizzie asked. Naturally, Michael and Georgiana had told her all about it.

"Oh no," Henrietta lied. "I was thinking of something else altogether."

Lizzie did not dispute it. "I'm sure at least one of the Vales will be at Miss Talbot's this afternoon, so we can inquire then. In fact, I am sure I have seen him at the pump room once or twice…"

Henrietta's stomach tightened. He had never been there when Henrietta went with Lizzie before. She wasn't sure she wanted him to be there now, though she *did* want him to be well.

As it transpired, they had not even got as far as the pump room before she caught sight of him.

Relief flooded her, for he stood in the street laughing with another young man, at whom Henrietta barely glanced. Her anxious gaze found no trace of illness or even weakness in Aubrey. He looked as he always did: handsome, elegant, refined, with just that edge of hunger that was so intriguing.

Despite his clearly amusing conversation, his gaze shifted suddenly beyond his companion and found her unerringly. For the tiniest instant, she glimpsed confusion in his eyes, some vulnerability she could not easily understand, and then he blinked, and a slow smile began to spread over his face.

He swept off his hat and bowed, drawing the attention of his much more expensively dressed friend, a young man who contrived to look even more dissipated than Aubrey. In fact, he seemed vaguely familiar.

Lizzie had already veered toward them. Aubrey's friend, after a quick, curious glance, had come back for a much longer, more admiring stare.

Henrietta sighed inwardly.

"Good morning, Mr. Vale," Lizzie said. "I trust we find you well?"

"Couldn't be better, my lady," Aubrey replied politely, replacing his hat with a flourish. "How do you do?"

His brow twitched as his friend nudged him urgently. "Don't be uncivil, Aubrey."

Aubrey said, "Allow me to present Lord Tranmere, ladies. Tranmere, Lady Launceton and her sister, Miss Gaunt."

Henrietta murmured politely. She found it hard to look away from Aubrey, who was smiling at her in a way that gave her butterflies, inviting her response as though it were a private conspiracy between them—and yet those dancing eyes, so full of life, were predatory, as she had first seen them, edged with a danger that made her want to come closer and escape at the same time.

"A pleasure to see you again, ladies," Aubrey said, touching his hat, and strolled away, taking Henrietta by surprise.

"Dash it, Aubrey!" Tranmere could be heard protesting.

Henrietta, confused and not a little piqued, understood the sentiment. Dazed, she walked on with Lizzie to the pump room.

Chapter Seven

THE AFTERNOON FOUND Henrietta accompanying Lizzie and Vanya to Miss Talbot's "at-home" in her hotel sitting room. Used to being hostess for her diplomat brother, Lord Linfield, Miss Talbot could hold her easygoing court anywhere and frequently did, always with perfect respectability. In her thirties but unmarried, she was generally accompanied by her widowed companion, the equally charming but rather quieter Mrs. Macy.

The Launcetons were the first to arrive, to the apparent pleasure of their hosts, and Henrietta was glad to talk and laugh over their days in Vienna. In a little, as more people arrived, she was introduced to Aubrey's sisters, Mrs. Maitland and Miss Lucy Vale, who were kind and friendly and deserved better than Henrietta's hasty glance toward the door in case any Vale brothers had followed them in. They hadn't, and Henrietta refused to ask after them.

A little later, she found Lady Alice and her sister Helen, which was pleasant, although Henrietta's restlessness seemed to have transferred itself to the other girls, who cast frequent glances toward the door. The reason became clear when Lady Helen's face suddenly lit up. At the same time, the room seemed suddenly to fill with tall men.

Sir Julius Vale had arrived, accompanied by his soldier brother, the major—and Aubrey.

Oh no, is Helen in love with Aubrey? Where did such a thought come from, and why should it even matter to Henrietta? Except that she liked Helen, and Aubrey was a rake.

On her other side, Alice seemed deflated.

While Helen's gaze followed Major Vale, now greeting Miss Talbot, it was Aubrey who came straight up to them and threw himself into the vacant chair beside Henrietta. His smile was dazzling.

"I hoped you would be here," he said, and raised his hand to Vanya, who was scowling on the other side of the room.

"Have you and Vanya fallen out?" Henrietta blurted.

"Oh, no. I never fall out with people. He's just moody."

Henrietta could not dispute that, although it was hardly Aubrey's place to point it out. "You look well," she said instead.

"Not as well as you. But I thought we weren't to notice looks."

"Don't be silly. I'm talking about health."

"Please don't. It's dull. Tell me, do you see much of Monsieur de Corentin?"

"Occasionally. He called on us once and I went for tea with Diane. Why?"

"He interests me. I see him in all sorts of odd places."

"I thought it was Diane who interested you."

He smiled and kissed his fingers like a toast to the other girl's beauty. At the same time, his eyes teased deliberately, and she knew better than to rise to the silent challenge.

"What of your other admirer?" he asked. "Lord Maynard."

"He calls. Sometimes I am out. But I had to go for a walk with him once."

Aubrey's lips twitched. "Did you take Dog?"

She found a responsive smile tugging her lips. "I wanted to, but I took Michael and Georgi instead."

"Don't let him marry you."

Henrietta blinked. "He is only just widowed. I think he regards me like one of his porcelain pieces, to be gazed at by way of comfort."

A frown flickered across his face and vanished. "Either you have some very odd ideas, or he does. Would you walk with me?"

"If you ever asked."

"I'm asking now."

"It would be rude to leave!"

"Miss Talbot wouldn't mind." He smiled beyond her, in the direction she had last seen Vanya, and understanding thudded into her chest.

This was nothing to do with her. Aubrey was here merely to annoy Vanya.

Without a word, she stood up and walked away. She didn't so much as glance at Aubrey, but somehow, she knew she had surprised him and was fiercely, bitterly glad.

AUBREY KNEW HE had been crass. Again. Along with his shame came the knowledge that he was making a spectacular mess of his plan to win Henrietta. Not only was he constantly frightening her away like a startled deer, but he continually showed himself in the worst possible light.

In two days, he had fallen at her feet like a gasping fish out of water, been seen in the company of the worst and possibly stupidest wastrel in the country, and used her to annoy her overprotective brother-in-law—and let her see it.

Had he forgotten she was no fool?

I must be the most inept rake in history.

Leaving Miss Talbot's, he separated from his brothers and went off on his own in search of distraction.

Despite recovering so well from his attack on the beach, it was affecting everything he did. The fact that she had seen it was intolerable. Well, now she knew he was intolerable in lots of other ways, too.

He didn't even know why he was so determined to annoy Vanya. He liked the man. Would Aubrey not behave in precisely the same way to protect his own sisters? And yes, perhaps Henrietta *did* need protecting from him. He might not wish to hurt her, but neither were his intentions strictly honorable.

In fact, his intentions confused him, so what chance did either Vanya or Henrietta have?

Avoiding the tavern, he had an expensive brandy in the hotel, then walked up to the inn for something cheaper. Here, he fell into the company of a couple of old soldiers, one of them an officer who was a friend of Roderick's.

An hour later, still ripe for trouble, he sauntered up to Mrs. Rhett's house and was not only admitted but invited to dine tête-à-tête with his hostess.

Oh yes. Distraction and relief in full measure.

Except his heart was not in the flirting. It came almost as a shock that he didn't want to be there. That he would rather go home than spend the night making love to this delightful woman. He was too restless, and he couldn't quite recall why he had found her so attractive before. Even though she was a generous and kindhearted lady…and she deserved better than him.

After dinner, he kissed her hand and her lips and departed. They both knew he would not be back. It made him sad, and he thought it made her sad too.

Angry with himself and confused by the conflicting, turbulent feeling, he was drawn to the beach and decided to walk home that way, since the tide seemed far enough out.

He didn't know how far he had gone before he realized dusk was falling. On sudden impulse, he whirled around and strode back the way he had come.

He knew which house in Graham Gardens the Launcetons had taken for the month because his lordship had pointed it out on their drunken evening together. He recalled how much fun Vanya was and how much he had liked him. That was the real route of his hurt over the man's warning.

Am I a child that I should behave so badly over it?

Realizing he had been so deep in his own thoughts that he had gone the wrong way, he doubled back and tried to take a shortcut along a narrow lane that, he was pleasantly surprised to discover, ran along the backs of the houses in Graham Gardens, a bit like a London mews.

It was dark now, with only a few visible stars and the lights from the houses to guide him. He counted along the houses, but from this side he could not be sure which was the right one. He paused, trying to work it out. And then wondered why he had come in the first place.

Not to apologize to Vanya. He had not wronged Vanya. And he could hardly call at this hour and ask for Henrietta. But some urge had propelled him here. There was no purpose in it, but he wanted to be near her. To lean over her gate and feel the soothing sweetness of her presence. Just the *echo* of her presence.

He was going soft in the head.

From the lane, he heard the odd murmur from voices nearby, the restive movement of a horse in a stable on the other side, the snuffle of some animal in the closest garden. He took a step onward and heard the low warning growl of a dog.

He stopped again and listened to the demented sniffing below the gate. The dog barked, and Aubrey would have moved hastily on except that a woman's voice said low, "Hush, Dog. Come here."

Aubrey's heart turned over. *There* she was!

Without further thought, he pressed the latch and opened the gate.

⁂

HENRIETTA HAD BEEN feeling unaccountably sad. On top of which, for the sake of her own pride, she wished she had not walked away from Aubrey quite so obviously. She should have talked civilly about the weather for another few minutes and then parted with politeness. Instead, she had surely betrayed her disappointment in him, and the fact that she had expected better.

And she had no reason to expect better. He had spent more time with Vanya than with her, and apart from gazing at her, he had no reason to value her. Whereas he must have regarded Vanya as a friend.

Over dinner, she had asked Vanya if he had quarreled with Aubrey Vale.

He had looked surprised. "No, why should I?"

"You were glaring at him at Miss Talbot's."

Vanya laughed. "Don't worry—Aubrey understands me perfectly."

Henrietta wasn't sure that Aubrey did. Though he gave every appearance of the sophisticated man-about-town, in fact he had very little experience of Society compared with most young gentlemen of his age.

"What should he understand?" Henrietta had pursued.

"To keep the line with you, of course," Lizzie had said.

Well, that was clearer, but it certainly did not cheer Henrietta. She was not used to such low feelings and had no desire to lie in bed with them. Restlessly, she had followed Dog out into the garden and sat with him on the step for a while, her arm around him and her head resting against his great, hairy body.

Both she and Dog had liked this, although inevitably, Dog got restive first, sniffing about the garden, growling and barking at the gate to the lane. For fear of his disturbing the household and the neighbors, she called him back as softly as she could. And then, before she could even stand up, she heard the sound of the latch lifting and a man walked out of the darkness into the garden.

Henrietta jumped to her feet. "Who is it?"

Not Vanya, who had retired early with Lizzie. Someone too tall to be Michael sneaking back from some mischief, or Misha, Vanya's servant.

"Me," said a male voice unhelpfully.

Her heart lurched. Dog danced happily around the approaching figure, but that was no guide. Dog loved nearly everyone. Poised for flight, Henrietta stood still until the intruder stepped slowly into the circle of light shining from the kitchen window and halted.

Aubrey.

"What are you doing here?" She wondered if she *could* run, though at least her voice was steady.

"I don't really know. I wanted... I didn't really expect to see you."

"Who did you want?" She had the impression they were just saying words, while some other meaning hovered just beyond their grasp.

"Oh, you, Henrietta. Only you."

In one smooth movement, he swept her into his arms and out of the light, and her mouth, open to object, was buried beneath his. She knew a moment of anger, even fear, before the stunning realization that there was a strange anguish in his kiss. She stilled for one fatal moment of surprise, and then she was lost.

In wonder, she let the sensual new feeling bombard her, entirely seduced by his tender, pleasuring mouth and the strength of his arms, the hardness of his lean, thrilling body. She gasped and clutched his coat. With trembling fingers, she stroked his rough cheek and kissed him back because she could do nothing else.

She never wanted it to end.

"Only you," he repeated against her lips. At which point Dog, who had been remarkably patient, reared up on his hind legs, pushing his large head under Aubrey's arm.

"And Dog," Henrietta said, a laugh trembling on her tingling lips.

"Not even him." Aubrey's arms fell away from her, though his eyes still glittered somehow in the darkness. "You are so good, and I...

I am not a good man. I wish—" He broke off with an abrupt, oddly bitter breath of laughter and strode away toward the bottom of the garden. He didn't use the gate but jumped it and vanished into the night.

Dog didn't try to follow him. He leaned against Henrietta's legs until she dropped her hand onto his head.

"What just happened, Dog?" she murmured.

An apology for this afternoon. Tonight, there had been only Henrietta and Aubrey, and the knowledge, the reality, was intoxicating.

She sat back down on the step with a bump and put both arms around Dog, who wagged his tail and licked her face.

"WHY ARE YOU so eager to dine with the Launcetons?" Diane de Corentin challenged her father, having found him asleep in his chair and wakened him in order to send him to bed.

"It is good for you to have friends when I am gone."

"Stop it," she said sharply. "Besides, I thought we had agreed it was a husband I needed, and there are none of those to be found at Lady Launceton's—unless you favor her fourteen-year-old brother?"

"There will be other guests. I believe Lord Linfield is unmarried. And Lord Maynard. Your birth is as high as theirs, even if your present circumstances are not."

"Then it has nothing to do with the fact that you have decided, on the basis of no evidence whatsoever, that Lord Launceton murdered my brother?"

"Nothing at all," her father said peacefully.

Diane did not believe him for a moment. She moved forward to catch his arm. "Papa. Even if it is true—it was war. The French army invaded his country. Would you not fight were your roles reversed?"

"It was not a fight," Papa snapped, his veil of amiability vanishing in an instant. "The fight was over and the French were leaving. Bonaparte had already gone. It was a senseless massacre of retreating men."

"Retreating *soldiers*," she corrected him. "Gaspard was a soldier, fighting for a country we left years before. In a war begun by your hero, Bonaparte."

"Be silent," he commanded. "And remain silent. You know nothing, a mere girl. I bid you goodnight."

"Goodnight," she returned wearily. *A mere girl*. Even alive, here and now, with him every day, it seemed she was of less account than her brother, whom he had not seen since childhood. Her future would still take second place to Gaspard's past.

Unless he was hiding the fact that he knew Aubrey Vale would also be at the Launcetons'. She hung on to that thought because she could not bear her father's final days to be spent in shame, in the betrayal of the country that had harbored him, perhaps even in prison.

But mostly because Aubrey filled her waking thoughts, and she wanted him with increasing desperation.

It had not always been like that. She had liked him, of course. She had been attracted to him ever since she first saw him. But this need, this hunger, was new, and stemmed, she thought ruefully, from the moment he had noticed the lovely Henrietta Gaunt.

Damn her.

She could not even dislike the girl, for she was unexpectedly intelligent as well as amusing and sunny. Diane was glad to have Henrietta as a friend, but the girl could not have Aubrey.

There, Diane drew the line of friendship.

Chapter Eight

LORD MAYNARD, FIGHTING his way through the storm to Graham Gardens, expected a quiet family dinner at Lady Launceton's, hopefully without children or dogs. But when he entered the drawing room, he found there were other guests. He did not mind—the numbers might even work in his favor, since those others were bound to distract each other and the family and so leave him more time with Henrietta.

Inevitably, his gaze went straight to her in all her exquisite beauty. The low evening sunshine beamed directly onto her dark chestnut hair, turning it to a fire that framed her perfect countenance. Her evening gown was simple, of palest pink muslin, but she could have worn rags and still have drawn all eyes.

Maynard did not allow himself to feast on the sight for more than an instant. Manners compelled him to greet his hostess. Lady Launceton hardly offended the eye, either, having a lively prettiness of her own, though she lacked her sister's awe-inspiring perfection. He was happy to bow over her hand and be introduced to the other guests—Lord Linfield, whom he knew slightly, and his sister, and an old émigré called Corentin and his daughter, whom Maynard had seen at the ball.

Henrietta greeted him politely but did not offer her hand. He liked her shyness. And, for now, he was happy enough just to gaze upon her.

"Vanya will be down directly," Lady Launceton informed him. "There was some crisis with the children. Or was it the dog?"

Ignoring the last, Maynard sat down in the chair nearest to Henrietta and accepted a glass of sherry from the servant. "Lord Launceton appears to have become like a father to your younger siblings. I hope one day to find a lady happy to mother my own children."

"How old are they, my lord?" Henrietta asked.

"Just eight and six."

"They must miss their mother terribly."

"They do, though my sister is doing her best with them."

The door opened again, and Lord Launceton entered in his usual impetuous and yet supremely casual style.

"My apologies," he said. "The dog was eating Michael's cricket bat. Miss Talbot, your servant." He kissed the lady's hand with far too much foreign flourish, in Maynard's opinion, before shaking hands with Linfield and turning to be introduced to the Corentins.

As Lizzie introduced the young lady, Maynard's attention slipped to the old gentleman, who was gazing fixedly at Launceton, his eyes blazing with some fierce, profound hatred.

Startled out of his usual, blinkered focus, Maynard murmured, "What does Corentin have against your brother-in-law?"

"Nothing," Henrietta replied in surprise. "Miss de Corentin is a friend of mine."

"Ah. Perhaps I misunderstood," Maynard said, although he knew he had not. For when Launceton turned to the old gentleman, offering his hand, there was a distinct pause before Corentin accepted it, and even then with almost insulting brevity.

However, the émigré smiled in his usual gentle way, and no one but Maynard seemed to find the incident odd.

To his annoyance, Linfield was placed beside Henrietta at dinner, though at least this meant Maynard could look at her across the table.

It also meant he was seated beside Diane de Corentin.

She was nothing like Henrietta. Although pleasing enough to the eye and undeniably attractive in her own way, she was not beautiful. Her features were too irregular, her expression a little too sardonic for comfort.

"Satisfy my curiosity, Miss de Corentin," he said quietly, when satisfied that everyone else's attention was elsewhere. "What is it your father dislikes in Lord Launceton?"

"Something that is not there," came the unexpected reply, although almost at once she smiled apologetically. "Forgive me, I was woolgathering. Of course my father has every liking and respect for Lord Launceton. Why else would we be here?"

"That is a good question," Maynard said. "You are a friend of Miss Gaunt's, I believe."

"I am. Are you her suitor?"

Maynard blinked. "You are very direct."

"Should I not be?" she challenged.

"Not when the matter is none of your business," Maynard said pleasantly.

The girl was not remotely cowed. "Nor are my father's friendships—or otherwise—any of yours."

Since that effectively killed the bout of conversation, Maynard turned with some relief to Lady Launceton.

The French girl was right, of course. He had no business inquiring into her father's opinion of their host, except, he supposed, in so far as he intended to marry into the Launceton family. In truth, his own interest in the matter surprised him. It had even distracted him, however temporarily, from Henrietta, whose beauty obsessed him almost to the exclusion of everything else in life, including his own grief and that of his children.

AMAURY DE CORENTIN, finally in the lion's den with the lion himself, began to see his way clear.

A short, gentle conversation with Launceton himself established little except he had been brought up in Russia and fought in the tsar's army under the name of Colonel Savarin, commanding a regiment of Cossacks. For a man who seemed so vainglorious, he was surprisingly reticent about his battlefield exploits.

But from Lord Linfield, Corentin learned that the tsar had personally rewarded Launceton for gallantry, specifically for his role in expelling the French in the winter of 1812. Oh yes, he had the right man.

His hand itched for a sword, to slide it between Savarin's ribs, to deprive him of life, as Savarin had deprived Gaspard, even fleeing. A stab in the back...

Forcing his expression to remain serene, Corentin reminded himself that he could do nothing that would land him in prison or shame Diane. Not unless she was safely married to Aubrey Vale. On the other hand, Aubrey might yet prove to be more useful than that, and he need never know...

The idea began to grow as the evening progressed. Lady Launceton and her sister played the pianoforte and sang an amusing duet, and while everyone, even the curious Maynard, watched the performers, Corentin watched Launceton.

At the ball, he had observed Launceton's conversation with Aubrey Vale and, from the latter's fury, gathered that Launceton had warned him off Henrietta. Which certainly suited Corentin's plans for Diane. But now, seeing Launceton's attention was not on his lovely sister-in-law but on his own lively wife, he realized something more.

This was the most important discovery of all. Launceton was in love with his wife.

Corentin's gentle smile widened. Now, at last, he had a weapon against Savarin-Launceton. He could both avenge Gaspard and help

Diane by making sure Henrietta dismissed Aubrey.

Being a man of subtlety, Corentin would rather have waited for the moment to happen naturally, as he had for his first meeting with his son's killer. But he was running out of time. Louis was increasingly impatient, and Corentin did not know how long his strength would last. But he needed to *see* Launceton suffer.

Accordingly, when tea was served, he made use of the movement in the room to sit by his host.

"I am having a most enjoyable evening, my lord. Your wife is a remarkable lady—so full of life and love that she infects all around her with the same spirit."

Launceton smiled. "She is remarkable in so many ways. Not least for putting up with me."

Corentin smiled. *"Putting up with you,* indeed! Her ladyship clearly adores you. A lady who holds out against the determined siege of a charming man—"

"What charming man?" Launceton said at once.

Really, this was too easy. He sounded amused, but there was nevertheless an edge to his voice.

"My lord, I tell you to prove your wife's adoration," Corentin protested.

"My wife needs to prove nothing to me."

"Needs to? No, of course not. But what husband, what lover, does not like to hear that his lady is indifferent to the blandishments of other handsome young men?"

Seeing that his skills were not entirely dead from lack of use invigorated Corentin. Launceton, frowning at him, finally got the message that Corentin was trying to warn him of something without actually bringing it into the open and saying it. An act of friendship, to preserve everyone's pride.

"I might like it, but I have no need of it," Launceton said. "I am well aware of my wife's virtues. Still, you had better give me a name. I have no qualms about punishing insolence or presumption."

Or anything else, Corentin thought bitterly while he patted the arm of his son's killer in an avuncular manner. "As we agree, there is no danger. I would have said nothing at all, except that I have had some dealings with the young man in question. He attended my daughter in much the same manner until your family came to Blackhaven." He lowered his voice even further to murmur, "Aubrey Vale."

Launceton laughed. "Oh, no, you have that wrong. If he pursues any of my family, it is Lizzie's sister, and I have already had a word on that score."

"Perhaps that word is what made him seek to annoy you in return, for it was definitely your lady wife I saw him sniffing around. He has a reputation as something of a rake."

"So did I, once." He did not sound pleased with himself.

Corentin had every hope that this would lead to considerable trouble. Because, just for a moment, Launceton's eyes betrayed a wealth of boiling emotion beneath.

Suffer, you murdering son of a whore, as Gaspard did—as I do.

THE DAY OF Lady Braithwaite's garden party at the castle dawned with great excitement, mostly because Michael and Georgiana kept fighting their campaign to take Dog.

"Only think how he would entertain the children," Georgiana said.

"And he would love all that time outdoors, with all those people..." Michael added.

Lizzie nodded. "And all those silk dresses and all that food, all those tiny children to knock over and terrify, all those flowerbeds to dig up..."

"We could tie him up," Henrietta suggested, eager as always to keep the peace. After all, Lady Braithwaite had been willing to include the animal. It was Henrietta who had advised against it.

"No," Lizzie said firmly. "This time, he really *has* to be left behind. Misha will look after him until we come back. It will only be a few hours."

Both she and Vanya were adamant, and Henrietta had to agree that kind Lady Braithwaite did not deserve the carnage that would inevitably follow Dog. She had been right in the first place to discourage it. In fact, the issue only tugged at the fringes of her awareness. Most of her was in turmoil because she knew the entire Vale clan was expected to be at the party.

She suspected Michael and Georgiana wanted Dog there to show off to the Vale twins, of whom they had heard but surprisingly never met. Henrietta sympathized. She both yearned and feared to meet Aubrey again.

She knew he was something of a rake. He had probably already forgotten the amazing kiss that had so turned her inside out. She had thought of little else, even dreamed of it, and now lived with constant butterflies in her stomach.

He was so erratic, on one encounter so attentive, on the next barely noticing her. Yet her resolve to forget him never quite worked. Perhaps because on some level deeper and quieter than the churning delight of his kisses, he *fascinated* her. The illness he had largely overcome, his troubled spirit, his joy in life that was so beguiling and spoke to her own. She had never met anyone so full of contradictions and surprises.

Most astonishing of all was the moment she realized she was gazing anxiously into her bedchamber mirror to see if she looked her best, if her hair and her gown were becoming enough.

Jolted, she whisked herself away.

What was the matter with her? She had always taken her looks for granted. In the last few months, she would even have masked them if she could. She had certainly never taken any care beyond tidiness.

Even her gowns were largely chosen by her siblings. And now... Was she actually *trying* to be beautiful for Aubrey?

Aubrey, with whom she had shared her hatred of the effect of her beauty, her humiliation that no one ever saw or heard anything more about her. Or wanted to.

What is the matter with me? Is it just because he is the only man who has not fallen instantly at my feet? Because I know that if I crook my little finger, any man I know will run to my side. Except him.

A lowering thought, a flabbergasting one. And yet as they squashed into the hired carriage for their journey up to the castle, her heart beat and beat with anticipation and a kind of delicious excitement she had never known before. Perhaps because there had never before been a man she wanted by her side...

Foolish. I barely know him.

She saw him almost at once. Georgiana and Michael had already been swept away with other children, while Lizzie and Vanya were walking around the building, Vanya enthusing about its military strengths. Henrietta was chatting with the earl's sisters when Aubrey sauntered out of the castle into the gardens.

Her stomach lurched. She didn't know why, and didn't much care, so busy was she assuring herself that he would ignore her and that she did not care. And indeed, he seemed to be heading for the noisy game of pall-mall on the lawn before she forced herself not to look.

Even so, from the corner of her eye she saw him swerve suddenly in her direction. Clearly he had already greeted the earl's sisters that afternoon, for he only smiled at them before speaking directly to Henrietta.

"Miss Gaunt! I thought you must be here when I saw Launceton manning the battlements. Would you care to play pall-mall?"

She grasped the suggestion with relief. "Why, yes, I would!" It seemed such an unthreatening pastime that she was glad to walk beside him, even to take his arm, for her fingers did not tremble.

Until he said, low, "I think of you all the time. I even dream about you."

"No you don't."

He blinked at her instant denial of such fustian, but he didn't seem to be angry. In fact, a definite glint of amusement sparked in his eyes. "I assure you I do. When may I kiss you again?"

God help me. This was bluntness with a vengeance.

"You may not," she said firmly.

"Not even if you win at pall-mall?" he teased.

"Not even if *you* win at pall-mall."

"You are afraid to wager your skill?"

"Since I would lose either way, yes I am."

He leaned closer, his lips almost tickling her ear. Her skin tingled and she forgot to breathe. "I can promise you would not lose."

She hoped her blush was hidden beneath her hat brim. A large, noisy game was in progress in one row of hoops, but with a few waves to participants, Aubrey picked up a couple of mallets and strolled on to another empty row close by.

To her relief—at least, she thought it was relief—he left off flirting in order to play. She had encountered men who used such opportunities to come too close, to pretend to be guiding her to a better shot. Aubrey did nothing like that. He played with a joyous sense of fun rather than competition. He laughed when either of them missed, cheered when they hit a good shot, and after a while, their game got tangled up with the larger game, with hilarious results.

Before they had even finished, the inevitable rain began. Aubrey seized her hand and, with everyone else, they ran for the cover of the castle's great hall. It stirred memories of childhood, playing in the rain, running with her siblings and dogs—a sense of uncomplicated happiness that was gone forever.

She *was* happy as they erupted into the castle, laughing. But it was highly complicated by complex adult emotions and uncertainties and the delicious, wicked stirrings of her body.

Warned by the atrocious summer weather up until now, the countess had clearly planned for rain, and most of the entertainments were indoors. Presenting Henrietta with a glass of champagne, Aubrey said, "Do you care for poetry? Paintings?"

"Both. Is not Simon Sacheverill meant to be here?"

"I believe he cried off, but Lady Helen will read the poems instead."

Lady Helen read them so beautifully that emotion took Henrietta by surprise. The pain of the poet's lost love made her throat ache and her eyes fill. She had to stare straight ahead and was aware of Aubrey watching her.

She smiled with deliberate carelessness. "I believe I shall go and look at some paintings."

Aubrey accompanied her quite naturally, without asking. Did he truly like her company? Or was this some rakish wager, whether with others of his ilk or with himself?

The paintings were upstairs in the gallery that ran around the great hall on three sides, the main attractions being paintings by the fashionable artist Lord Tamar—who was, in fact, the Earl of Braithwaite's brother-in-law. Henrietta had seen his work before, in London, and loved the depth of emotion he somehow created, whether in portraits or landscapes, beauty or ugliness.

A slightly tousled man sat on a stool at the end of the gallery, observing her. He had a sketchbook open on his knee but seemed to be doing nothing with it. Instead, all his attention was fixed on Henrietta.

Seeing that she noticed, he smiled, quite without embarrassment, and Henrietta moved hastily away.

"Look at these," Aubrey said. "Watercolors by Lady Helen."

"They're beautiful," Henrietta said after a few awed moments. "She has a wonderful talent. I so envy her that."

"Watercolors are not your strength?"

She wrinkled her nose. "I don't have a strength. Lady Alice plays the pianoforte as well as any professional musician I heard in Vienna. Helen paints like this... I so admire them."

"You never did tell me your ambition," he said.

She shrugged. "I don't have one. My old one was naïve and childish, and I have no talent or desire to take its place."

His expression changed. "You wanted a husband and family."

Appalled to have been found out, she blushed furiously. "It's what all girls are trained for. I accepted it far more wholeheartedly than Lizzie did."

"And yet Lizzie is a wife and mother."

Henrietta smiled. "Yes, but they have adventures. She has an adventurous soul."

"Don't you?"

She considered, and then, remembering her childhood, and then Vienna and Russia, she laughed. "Perhaps I used to. Now, I feel it bound and shriveled."

"Then we must free it. Let us plan."

The man at the end of the gallery was no longer staring at her but at his sketchbook while his fingers gripped a length of charcoal and flew across the page.

"You are Miss Gaunt," he said without looking up.

Henrietta paused, glancing at him uncertainly. "I am. Have we met?"

"No... But we have the same surname. I wonder if we are related?" He dropped the charcoal into his pocket and looked up at last. He even stood, grasping the sketchbook in one hand. "I'm Tamar. Otherwise, Rupert Gaunt."

Henrietta, liking his informality, found herself offering her hand, which Lord Tamar bowed over with careless gallantry. "Henrietta Gaunt. And this is Mr. Aubrey Vale."

"Ah, another Vale. I've met some of your siblings." Tamar shook hands with equal friendliness. "So are we related, Miss Gaunt? I confess, the family genealogy is lost to me—physically lost, I mean. Bad blood in our branch, I'm afraid. But someone said you are the Launceton Gaunts."

"Yes, we are." She frowned. "And actually, now you mention it, I believe there *was* some distant connection to Tamar, many generations ago. Lizzie, my sister, might recall it. Or my other sister, Georgiana—she studies such matters."

"Then I look forward to meeting them," Lord Tamar said. "How does Lord Launceton fit into all this?"

"Oh, he is a distant cousin who inherited the title and estate. His grandfather was the family black sheep who ended up in Russia and made his fortune there. We met him by accident in Vienna, and he married Lizzie. Which worked out very well."

"Vienna, eh? I don't suppose you met *her* in Vienna?" He swiveled and pointed at the portrait of a dark, enigmatic young lady who seemed to blend into the background at first glance but, at the second, never could.

Memory stirred. "Actually, yes! Madame de Delon! She is French, is she not?"

"Well, her husband is. She is my sister." He sounded distracted, and brought up his sketchbook once more. "It will have to do. I couldn't quite catch you." He tore out a page and handed it to her. "Would you sit for me some time?"

"Oh, no," she said, appalled.

"Tell you what, I'll ask Lord Launceton, shall I? I don't suppose you'd care to introduce us?"

"Well, I will if you like," Henrietta said. "But I still don't want to be painted. Not even by you."

"Take your time to decide," he said. He glanced at Aubrey with a rather charming, apologetic grin. "Sorry to steal her away. Privilege of rank. Or at least brazen impudence."

Aubrey's grin was slightly crooked, but he stood aside and bowed with a mock flourish. On impulse, Henrietta held out the sketch to him. She still had not looked at it. He took it from her wordlessly, and then she walked away with Lord Tamar in search of Vanya.

Chapter Nine

Henrietta glimpsed Vanya in the hall, laughing at something Major Vale said to him. A moment later, he sauntered outside. Henrietta tugged the eccentric marquis after him. Aubrey's friend, Lord Tranmere, in conversation with a group of people she didn't know, ogled her shamelessly as she walked past. She pretended not to see him.

"Vanya!" she called once they were in the open, and her brother-in-law, who was striding across the lawn in the direction of some small boys playing football, swung around and came back to them. Tamar tensed, as though determined to get some duty over with.

"My brother-in-law, Lord Launceton," Henrietta said formally. "Vanya, this is Lord Tamar, the artist. Madame de Delon is his sister." She took a half step back, as though leaving them alone, but curiosity kept her from moving further away.

"Intriguing lady," Vanya said as the two men shook hands. "Elusive."

"Sounds like Anna. I had a cryptic letter from her yesterday." Lord Tamar smiled crookedly. "I can count the number of letters she has ever written to me on one hand, so when I receive one, I pay attention. Thing is, she mentioned you."

"Me?" Vanya said in surprise. "Why?"

Lord Tamar looked awkward for an instant. "She knew I was coming to Blackhaven and had heard a whisper that a few unsavory characters were heading this way. And that if you also turned up in Blackhaven, I should warn you to stay away from Frenchmen."

Vanya blinked. His lips twitched. "It would have been sound advice a few years ago. Perhaps your letter was delayed."

"I know it sounds foolish," Tamar said ruefully. "Thing is, Anna *isn't* a fool, and if she took the trouble to warn you, you should heed it."

"How can I if I don't know what it's about?"

"Old Bonapartists," Tamar muttered. "Fanatics who won't give up. And something to do with Russia. You've been there, have you not?"

"Yes." Vanya tugged one ear. "In fact, up until a year ago, I regarded myself as entirely Russian. Now, I am half English. Why would Bonapartists come after me? I was colonel of a ragtag Cossack regiment. I never had any influence."

"There, you have me. But you look to me like the kind of man people notice. So don't dismiss the warning. And call on me if you need help."

In other circumstances, Henrietta might have been delighted to realize she had been ignored for the length of this discussion. Now, unease coiling in her stomach, she took herself off before they noticed her.

Since the shower had stopped, she walked across the terrace toward the lawn, where she ran into Michael and Georgiana with a pair of obvious siblings of around Michael's age.

"Henri, these are the Vale twins, who are eager to meet you," Georgi said happily. "Leona and Lawrence."

"How do you do?" Henrietta said, eyeing them with as much curiosity as they exhibited toward her. "Though I'm sure Georgi exaggerates your eagerness!"

"Oh no," Leona said. "You're Aubrey's friend, aren't you?"

Annoyingly, Henrietta felt heat seep into her face. "I hope so. But then, your brother has many friends."

"Not like you," Lawrence said.

Somehow, Henrietta found herself walking between the twins.

"He needs true friends," Leona added. "He has had a rather lonely life until now."

"Because of his illness," Henrietta said. "So I gathered."

"He is not ill anymore," Leona said. "In fact, he has so much energy now, he doesn't know what to do with himself. He's a bit...*wild*."

"But he isn't a true rakehell," Lawrence said. "He isn't selfish enough. He pays attention to people."

"He does seem to," Henrietta said. When he wasn't ignoring her. "Are you trying to convince me to like him?"

Unabashed, they flashed her grins that were startlingly alike.

"Do we need to?" asked Leona, steering her in a particular direction.

"No," Henrietta said honestly.

"Do you know our sister Lucy?" Lawrence asked.

"I believe I met her once, but I don't believe I—"

"This is Lucy."

Henrietta blinked at the young lady before her. She was about Henrietta's own age and seemed vaguely distraught, though she summoned a bright smile.

"She is a friend of Aubrey's," Leona said, fixing her sister with an intense gaze.

"Of course she is," Lucy said wryly. For an instant, her distracted eyes cleared as they looked into Henrietta's. Another, more natural smile dawned. "I'm very pleased to meet you. Excuse me..."

"She likes you," Lawrence observed. "Will you please excuse us? We need to see to something else..."

As the twins ran off back in the direction of the castle, Henrietta felt bemused. "What just happened?"

"Apparently Lucy can tell a person's character immediately," Georgiana said. "She seemed to like you. Aren't the twins funny?"

"I don't know. Were they *testing* me?"

"They're worried about Aubrey," Michael said. "I think it's going to rain again. Let's go back to the castle."

AUBREY, ABANDONED WITH a mere sketch of Henrietta, glanced down at it idly, then blinked, regarding it more carefully.

Tamar had caught her beauty, whatever it was that turned a mere collection of pleasing, regular features into loveliness. And yet that beauty was somehow secondary. The way she held her head, her distracted gaze, the implied movement of her hands—all lent her a look of restless loneliness behind her smile. Though her smile was real enough. He wished he'd inspired the smile. He wished he could assuage whatever unhappiness Tamar had somehow seen in her, because the man was right. It was definitely there.

But she smiled. She smiled *at* him. She had kissed him back the other night with such passionate sweetness that he'd had to run to preserve her safety. Or his.

Henrietta was looming too large in his life. He should run.

"Mr. Vale," said a light voice beside him.

He glanced up and beheld Henrietta's sister, Lady Launceton. He bowed. "My lady. What do you think of this? Lord Tamar just dashed it off while we were admiring his paintings."

Lady Launceton took it from him, her eyes widening. "Goodness. He has caught something of her, has he not?"

"He wants her to sit for a proper painting. She is not keen."

"No, she wouldn't be," Lady Launceton said ruefully.

In silent agreement, they had begun to walk together toward the staircase.

"Why is that?" he asked. "It's as if she hates to be reminded of her own beauty. A trait I have never encountered before."

"Some of it is my fault," Lady Launceton admitted. "You see, she was always lovely, even as a child, and as she grew, everyone teased her that she would make a brilliant match. And then, when my father died and we were left penniless, this brilliant match became a serious plan. We all took it for granted, even Henrietta, who was quite content—proud, even—to save the family in such a way."

At the bottom of the stairs, Aubrey lifted two glasses of wine from the table and presented her with one of them.

"Of course, life moved on. I married Vanya and Henrietta's brilliant match was no longer required. Don't scowl at me—I know we were naïve in the first place. But in our original plan, our rich suitor would have fallen in love with Henrietta, and she with him. For she is extremely sweet-natured, and after all, who would *not* fall in love with her?"

Lady Launceton sighed and sat down, and Aubrey, fascinated, joined her. In the background, a pianist was playing a rather wonderful piece of music he did not recognize. But he was more fascinated by Lady Launceton's tale.

"The damage was done," she said. "Men could not help staring at her, courting her to the extent that even she noticed and grew uncomfortable."

"And blamed the discomfort and the rude stares on her beauty," Aubrey said, frowning. "No wonder she feels so…*invisible*."

"And she is right in many cases. Much of the world truly is that shallow. We are all judged on our appearance, no one more so than Henrietta, whom men desire and women hate because she casts them all in the shade."

Aubrey shook his head in impatient denial.

"Please," Lady Launceton said dryly. "Tell me you did not approach us at the ball simply because Henrietta was the most beautiful woman you had ever seen?"

"I did," he agreed. "It is undeniably part of her, but it's not what keeps…"

A smile flickered in Lady Launceton's eyes. "What keeps you coming back?"

He felt heat rise to his cheeks. He remembered Vanya's warning and no longer knew whether or not to be angry. "She has everything out of proportion."

"Yes. Perhaps you can help with that."

"Perhaps." He shifted restlessly and sipped his wine. Lady Launceton had a beguiling manner and a vital beauty of her own. "Tell me about Vienna," he said.

Five minutes later, he was laughing with delight when Lord Launceton walked into the hall and fixed him with a look of such steel that the smile died on Aubrey's lips.

AFTER THE MUSICAL recitals—at which Lady Alice, the earl's sister, dazzled—there was an invasion of children and young people, among whom Aubrey glimpsed the twins with Henrietta's little brother and sister. They spared him a grin as they led a raiding party upstairs. Clearly, mischief was his only worry there, but by then the rest of his siblings were bothering him. Delilah was worried, Lucy was flirting atrociously, Julius had turned cold once more as though he'd had enough of life, and Roderick looked ripe for trouble.

Obsessed with his own life, he had been oblivious to theirs. Now he felt both guilty and uneasy. It was past time he got over the selfishness of the invalid.

After tea, there was dancing. He was waltzing with Diane de Corentin before he saw Henrietta again. Tranmere had accosted her, damn him, and was standing too close to her. She did not appear to notice, merely walked with him to join the dancers. When she caught sight of Aubrey, her lips curved into a quick, spontaneous smile before she twirled out of his vision.

"She draws all eyes, does she not?" Diane said lightly. "It strikes me a man would never be at peace with a wife quite that beautiful."

"Jealousy, you mean?" Aubrey said, having just discovered with some shock that he was not immune to that ugly emotion. "Why should beauty make a woman more likely to stray?"

"Because she is offered more temptation," Diane said cynically. "Just as you are offered more temptation than, say, that gentleman with the bulbous nose."

Aubrey batted his eyelashes. "You mean I am beautiful?"

She laughed. "In your own way."

"So are you," he said, "in all ways."

"Liar. I am merely passable, but I know how to please a man and make him comfortable."

He regarded her. "Do you know, I have never thought of you as comfortable?"

"But you are comfortable in my company."

"That is true. And you in mine. We are friends."

"We are."

Was this a mutual acknowledgement that the flirting was over? It was for Aubrey—had been, really, since the night of the ball when he met Henrietta. But he liked Diane and was glad of her friendship.

Still, it seemed nothing could compare to the glow in his heart when Henrietta all but rushed at him as soon as the dance had ended.

"I want to talk to you," she said bluntly, and took his arm before he even got around to offering it.

※

DIANE WATCHED HIM go, a wry smile inside her. She no longer felt quite so certain of winning him in the end. She had cause to know that Henrietta's beauty was more than skin deep, and Aubrey, while he might be ruled by his nether regions as much as any man, was observant enough to recognize that. Henrietta was a rare and unbeatable rival, and Diane could not even dislike her. She could only wait and hope that Henrietta would dismiss him.

"Bereft, Miss de Corentin?"

She glanced up to find Lord Maynard at her side. She hadn't expected him to be present. "No more than you, my lord. I gather you could not stay away—another moth to the flame of Miss Gaunt's beauty."

"She is exquisite."

"She is." Diane eyed him curiously. "Is that why you want her? To add to your collection?"

His eyes froze over. "I find you impudent."

"You find me honest, which is why I tell you she will never sit in your display cabinet."

"Now I find you offensive."

"Do you? I find you obsessive, unobservant, and rather obvious."

His nostrils flared. For once, she had his full attention, though he said nothing. She liked that he did not even try to bluster.

"Still," she said, "it is possible we might be able to help each other. If you take the trouble to actually listen to her—try closing your eyes so that you are not distracted by her face—she might look at you afresh. Try to interest *her*. A novel concept, I know, but believe me, it works wonders on many women. I might even drop a few words in your favor."

"And in return? You believe Aubrey Vale will give up on the unattainable and turn to you?"

She shrugged. "It is not unlikely. At the moment, I doubt he is even thinking of marriage."

"Only about…shall we say, *gratification*?"

"Precisely."

"And you are content with that?" he asked, frowning.

"Oh, there is much more to Aubrey than that," she said, annoyed to be defending him. "Leave me to concentrate on him. You turn your *full* attention to Henrietta, or you will never stand a chance with her."

⁂

HENRIETTA, AFTER A long walk on her own, had come to the conclusion that Vanya's danger, as reported by Lord Tamar, was not something she should discuss with Lizzie. Nor could she involve her younger siblings in something so dangerous.

Just why Aubrey should be the right person to talk to, she didn't know, but instinct said so. She did not even mind taking him from Diane with no more than a smile, for she knew now that Diane did not love him. She was too detached.

As soon as Henrietta and Aubrey were outside in the fresh air, she poured out what Tamar had told Vanya.

Aubrey listened without interruption and, when she had finished, scratched his head in a thoughtful kind of way. "I can see it worries you, but I wouldn't let it. Vanya seems to me the kind of man who can take care of himself. He fought some of the most arduous campaigns of the war and came out of Waterloo relatively unscathed. Dash it, he even wears his sword in public. If ever a man was prepared—"

"Yes, but that was *war*," she interrupted. "He only wears the sword now to annoy English people who consider him a barbaric foreigner. Vanya is reckless by nature and would never give in to some vague threat, especially not one reported thirdhand via a woman he hardly knows."

"That's another point. How would Tamar's sister know such a thing?"

"Her husband is French. He was with the Prince de Talleyrand in

Vienna. You might think the threat is silly nonsense—I'm pretty sure that's what Vanya thinks—but what if it isn't?"

He met her gaze. "It truly bothers you."

"Lizzie would be devastated if Vanya died. We all would."

"I'd like to tell you it's nothing and not to worry," Aubrey said slowly. "Though that never helps anyone, does it? The only French people I know in Blackhaven are Monsieur de Corentin and Diane. And I did once come across him in the tavern, speaking French to another man. He gave him something. Letters of some kind."

She frowned. "The tavern where you and Vanya got into a brawl?"

"That's the one. Horrid place, really. I wondered at the time what a refined gentleman like Corentin was doing there. He didn't look quite so refined at the time, which was why I pretended not to see him."

"Did he see you?"

"He might have done. I was with Tranmere and a few others, but he left before we did. I wish I'd kept a closer eye on the other Frenchman. But Corentin is an émigré, been here for ages. He lost everything in the revolution. I can't imagine his being a Bonapartist."

"We only believe he lost everything in the revolution because he told us so," Henrietta pointed out. She halted, her eyes widening. "And actually, Tamar never said this Bonapartist was a man. What if it is Diane?"

"She definitely wasn't in the tavern," Aubrey said flippantly.

"Which is the only place Bonapartist assassins frequent?"

"Clearly. To be honest, I cannot imagine either Corentin in such a role."

"No," Henrietta agreed, walking on. "But there is something odd there. Corentin's son died in the Russian campaign, during the retreat from Moscow."

"So the son fought for Bonaparte? That *is* odd."

Henrietta nodded. "According to Diane, she and her father fled when she was small. Her mother and brother were elsewhere in France at the time and were prevented from escaping. In time, I suppose Gaspard—Diane's brother—would just have done what he saw as his duty and fought for his country. As Vanya did for his. But Gaspard is a link to him."

She swung around to Aubrey once more. "Vanya will never talk to me about what he did in the war, but perhaps you could ask questions, see if he ever came across Gaspard?"

"Hmm. Not sure he's speaking to me."

She blinked. "Vanya? Why not?"

"He's afraid I'll seduce you."

Her face burned, but she would not allow mere words to overwhelm her. She met his gaze. "Would you?"

His eyes seemed to have darkened, intensified, and yet something glinted there too—little imps of mischief. Or desire. "Would you like me to?"

"No. Then Vanya really would kill you."

"I might kill him," Aubrey countered, "and then we could all run away together."

"Including Lizzie and the children and Dog? None of them would speak to you again if you killed Vanya. Neither would I."

"Poor seduction technique, then. I would settle for a kiss."

"You are more likely to win a punch in the nose."

He sighed ostentatiously. "Vanya again."

"No, me."

His eyes kindled with fresh delight. "Shall I teach you how?"

"I already know how. Michael taught me years ago."

He let out a shout of laughter, which turned a few heads in their direction. "Then we must have a sparring contest one day."

He halted suddenly by an ancient oak tree, and she realized with a leaping heart that they were now hidden from those gathered on the terrace. He could take her in his arms. He could kiss her unseen. The very thought turned her insides to liquid.

His eyes were full of laughter—strangely tender laughter that sent the butterflies in her stomach soaring. He lifted her gloved hand to his lips and kissed her knuckles. His mouth lingered too long, even by foreign standards. His breath was hot, seeping through the fine cotton fabric to her tingling skin. She forgot to breathe.

"One day, Henrietta," he said with odd huskiness. "One day."

He replaced her hand on his arm and strolled on, away from the tree's dangerous protection, leaving her to wonder, among other things, whether *one day* referred to the sparring contest, the kiss, or the seduction.

At that moment, she was afraid she would have welcomed any or all of them.

Chapter Ten

"I THOUGHT," LIZZIE said to her husband as she prepared for bed that evening, "that we might invite some of the Vales for dinner."

Vanya, in his shirt sleeves, was prowling restlessly about the room, but stopped to gaze at her without warmth. "Which Vales?"

"Well, the twins to begin with. Michael and Georgiana have never agreed on anything in their lives before, but they both agree the Vale twins are wonderful. We could all dine together for once, if we just have Aubrey and Roderick, who is—"

"What do we want Aubrey for?" Vanya snapped, scowling.

Lizzie blinked in the looking glass as she picked up her hairbrush. "Henrietta, largely."

"Henrietta?" he demanded in frank disbelief.

"Yes, I believe she actually likes him, and he seems rather sweet—in a slightly dangerous kind of a way."

"You liked that in me when we first met."

She laughed. "Perhaps. Why do you look so ferocious? I thought Aubrey was a friend of yours? He and Roderick both."

"Roderick can come," Vanya said generously. His turbulent gaze met Lizzie's in the mirror, and he moved toward her with some purpose. "Damn it, bring Aubrey too." The rest of his words were muffled as he buried his mouth in her hair, her throat, and then her lips. But they sounded like, "At least I can keep the rat in sight."

Lizzie opened her mouth to pursue this oddity, but Vanya was so intent upon seduction that she was enchanted and forgot everything else.

ONCE AGAIN, HENRIETTA was piqued by Aubrey's failure to call the day after the garden party. They had agreed they would investigate Corentin and his mysterious French contact together as a matter of urgency, and yet he did not even turn up to talk about it.

Michael and Georgiana, returning from walking Dog on the beach, gave her some clue as to Aubrey's distraction.

"The twins were helping recue Mrs. Macy from pirates! Georgi exclaimed.

"Smugglers," Michael corrected her. "Mrs. Macy is engaged to Sir Julius Vale, and all of them piled down to the harbor—along with half the town—to make sure she and Sir Julius came home safely. They're all at the hotel now, having a tea party to celebrate the engagement."

Grudgingly, Henrietta forgave Aubrey his failure. But the following morning, leaving Michael and Georgiana in charge of Dog on the beach, she slipped away to call on Diane de Corentin.

Diane herself opened the cottage door. If she was embarrassed to have no servant for such a task, she did not show it, merely invited Henrietta inside.

Voices drifted from the parlor on the left, where Diane led her guest. By then, Henrietta had recognized Aubrey's voice with a hint of both panic and pleasure. Had he begun their investigation already? Or was he here simply here for Diane?

Both gentlemen rose as she entered the room and bowed, looking politely pleased to see her.

"They have just been abusing your brother-in-law," Diane said with a hint of malice. "Since he appears to have taken a dislike to Aubrey."

"Don't be silly," Henrietta told Aubrey. "If he disliked you, why would he invite you to dinner?"

"To do away with me," Aubrey said, showing so little surprise that Henrietta assumed he had already received Lizzie's invitation.

"Indeed, who could blame him?" Henrietta said, and Diane laughed.

Talk was general while Diane went to "arrange" tea. Everyone knew she would make it herself, but Henrietta allowed the girl her pride by squashing her instinct to help. Once Diane returned with the tea, Henrietta found herself seated beside Corentin, leaving Diane free to talk quietly with Aubrey.

Henrietta disliked the sting of jealousy. They were too comfortable together. Beside Diane, he must find her a naïve bore.

But she was not here for such trivial reasons.

When opportunity arose, she said to Corentin, "Do you think you will ever go home to France? Now that the king is restored?"

"My home has been here for so long that France would seem strange to me now. Besides, the king is in no hurry to return my lands. At least here I can earn a pittance teaching French to children."

"You could always teach English to French children."

He smiled. "Perhaps I could. What of your family? Will you stay here or remove to Russia?"

"Vanya wants to do both. Live half the year in Russia and the rest here, but who knows how this will work out now there is little Jack and the new baby to consider? Russia is certainly a fascinating country, is it not?"

"I have never been," Corentin said.

"Indeed, you have no cause to. Do you have many friends in similar situations to you? Have they returned to France?"

"Some have. Some have not," Corentin said, and then changed the subject. There was no more she could ask without arousing suspicion, as she told Aubrey when they finally left together.

"No, and our theory is probably entirely wrong anyway. He betrayed no animosity toward your brother-in-law, even when I led the way, abusing him quite freely. On the other hand, he was about to speak about his son's death in Russia when you arrived and distracted him."

"Then you should have kept our agreement and told me what you were doing," she retorted.

"Why, what are you doing?" he asked, his eyes smiling as she marched toward the beach.

"I am going back to the beach to find my brother and sister."

"And Dog?"

"I hope so, or there will be trouble. You need not come."

"But it is my ambition to make better friends with Dog before I dine with you tomorrow evening. Alas, Roderick is away from home on some matters of business, and he will not be back in time, but the twins and I are delighted to accept."

She nodded as if it made little difference to her life. "I believe the twins met Dog yesterday and were suitably impressed. Oh, and pass on our congratulations and good wishes to Sir Julius. I've always liked Mrs. Macy and her scamp of a son."

"It's funny—I've never seen Julius so happy. The twins were right."

"About what?"

"Oh, they always have plans and schemes," he said vaguely.

"What is their plan for you?"

"God knows. I like to think I'd foil it, but I suspect I have as little chance as anyone else."

They had reached the harbor, and Aubrey was examining each ship and boat tied up there.

"What are you looking for?" she murmured. "French vessels?

Would they not be a little obvious?"

He shrugged. "We are no longer at war with France. But I agree, the route is more likely to be a secret one, such as the brandy smugglers use. And Julius's gun smugglers who tried to take Mrs. Macy yesterday. Shall we walk along the beach? There are smugglers' coves—and caves—all the way along the coast. That's how Julius discovered the arms."

By the time she had heard that exciting story, they were at Black Cove, happily investigating rocks and little caves half hidden in the cliffside.

"I can't really see Monsieur de Corentin climbing in here to hide weapons with which to murder your poor Launceton," Aubrey said, backing out of a hollow and sitting down on the rock beside Henrietta. "We should think about this. Was the warning from some organized group of Bonapartists? Or one man set on his own revenge?"

"I could more easily believe in the latter," Henrietta said. "Though even that seems unlikely in his company. But if he is alone in the matter, who is the other Frenchman you saw him with?"

Aubrey shrugged. "Perhaps just some old friend fallen on hard times, an old servant, even, who now makes his way as a seaman."

Henrietta nodded, then frowned suddenly. "He is a subtle man, is he not? Like the Prince de Talleyrand."

Aubrey considered. "I never met the prince, but certainly, I would say Corentin is subtle. So is Diane."

Henrietta gazed out to sea, letting her conflicting loyalties fight.

"Diane does not love you."

He looked neither surprised nor devastated. Instead, he turned his head toward her, his gaze curious. "I know. Her standards have dropped. A younger son with no prospects but a supportive family is better than destitution."

"You don't mind?"

His lips tugged into an unhappy smile. "I don't love her either. I like her, though. I would hate to discover she was working against us, even to the extent of revenge for her brother."

"I don't believe it is Diane," Henrietta said. "She does not even remember her brother. If anything, she is jealous of her father's affection for him." She turned her head to look at Aubrey. "Did you ever mean to marry her?"

"No. I'm merely an unhelpful distraction, aren't I? I should stay out of her way." He moved suddenly, catching her gaze. "I should stay out of yours too."

"Oh, you are quite safe with me," Henrietta said, jumping up just a little too quickly. "I don't want to be married either."

The words were a matter of pride, but only when she said them did she realize the magnitude of the lie. He already knew her early, childish wish for a husband and children to love. The more adult complications of acquiring them might have made her wary of men and marriage, but Aubrey...

Her mind, her awareness, were suddenly full of Aubrey, the way he talked and laughed, the feel of his mouth on hers, the touch of his body, the urgent grace of his movements, the way his eyes danced and teased, his sheer hunger for life mixed with odd moments of vulnerability...

How would it be to be married to such a man?

There is only one such man...

Her imagination took flight. To live with him, love with him, share his bed and his life, his ambitions, successes, and failures, bring him comfort in bad times and receive her own... Such intimacy, such excitement and joy and...

He was not walking beside her. She realized she had rather bolted from the rock, striding back along the beach toward the town, and he was letting her go alone.

Well, it hardly mattered. She was perfectly capable of going alone, and in any case, she had no idea how to face him now. But she was afraid she had repelled him by saying the wrong thing, fleeing from him for no reason.

She wasn't fleeing from him. She just could not be still while all these images and feelings washed over her. And now, with the salt breeze whipping strands of her hair from its pins, the rush of the sea filling her ears, and the seagulls crying above, she missed him.

She wanted to weep, though she had no reason except the emotions bursting inside her.

At first, she thought she merely imagined him walking at her side. But no, he was real. She caught the faint scent of his soap. His arm brushed against hers. And then his fingers closed around her hand. Like happiness.

She gasped into the wind, and he pulled her behind a ridge of rock for privacy, for they were nearing the town now and there were more people who might have seen them.

"You're safe with me, too," he whispered, His hand, still holding hers, was at her back. His other cupped her cheek. "I won't hurt you." And then his face blotted out the sky as his mouth took hers and everything in her leapt and soared.

His thumb stroked her cheek. "Your face is wet," he said unsteadily.

"It's raining."

"No it isn't." He kissed the foolish tears from her skin, then returned to her lips, and she grasped his hair in wonder, stroking and tangling.

I love you, Aubrey Vale. I love you...

But they could not linger here, where anyone might see them in so shocking a pose. They drew apart, and she took his arm more decorously as they walked on toward the town.

In all her excitement, she had almost forgotten Vanya's danger. Until a roughly dressed sailor sprang up the harbor steps in front of them and strode off in the direction of the market.

"That's him!" Aubrey exclaimed.

"Who?"

"The other Frenchman from the tavern."

"Are you sure?"

He didn't answer. He was peering over the harbor wall to see which vessel had brought the Frenchman ashore. "He came in a small rowing boat, I think. Come on, we don't want to lose him."

Excited now for a different reason, she hurried with him across the quay after their quarry.

"He's probably gone back to the tavern," Henrietta said when there was no sign of him around the market stalls.

Aubrey cast the tavern a glance she could not quite read. "Last resort. Let's see if we can find him further on."

A few minutes later, they were rewarded by a glimpse of him in the high street. When he turned right past the theater and seemed to double back toward the sea, Henrietta began to feel uneasy.

"He's going toward your house," Aubrey said.

"I need to go home," she blurted. "He's after Vanya."

"He can't just storm in and attack him," Aubrey said reasonably. "If he tried, I'm fairly sure he'd come out in pieces, if at all. Besides, we don't even know if Launceton is at home. Do you know his plans?"

"They were going for a walk with the baby, but I don't know if they've left yet. Oh, Aubrey, what if he lies in wait for them?"

"He's gone into the back lane," Aubrey observed. "I think he's reconnoitering."

"Miss Gaunt, well met," said a totally unexpected voice behind them.

Lord Maynard.

Henrietta turned, inclining her head civilly. "My lord. I believe you know Mr. Aubrey Vale."

The two men exchanged distant acknowledgements.

"I was on my way to call on your family," Maynard said. "Allow me to escort you."

Henrietta was about to point out that she already had an escort when Aubrey swiped the metaphorical carpet from under her feet.

"Very kind of you," he said, removing Henrietta's hand from his sleeve and placing it on Maynard's instead.

Speechless, she glared at Aubrey.

"I have an urgent appointment," he said apologetically. "And I believe we may trust his lordship to see you safely home."

Surely there was significance in his words... Maynard was her protection, while Aubrey's urgent appointment was no doubt with the French sailor now skulking in the back lane. Nevertheless, being palmed off on Maynard felt like a betrayal as well as an annoyance. She would far rather have gone in pursuit of their quarry.

However, she could hardly say so without making an absurd fuss. She contented herself with a contemptuous sniff in Aubrey's direction and a cold "Good day, sir," before stalking off with Maynard. Who looked inordinately pleased with himself.

Chapter Eleven

IT WAS AN undeniable wrench for Aubrey to abandon Henrietta to Maynard, not only because he knew the man distressed her, but because the claws of mindless jealousy were digging into his ribs. Nor did he care for the glare of mingled hurt and outrage she threw at him as she went.

On the other hand, he needed to see what the Frenchman was up to, and he did not want Henrietta going into his vicinity alone.

Accordingly, he strode away from them and slipped into the mews lane, striding along as if he had every right to be there. And indeed, it was a local shortcut to the inn, avoiding as it did the wide bend down to the sea.

Keeping all his senses alert, he looked constantly around him for signs of his quarry or any other danger. If he was honest, he had not truly given much credence to the warning from Tamar's sister, let alone to the theory that Corentin was conspiring to harm Lord Launceton. Until this sailor, or whatever he was, had turned into this lane.

Now he was uneasy in the extreme.

There was no sign of the sailor ahead, but there was a comforting number of other people around, maids and grooms gossiping, two women with baskets hurrying along toward the inn, a saddled horse being led round to the street, an open carriage being pushed under cover, gardeners hard at work.

Although he glanced into all the gardens he could, he paused at the Launcetons' gate for a longer look. There was no sign of Dog today, nor Henrietta's siblings. The sound of sweeping reached his ears, so he moved on to the next garden—and there was his Frenchman, head down, sweeping mud and earth off the path to the main house and the outhouses.

Aubrey walked on without pause, as though uninterested. Had he got it wrong? Was the man merely doing odd jobs? Or even employed by this householder? Or was he pretending in order to keep watch on Launceton's house and movements?

A little further on, Aubrey paused to talk to a pretty maidservant, going through the motions of flirtation while he watched to see if the Frenchman would emerge from the garden.

He didn't. And when the maid reluctantly scuttled back to her duties, Aubrey walked on to the end of the lane. He then strode all the way around Graham Gardens and entered the lane again. It had begun to rain, and the people he had seen before were mostly gone. The Launcetons' garden was still empty. And now so was the one next door. The Frenchman had vanished.

Well, who sweeps mud in the rain?

Thoughtfully, he wandered on, meaning to return to the harbor and inquire about the rowing boat that had brought the Frenchman ashore. He went via the pump room and contemplated asking questions at the tavern.

In truth, mindful of Dr. Lampton's strictures, he was reluctant to return there and risk another attack. Such restrictions irked him, and yet he could not have everything just because he wanted it. He already had far more in terms of life and fun than he had ever dreamed possible from his sickbed.

As he sat alone in the pump room, he let the voices of the middle-aged ladies comparing nerves and palpitations wash over him. He acknowledged that he was dwelling on Launceton's problems and his own health largely to avoid thinking about Henrietta.

"You are quite safe with me," she had said. *"I don't want to be married either."*

The words had stunned Aubrey, so much so that he had sat there paralyzed for almost a whole minute before he realized she was getting away from him. He had run after her, self-knowledge battering at him in a chaotic yet curiously happy manner.

Not because she had pierced his foolish pride by pointing out that every woman didn't long for marriage with him. He already knew that. What threw him was the sudden realization that *he* really wouldn't mind marrying Henrietta.

Of course, he was immediately assailed by erotic visions of her naked beauty in his arms, writhing with passion beneath him. There were so many things he wanted to do to her that he heard himself growl. Which had made him laugh and recall the fun of her presence. How sweet, how wonderful it would be to have her there with him all the time. To care for her, have children with her, make her happy.

It wasn't terrifying at all.

It was beautiful and joyous, and he wanted it with a strength that totally confused him.

Oh no. I am the family rake, sowing my wild oats. I am not marriage material! I would be an atrocious husband, neglectful, faithless…penniless.

Relief had seized him by the throat, and he had jumped up and hurried after Henrietta. He was in no position to offer marriage to anyone. He was saved.

And yet Henrietta had looked so sweet, so vulnerable, when he took her hand. She had not even known he was there, assuming he had abandoned her. What a funny, contradictory little creature she was. Consumed with tenderness, he had given in to his need to kiss her and rejoiced in her instant response.

He had promised her safety, but there was no harm in a few stolen kisses.

The trouble was, those kisses fed his obsession. He hoped she had not spoiled him for all other women.

In the doorway of one of the cottages opposite the harbor, he found an ancient fisherman mending nets and paused to exchange pleasantries about the weather in general and the damage caused by last week's storm in particular.

"Do you know if anyone is prepared to hire out a rowing boat for a couple of hours?" Aubrey asked. "Supposing the sun shines for so long!"

"I'll lend you mine if my grandson isn't using it."

"Thanks, that's very civil of you. That's not yours tied up at the foot of the steps, is it?"

"No, that's from a cargo vessel that anchors out there sometimes." The fisherman nodded out to sea, where one ship, sails furled, did indeed seem to be anchored. "Waiting for cargo round at Whalen, I expect. Captain must be restless with nothing to do, keeps his lads busy sailing up and down." He grinned. "Just like those Captain Alban and Captain Vale caught the other day."

"Not *just* like them, surely? Are you saying this cargo vessel is up to mischief too?"

"Don't know anything about it," said the old man. "Just guessing."

"Do you know the fellow who came ashore today in that boat?"

"He don't talk. Seen him at the tavern once. He don't talk there either."

Because he couldn't speak English? Or because he didn't want his accent recognized?

There was a lot to think about as Aubrey walked home.

❦

AUBREY DISCOVERED HIS brother Roderick in his bedchamber at the top of the house, packing to leave for his trip. There was a new energy about Roderick these days, made more of purpose than restlessness. Or so it seemed to Aubrey.

"All well?" Roderick asked, pausing to peer at him. They did not often venture into each other's territory.

"Yes, of course. I just wanted to pick your brains while you're still here. You're a friend of Launceton's, aren't you?"

Roderick shrugged. "Acquaintance. I'd only heard of him before we came back home. Why?"

"Just curious. What had you heard of him?"

Roderick smiled slightly. "He was a mad Russian, commanded some wild Cossacks who turned up in Vienna to protect the tsar. He had a heroic reputation in war and a reckless one in his private life."

"Deserved?"

"So far as I know. He was Colonel Ivan Petrovich Savarin in those days."

"Then you never heard anything…unsavory about him?"

Roderick stared at him. "Such as what?"

"I don't know." Restlessly, Aubrey paced to the window, then turned to face his brother. "Such as the mistreatment of prisoners or unnecessary slaughter, especially during the French retreat from Moscow."

Roderick continued his packing, throwing a razor and a cloth into his saddlebag. "He was certainly involved in harrying the French out of the country. Freed a good many Russian prisoners in the French train. I don't know with what slaughter. I never heard anything against Savarin. But it's different with the enemy in your country, isn't it? I wouldn't like to judge."

"Neither would I," Aubrey said. "Having never raised a hand in anger. Or faced one."

"Not entirely true," Roderick said. "I'm sure we all thrashed you at one time or another. Just for fun."

"I must have been asleep."

"Be grateful," Roderick said, hefting the bag over his shoulder. "And don't go picking fights with Launceton. He also had a reputation for dueling at the drop of a hat."

Aubrey next bearded Julius, his eldest brother, who was in the drawing room pouring himself a glass of brandy. Seeing Aubrey, he poured another.

"Do you still have the loan of that ship from Captain Alban?" Aubrey asked.

"I do."

"Can I borrow it?"

"No," Julius said, pausing before releasing the glass into Aubrey's hand. "Why would I do that?"

"I might want to check on a ship that potters up and down the coast, a bit like your gun-smuggling vessel."

"Leave it to the revenue cutters."

"Like you did?"

"I can sail."

"You can come with me, if you like. You can even bring Antonia."

"I'll think about it."

Aubrey grinned and clinked glasses with him. "Next question—what do you know about French spies?"

"Nothing. Not much point now the war is over."

"Then no one is bent on freeing Bonaparte from his island prison in the Atlantic?"

"Not unless they're delusional."

Aubrey rested against the sofa arm. "Who around here would know about spies and covert kinds of things?"

Julius stared at him. "Aubrey, what the devil are you up to?"

"I don't know. Probably nothing. But I think I need to know."

"I'll take you to see Captain Alban tomorrow, if you like. Interesting fellow. And his wife is lovely."

"Will I be back in time for dinner?"

"Oh yes. You're taking the twins to the Launcetons', aren't you?" Julius looked amused. "What an exciting day for you."

LORD MAYNARD HAD taken to calling upon the Launcetons every second day. Since he had come to tea the day Aubrey abandoned her to his escort, Henrietta was taken by surprise when, the following day, he appeared in his driving coat, offering to take her to the ruined abbey.

"What a charming idea," Henrietta responded, covering her dismay. "Michael and Georgi would love it, too."

"Alas, I am driving my own curricle. There would not be room."

"I hope it will not rain," she said feebly.

"Then hurry," Lizzie said unfeelingly. "Make the most of the sunshine!"

There was nothing for Henrietta to do but fetch her bonnet and go. She only hoped it would not take too long. But at least if he was driving, he would need to pay more attention to his horses than to her.

"It will probably be a little too far to go all the way to the abbey," Maynard said as he handed her up into the carriage. "But I have been told of a place closer at hand from where we might get a spectacular view of it, even if from a distance."

To Henrietta, anything that shortened the expedition was a blessing.

"Lady Launceton tells me you met the eccentric Mrs. Fawcett in Vienna," he said as they drove through the town, surprising her for the second time that day. "How did that come about?"

He even listened to her reply, for he frowned and asked questions. She was fairly sure he did not approve of such adventures, involving shootings and secret police, which also suited Henrietta. With luck, by the end of the journey he would have decided she was entirely unsuitable.

She asked him about his children. He seemed to know very little beyond their names and ages, though he did betray a spark of affection that seemed to puzzle him, and he did say they needed the care of a mother. At which point Henrietta changed the subject.

He asked her about the architecture of Vienna and the emperor's palaces, and she chattered about what she had seen for another few minutes.

"You would appear to have a good eye for art," he said.

"Oh no," she said hastily. "Just what is pleasing and comfortable to be around."

An odd, arrested expression flitted across his face, and then, unexpectedly, he smiled, the first smile she had ever noticed on him. It made him surprisingly human.

"Perhaps you have the same taste when it comes to your own home."

"Well, we can hardly aspire to the treasures of the Hofburg, but Lizzie does ask my advice sometimes about Launceton House."

"Do you enjoy such matters?"

"Oh yes," Henrietta said fervently.

"How interesting," he said warmly. "I always imagined you were too young and beautiful and giddy to care."

Discomfort swamped her, and she looked hastily away. And fortunately found a distraction. "Oh, look, there is the abbey ruin! It is just like Lady Helen's watercolor, don't you think?"

⚜

AMAURY DE CORENTIN felt that his plans were incomplete and just a little trivial.

The realization made him uneasy as he sat outside the pump room, making the most of the day's glimpse of sunshine while he drank the water that would never cure him.

He could make Launceton miserable, cause the world to ridicule him as a cuckold, but that was hardly fit punishment for his heinous crime. The taking of his life was certainly fitting, but would the man even know who and what was responsible for his death?

Of course Corentin had to be careful. He had to consider Diane in all of this. He must be sure that only Launceton knew the instrument of his misery and death.

Grief and fury swamped him all over again. It wasn't enough. Nothing was ever enough to ease the pain of his loss. Blindly, he raised the glass to his lips, and over the rim, he saw his enemy himself.

John Gaunt, the sixth Baron Launceton, also known as Count Ivan Savarin, swaggered toward the pump room, his laughing wife at his side, a wriggling child of less than a year in one arm. The baby was gurgling and clutching little handfuls of Launceton's face.

Lady Launceton caught sight of Corentin and waved. "How do you do, sir? No, no, please don't get up. I am about to sit."

"May we join you?" Launceton asked, with absolutely no concept of his danger.

Corentin smiled. "Of course. I should be charmed." He watched as Launceton handed his wife into the seat next to him. "And is this your son and heir?"

"He is indeed," Launceton said with a grin. "The Honorable, and entirely exhausting, Jack Gaunt. Say good morning to Monsieur de Corentin."

Jack, plonked onto his mother's knee, bounced and chortled.

"I'll fetch your water," Launceton said to his wife. "Sir, may I bring you anything?"

"Thank you, no, I am quite content."

Quite, quite content, Corentin thought as Launceton strode off into the pump room, leaving his enemy alone with the two people he surely loved best in the world, his charming wife, and his strong, healthy baby son. His heir, his firstborn.

Now, *now* Corentin had a worthy goal, one so right he should have seen it from the beginning. The child who was so clearly the center of his parents' universe.

Oh yes, Corentin would take everything from the man who had murdered his son.

Chapter Twelve

THE FAMOUS—OR INFAMOUS—CAPTAIN Alban lived in a pleasant manor house by the sea, a little like Black Hill House, within sight of the sea. Having ridden over with Julius, Aubrey was welcomed in an amiably casual manner by a tall, lean man with sardonic yet perceptive eyes.

"My brother Aubrey," Julius introduced him. "Aubrey, Mr. Alban Lamont, still known to the world as Captain Alban."

"How did that come about?" Aubrey asked in surprise, shaking hands with his host.

"Oh, a misguided effort to save my family embarrassment from my more disreputable exploits."

"But you are a national hero."

"That was hardly my intention. Or just reward. But it scares off the pirates. Come inside. My wife is resting, and will be down shortly. What is it I can do for you?"

"I'm not sure," Aubrey admitted, taking the comfortable chair offered by Alban. *Lamont*, he reminded himself. "But I'm afraid there might be something havey-cavey going on in Blackhaven."

"Isn't there always?" the captain murmured. "What in particular troubles you?"

"French spies or assassins, conspirators who might want to free Bonaparte and put him back on the French throne."

Aubrey expected ridicule, but the captain only held his gaze inquiringly, waiting for more.

"You haven't laughed me out of the room," Aubrey remarked.

Alban shrugged. "It will take time for such characters to vanish. Fanatics and idealists remain. They have no support to do much damage. Exactly what is your suspicion?"

"Well, that's the thing," Aubrey said. "It isn't really *my* suspicion. It came to a friend of mine via an unlikely source that he was in danger from some Bonapartist plot."

"How unlikely a source?"

Aubrey shifted in his chair. "Lord Tamar's sister."

"Then absolutely take it seriously," Alban said, without even blinking. "Your friend should take extreme care."

"He won't. It isn't in his nature. I don't suppose you know anything about an émigré called Amaury de Corentin? Or his daughter Diane?"

Alban frowned. "Corentin. I'm not sure. I deal more with action than investigations, but occasionally I—er…retrieve documents that have proved useful. I'll look into it. Do you believe he somehow threatens your friend?"

"I have difficulty. He is old and unwell. In fact, I think he is dying. But he has an acquaintance—also French, I think—associated with a ship anchored at Whalen."

Alban's eyes narrowed. "You fear this other man is an assassin?"

"It crossed my mind. No doubt foolishly."

"No doubt," Alban agreed. His rather hard face softened, and he rose to his feet as a lady entered the room. "Here is my wife. Bella, you know Sir Julius. This is his brother, Mr. Aubrey Vale. Sir, my wife, Lady Arabella Lamont."

Lady Arabella was an unexpected wife for such a man. She was a gentle lady with weak eyes and a shy manner. She was also heavily pregnant and hospitable, inviting Julius and Aubrey to stay for luncheon.

While Julius and Alban fell into discussions about the sea, Aubrey admired the flowers visible from the window and told Lady Arabella about their efforts with the Black Hill gardens.

"Well, come and see what we have done here, if you like," she offered. "It might give you some ideas. I stole several from friends!"

In fact, there was an informal delight about her garden that Aubrey liked very much, though he doubted it was the same vision as Delilah's. But then, Antonia would be lady of Black Hill very soon…

"Are you the invalid brother?" Lady Arabella asked suddenly.

Aubrey's smile died. "I used to be so known. Now, I believe, I am the badly behaved brother."

Color stained her cheeks. "I'm sorry, I should not have blurted out such a thing. Believe me, no one understands the stigma more than I. I was always so regarded too, being a sickly child myself, which is why I wanted to say to you… Oh dear, this is coming out all wrong."

She looked so agitated that Aubrey found himself handing her onto a bench and sitting beside her.

"I thought I was dying once," she said abruptly. "We all thought it. Because of my sickly childhood, I was smothered in the care of my family, a victim, if you like, of benevolent tyranny. As an adult, I was subject to attacks that made me cough so badly I was told I was consumptive. And then one day I spoke to a different doctor who blamed it all on anxiety of the mind."

Aubrey blinked. "This…doctor said anxiety of the mind gave you consumption?"

She smiled. "No, quite the opposite. I didn't have consumption at all, nor any other dangerous malady. I merely…panicked in certain stressful situations. Situations that were not remotely trying to other people. But now, I hardly ever cough and my lungs remain quite clear. Which is why I wanted to advise you to embrace the current improvement in your health. Dr. Lampton is very good, but if would care for the opinion of another, Alban will happily arrange for—"

"I have asthma," Aubrey interrupted. "It was very severe in childhood, and I almost died several times. I was coddled and confined for fear any exertion would see me carried off. But even before we came to Blackhaven, I was improving. Believe me, I am now very happily embracing life."

"Hectically," she said vaguely.

"I beg your pardon?"

"You are *hectically* embracing life. From what I hear." She met his gaze with odd seriousness, suddenly not vague at all. "You are afraid health will be taken away from you again and are trying to cram a lifetime's natural wildness into a few weeks."

Aubrey stared at her. He closed his mouth and swallowed. "Perhaps."

"I am not criticizing," she said. "I just… It can feel lonely. Sometimes, we just need a friend who listens. Alban listened to me. To more than I ever said. If you see what I mean."

Henrietta's image swam before his mind. The girl no one heard because they were all too busy looking. And yet *she* listened to him, to more than *he* ever said.

"You are welcome here any time," Lady Arabella said in her shy way.

It was, he realized, an offer of kindness, understanding, and friendship. Even more surprising, he valued it.

He smiled, and she looked both grateful and relieved. "Thank you. I would love to visit again."

※

AUBREY AND THE twins arrived with something of a roar.

The roar was made up of delighted laughter, enthusiastic greetings, and shouted, if futile, commands to Dog, who broke loose from

Georgiana on the stairs to hurl himself at the newcomers.

Aubrey, from experience, sidestepped smartly and allowed Lawrence to take the full brunt. As everyone charged to the rescue and howled with laughter, Aubrey stepped over his brother to take Lizzie's hand.

Oh yes, Aubrey had a certain style, Henrietta allowed with amusement. He took the chaos of her family in his stride. And his eyes were still warm and conspiratorial as he turned to greet her. Her stomach somersaulted.

"Manners, twins!" he called over his shoulder, and there was a mad scramble below as said twins, aided by Henrietta's grinning siblings, extricated themselves from Dog to greet their hosts and Henrietta.

Dog then remembered Aubrey and thrust his big head under his hand to have his ears scratched. He didn't jump up. Belatedly, Henrietta began to worry that proximity to the dog would bring on another of his attacks, but Aubrey himself seemed oblivious to the danger.

"Michael, why don't you take you take Dog upstairs for now?" she suggested.

"Good plan," Lizzie agreed. "Come into the drawing room, Mr. Vale…"

"Please, just call me Aubrey. There are altogether too many Mr. Vales."

"Then we are Lizzie and Vanya." Lizzie, who had never been good with formality, sounded relieved.

At that moment, Vanya appeared in the drawing room doorway. Just for an instant, Henrietta glimpsed the steel in him. There was a dangerous edge there that she rarely saw but knew existed. She suspected it had always been there. Honed by war, he had given it full rein in the past. Nowadays, it came to the fore only in protecting his family.

For a moment, the two tall men regarded each other, the one

hardened in battle, the other a recent invalid, yet strengthened by his own kind of suffering, afraid of no one. Neither would back down.

That glimpse of Vanya's devil dismayed Henrietta. And then it vanished. With a slightly rueful smile, he held out his hand to Aubrey.

"Welcome to Bedlam. Sherry or brandy?"

"Brandy, if you please."

And the difficult moment passed.

In fact, from then on, the banter between Aubrey and Vanya revealed what had drawn them to each other in the first place—irreverent humor and appreciation of the ridiculous. Henrietta found their interactions entertaining, although it meant they were going in to dinner before she had the chance to have any private conversation with him.

Even then, as she took his arm, he said only, "Do you know who lives next door to you on the right?"

"Mrs. Hamley. She is very kind and baked us a beautiful apple pie the day we arrived. Her husband does not like Dog, however. He jumped the fence into their garden—Dog did—and dug up his carrots. Why?"

"Ah, then he is a keen gardener? Does he employ someone to help?"

"I would be surprised. He is too jealous." She considered. "Or zealous. *Why*, Aubrey?"

He dropped his head a little closer, causing a frisson down her spine. "I found our quarry sweeping their garden path. I suspect he was merely hiding, but I don't like that he feels free to do so quite so close."

"Nor do I, but I don't believe he lives there."

"No, I think he lives aboard a ship anchored in Whalen. Mostly."

"Then we must make an expedition," Henrietta said firmly. "Perhaps I need a different dressmaker. Tomorrow?"

His eyes gleamed, making her warm and breathless. "Why not? It's a fine excuse to be near you. We'll take the children, but not Dog."

Since dinner was informal, the adults and children ate together, although baby Jack had been banished to his cradle by then. The twins, while entering with enthusiasm into Georgiana and Michael's nonsense, were also curious about the adults and had no hesitation in asking blunt questions. They also observed in a curiously adult way.

I doubt anyone can keep secrets from them, Henrietta thought. Although why would anyone want to? There was nothing malicious or spiteful about them. In fact, Henrietta rather liked the affection that stood out so clearly when they teased Aubrey and accepted his bantering retorts with delight.

In all, the evening was fun, like a less fraught continuation of the new emotions she had experienced on the beach with him yesterday.

I could live with him, she thought in wonder. Then, *Oh, I want to live with him…*

Not living with him would be the real tragedy. Her world seemed to be opening, unfurling in such new and surprising and wonderful ways.

And if Vanya occasionally gave the impression of a cat watching a mouse, well, Lizzie clearly had that well in hand. For when Aubrey finally rose to take his leave and Henrietta moved to accompany him, Vanya also started toward the door, until Lizzie took his hand and he was still.

Misha, Vanya's servant since childhood, had already herded the twins into the waiting carriage. Georgiana and Michael, with Dog jumping up to peer in the window, were still saying goodbye.

Just for a moment, if they stepped behind the open door, no one else could see them. Henrietta felt as if her heart was bursting. Smiling, Aubrey took both her hands, and she drew him out of sight. She stood on tiptoes, trailing her fingertips across his jaw, and pressed her lips to his.

His moved in instant response, then curved into a smile as he took her into his arms and prolonged the kiss so blissfully that she was taken by surprise when he stopped.

She opened her eyes. He was gazing down at her, his face so lost in shadows that his expression looked no longer tender but oddly desperate.

"Until tomorrow," she whispered.

"Tomorrow," he agreed. He swooped and took a last brief, hard kiss, and then he was gone.

She stood by the door, no doubt smiling foolishly while she let all the wonder and excitement flood over her. Dog, bounding into the house ahead of the children, and Misha, took her by surprise, and she laughed with pure joy.

AUBREY ALL BUT ran from her down to the carriage, appalled both by his own behavior and the mess he was getting himself into. He was behaving exactly as Vanya had suspected when he warned him off at the ball. What was more, one could not go around kissing well-born girls without eventually paying the price of marriage.

True, there was a strange allure to the notion of marriage with Henrietta, but Aubrey was far from ready for such a step. There was too much hell to be raked, wine to be drunk, women to be enjoyed.

He needed to wash away his craving for Henrietta, erase her smile and her sweetness, the scent of her skin, the trusting passion of her lips.

"Damn it," he said, wrenching open the carriage door. It was the better of the Vale carriages, and the twins, regarding him from the back-facing bench, looked perfectly comfortable.

"Damn what?" Leona asked, clearly more intrigued than offended by his language.

"Me," Aubrey said. "I forgot something. Hal will drive you home, and I'll follow in an hour or so."

They turned matching scowls of disapproval on him. He shut the door on their retort, which might have been "Aubrey, don't!" Paying no attention, he gave Hal the coachman his orders and was already striding along the road when the carriage passed him, two identical disapproving faces glaring from the back window.

Aubrey laughed and turned toward the inn in search of some convivial company. Here, he was in luck. His name rang out in a welcoming chorus. In no time, he was happily ensconced with a large glass of brandy, the center of a very jolly group. Even more luck followed with the arrival of two of his favorite actresses celebrating after their successful show at Blackhaven's theater.

Violet, whose bed he had already warmed on a couple of memorable occasions some weeks ago, was delighted to see him and pretended to fall into his lap. More than happy to co-operate, Aubrey quickly lost himself in entertaining and flirting. If there was a hectic element to his enjoyment—as Captain Alban's gentle wife had guessed—he didn't care. In fact, he embraced it, longing for the simplicity of behaving badly and hurting no one except himself.

It was if he were proving to himself that nothing had changed, that he was still the same man who had first come to Blackhaven rejoicing in his newly found health and strength.

In time, Trent the innkeeper threw them out, and they all repaired to Violet's lodgings for a little more brandy and a promising night of sensual debauchery.

ON THE MORNING after the dinner party, Vanya lay awake beside Lizzie, deep in thought.

In the almost two years since his marriage, he had mellowed considerably from the hotheaded rakehell of his youth. But he was well aware that he would still kill any man for touching Lizzie. Aubrey Vale, so amiable and charming, could have had little idea how close to death he came.

That, Vanya told himself, was the sign of his new maturity. He no longer started a fight without evidence, and he had always been capable of observation. Aubrey liked Lizzie—Vanya despised anyone who did not—but his gaze had strayed most frequently and most warmly to Henrietta.

And Henrietta was touchingly different with him. There was no sign of the rigidity she displayed with Maynard, or the utter indifference she'd shown her many suitors in London. Lizzie was right, as she often was, that there were possibilities for Henrietta there.

Where on earth had Corentin got the idea it was Lizzie that Aubrey pursued? Vanya had seen no sign of it. More to the point, Lizzie had treated him much as she treated Michael or Lawrence Vale. There was no romantic interest there at all. Lizzie was still Vanya's.

He smiled at her sleeping face and, as she stirred, drew her into his arms.

It crossed his mind to wonder why Corentin had planted such a false seed.

"Why would Corentin dislike Aubrey Vale?" he said.

"He doesn't. He wants Aubrey for his daughter," Lizzie said sleepily. She snuggled closer, and Vanya forgot about everything else.

⁂

AUBREY WOKE ON a strange sofa, his legs dangling off the end. Where the devil was he? Surely not still at the inn? His head certainly ached enough for that, though he couldn't imagine Mrs. Trent tolerating his untidy presence in her taproom all night.

He sat up and reached for the nearest bottle. His head spun. Sniffing the bottle, he was relieved to find it was water, not gin, and necked a significant quantity to slake his raging thirst.

Now he remembered. He was at Violet's lodgings. A quick survey discovered he was without his coat, cravat, and boots. The rest of his clothing remained in place.

Of course. He had passed out on the sofa.

He had a vague recollection of Violet, laughing, tugging him by the hand to get him to join her in bed. It was what he had come for, was it not? To indulge in some fun, carefree lusts of the flesh, to free himself from Henrietta's bizarre hold on him.

He hadn't been so very drunk that he could not have played his part. And yet he had chosen not to. Pretending to be asleep, he had stayed where he was, and Violet had shrugged, thrown a blanket over him, and left him to snore.

He probably had, shortly thereafter.

He took another mouthful of water and set the bottle back on the table. That would count as his day's ration of water. There was something else he needed to do today.

Go to Whalen with Henrietta to investigate the Frenchman's ship.

Which meant he had to go home and wash and change. He suspected brandy was leaking from his pores. A brisk walk, coffee, and breakfast and he would be ready for anything. Still, he must draw back from Henrietta, stop kissing her and misleading her. He could not take her and he could not marry her, so he had to leave the girl alone.

Guiltily, he realized she already liked him too much. It would take a great deal of self-restraint and effort to return their relationship to friendship. Or he could go away somewhere for a few weeks until her family left Blackhaven. Once this threat to Vanya was dealt with, of course.

Rummaging among the cushions, he found his cravat, which he knotted loosely about his throat, and his coat, which lay in a crumpled heap, as though someone had been sitting on it. He shook it out and shrugged into it. Wondering why he should be glad not to have romped with Violet last night, he located his hat dangling from a twee picture of a child with a kitten and ambled to the door.

He paused, frowning. This had happened before, hadn't it? With Violet, in fact.

And the delicious Mrs. Rhett.

Damn it, Henrietta was ruining him for other women. He just didn't seem to want them anymore. And yet he *liked* being a rake.

Didn't he?

A conundrum to be contemplated on the long walk home. He opened the door and was on the front step in the early morning light when Violet called his name and came running after him.

He turned and smiled at her. "I didn't want to wake you," he said truthfully as she wound her arms around his neck.

She pouted. "Do you have to go so early?"

"Afraid I do. I have an appointment and I smell like the inside of a barrel." Wrapping his arms around her, he kissed her a hearty goodbye, then jumped down the last of the steps, almost landing on a passerby with a large dog.

Henrietta, her eyes wide with shock. And Dog, nudging him enthusiastically with his large head.

Blindly, mechanically, Aubrey patted the dog. Most of him was too appalled by the shock, the pain in Henrietta's face, to see anything else.

And then she whisked away from him, tugging Dog with her. For once, Dog obeyed.

Aubrey opened his mouth to call after her, but his voice didn't work, and in any case, what could he say that wouldn't sound like the clichéd excuse of a farcically unfaithful husband?

"I wouldn't right now," Violet said ruefully. "Give her time to calm down. Go home, Aubrey."

Chapter Thirteen

HENRIETTA WALKED AWAY because she could not bear what she had just seen. She could not think for the shock, merely kept moving from instinct.

He will come after me and explain. It can't be what I am imagining…

But he didn't come near her. At the corner, she turned and glanced back. There was no one in the street at all except Henrietta and Dog.

She walked on blindly, letting Dog decide the direction, while disappointment warred with reason in her head. She had always known what Aubrey was—a joyous rake. A man could not change so quickly.

Vanya did, for Lizzie.

Aubrey is not Vanya. I am not Lizzie. And I will not cry…

But her eyes were too full. A tear trickled down her cheek. There was no one to see, so she left it there.

She had so quickly grown used to thinking of Aubrey as her friend. She had been so sure that his kisses meant he cared for her, that in him she had found the elusive being who could not only be her husband but her love. All those hopes built on nothing. For Aubrey had gone straight from kissing her to a night in that woman's arms. She was not naïve enough to believe anything else of what she had just seen. The intimacy of lovers.

No other loss had ever been as painful as this, not even the deaths of her parents nor the loss of their home. This clawed at her stomach with anger and humiliation and a sadness so profound that she felt lost. All her bright, foolish hopes, her silly dreams, gone again. Life without love, without Aubrey, stretched out before her in bleak desolation, made all the worse because it had seemed within her grasp.

It never had been. It had only ever been her foolish fantasy. She gasped, her throat aching, and wished Dog had woken Michael or Georgi or Vanya. She hadn't needed to bounce out of bed as she had, eager to greet the day and the next expedition with Aubrey. If she had only pretended to be asleep, Dog would have moved on to someone else, and Henrietta would never have seen Aubrey emerge from that house, never have seen him embrace that tousled, yet beautiful, woman…

A door opened and closed nearby. Blackhaven was awakening, and she needed somewhere to hide before her grief exploded. Dog made one of his sudden halts, jolting her to a standstill, and she realized he had brought her home. All she had to do was open the door and stumble inside.

So she did.

"You smell like last week's ale," Delilah greeted him in the kitchen as he hacked a slice off yesterday's loaf.

"I'm largely *made* of last night's ale," he confessed. "And brandy. Lots of brandy. I'm going to stick to claret from now on."

"I doubt it will smell any better when it sticks to you." She watched him slather butter onto the bread, then raised her gaze to his face. "Rough night?"

"No," Aubrey replied. "The night was fun. It was the morning that sank me. I'm going to have to work dashed hard to get over *that* mistake."

"Spoken with feeling," Delilah observed. "I could almost believe you mean it."

"So could I. I think I might be a bad person, Delly."

"I've never found you so."

"Only because I couldn't be anything else tied to my couch of sickness. Oh God, I've started to whine, too. Shoot me."

"Not so early in the morning. People need their rest. Including you, by the look of you."

"I can't. I have an appointment to keep and a lot of groveling to do to make things right." He scowled at her. "What are you smiling at?"

"You, groveling to put things right. I'm glad you care enough." She patted his shoulder on her way out. "Go forth and grovel."

Delilah had a habit of making one feel better. She had always done that, as long as he could remember. With little more than humor she somehow put troubles back into manageable proportions so that they no longer seemed insurmountable. She made one see there was hope.

Of course, Delilah did not know the whole of it.

In fact, neither did Aubrey. If his aim was to take a step back from Henrietta, the little scene outside Violet's rooms had surely accomplished the job better than any words. Except that he wanted Henrietta's friendship. He *liked* her. He didn't want to lose her from his burgeoning world.

Your trouble, Aubrey Vale, he lectured himself as he went up to his room, munching his bread and butter, *is that you want your cake and to eat it too. And if your head wasn't quite so thick, you might be able to work out how to achieve it.*

Without hurting Henrietta. Because that was the damnable thing, the guilt that would haunt him until he made this right.

Half an hour later, thoroughly washed, scrubbed, and brushed, dressed in his not-quite-shabby blue morning coat and favorite pantaloons, he winkled out the ancient gig used mainly by the staff and drove himself back into Blackhaven.

The Launcetons' front door was opened by the Russian servant, Misha. Aubrey, quelling his unaccountably nervous stomach, greeted him cheerfully.

"Good morning. Is Miss Henrietta at home?"

Misha shook his head. "No. She has gone out for the day."

"The whole day?" Aubrey exclaimed. "But she was—" He broke off. "Can you tell me when she means to return?"

"No," Misha said. He had a black scowl, probably learned from Vanya.

"Perhaps Lady Launceton is home, then? Or the younger people?"

"No. The children are with Miss Henrietta. Lord and Lady Launceton *may* return in the afternoon."

Aubrey was temporarily flummoxed.

"I'll leave a note," he decided, and Misha—reluctantly, it seemed—admitted him to the reception room on the ground floor, where he found a desk furnished with paper, pen, and ink.

Pen in hand, his mind went blank. What on earth could he write that Lizzie or Vanya might read too? The impossibility of making everything right again with a few scrawled words almost swamped him.

Under Misha's impatient scowl, he sat down to give himself a moment's thought, then wrote.

Dear Henrietta,

Sorry you went without me. Will call tomorrow morning at 11 and look forward to our talk.

I remain your servant,
Aubrey Vale.

As he folded the paper and inscribed her name, he knew the note was unsatisfactory to say the least. God knew what she would think of it, but at least she would know he had called and would wait for him tomorrow—when he might, in any case, be in a better condition to plead his case.

Whatever his case was.

Accordingly, at eleven the following morning, Aubrey again presented himself at Graham Gardens and asked for Henrietta.

At least it was the maid who answered the door this time.

"I'm sorry, sir, Miss Gaunt is not at home. Perhaps you would like to see Lady Launceton?"

There was a distinct pause before the flummoxed Aubrey said, "Yes. Yes, I would, thank you."

Lizzie was discovered in the drawing room playing with baby Jack, who was on his feet, holding on to the sofa and screaming with laughter as he shuffled from one end to the other and she pretended to chase him.

"Good morning, Aubrey," she said with some surprise.

"I seem to be unexpected. Perhaps Misha forgot to pass on my note."

"He gave it to Henrietta," Lizzie said without much interest. "She must have had a previous engagement, though I'm surprised she did not write to tell you so."

"Perhaps I can catch up with her," Aubrey said as evenly as he could. "Where did she go?"

"I'm not quite certain," Lizzie said, sparing him all her attention for the first time. "She went driving with Lord Maynard."

"Thank you. I won't take up more of your time."

"I expect we shall see you at the masquerade ball at the castle on Friday."

"I expect so. Good morning." He bowed and somehow got himself out of the house.

His head was reeling.

Henrietta had chosen Lord Maynard, whom she loathed, over him.

There could only be one reason for that. She was not giving him the chance he had assumed was her nature and his right.

He had lost her.

And quite suddenly, he realized all that entailed.

On the front step, he walked straight past someone before realizing, some fifty yards on, that it had been Vanya.

Lord Maynard was indebted to Diane de Corentin for her sound advice about Henrietta. Gazing at her had always been enough to feed his love of beauty, but he took Diane's point that it might not be the best means to win her.

Even so, having asked his questions at random, merely to be able to listen to the answers, he discovered he was often interested, even intrigued by what she said. There was a lot of nonsense in there too, of course, which reminded him more of his children than his late wife, but then, Henrietta was still only seventeen or so. Besides, the way her face lit up when she told him of some quite unsuitable exploit in Vienna or St. Petersburg was utterly exquisite.

And today she had made no excuses not to accompany him on his drive along the coast. She had merely smiled and fetched her pelisse and bonnet. She had seemed quiet and distracted, and yet when he found a question to ask, she seized upon it with alacrity, almost desperation, and then asked him about his collections.

He was careful not to prose on for too long about his favorite subject, especially once he saw that look of distraction glaze her eyes. He forced himself to stop, asking instead, "Do such things interest you?"

"Oh yes," she replied vaguely.

He smiled upon her. "Does it not seem to you that we are rather well suited in such appreciation?"

"Yes indeed."

"You would like to have a home of your own, I daresay. And I confess I am sorely missing a helpmeet. I can imagine no wife more beautiful or more suitable than you."

"That is true," she murmured, nodding.

Slightly surprised but not displeased by this speedy agreement, Maynard said, "Then you will marry me? Should I call upon Launceton tomorrow for his consent?"

"Yes, I think so."

"How delightfully clear and honest you are. I assure you I shall do all in my power to maintain your happiness."

"Of course I am happy," she said with an unexpected hint of sharpness. "I have no reason not to be. Is it beginning to rain?"

"I fear it is. I can turn the horses in a moment and we can spring them."

Despite the rain, he remained jubilant as he handed her down from the curricle at her front door. He pressed her hand as he bowed over it. "Until tomorrow," he said tenderly.

A faint frown tugged at her brow, and she looked as if she would say something. But the front door opened and she merely smiled and ran up the steps and inside.

Maynard leapt back into his seat and jauntily drove the horses onward to the hotel. He truly was engaged to be married to that lovely creature, who would grace his home and care for his children. Or at least he would be tomorrow after he had spoken to Launceton. He foresaw no problem in obtaining agreement.

<hr />

HENRIETTA, HAVING CHANGED into dry clothes, could not make up her mind whether to stay in her room for the sake of peace, or seek out company in the hope of further distraction. Maynard's company had done little to pull her out of her own thoughts, even when she tried. She just kept thinking, *I wish he were Aubrey…*

For which she hated herself. Perhaps she and the children could take Dog for a walk? Except Dog only reminded her of yesterday's early morning walk and seeing Aubrey with that woman.

I need to pull myself out of this idiocy. I am being a stupid bore…

A brief knock heralded the entry of Lizzie, a welcome if slightly too perceptive a distraction.

"An enjoyable drive?" she asked, seating herself on the edge of Henrietta's bed. "Even if a wet one!"

"It was something to do." Henrietta frowned, new insight appearing from nowhere obvious. "I think he is lonely."

"Probably. His wife is not long dead. Aubrey Vale was here again. He said he had arranged to call at eleven this morning."

"He didn't arrange it. He informed me of it."

"Upon which, you arranged to be deliberately elsewhere?"

Heat seeped into Henrietta's face. "Something like that."

"You have quarreled with Aubrey." It wasn't a question.

"No." Henrietta moved restlessly to the mantelpiece, blindly picking up a small, empty vase, examining its bottom, and setting it back down. "I just don't wish to live in his pocket. He is too much the rakehell for me."

"He is four and twenty years old and was an invalid for at least twenty of those, from all I can gather. Is it so surprising if he runs a trifle wild?"

"No." Henrietta paced to the window, where she turned to face her sister. "But neither is it surprising I should wish to distance myself from such a man."

Lizzie hesitated. "Even Vanya allows that his heart is good."

But it is not mine. "All rakes are not Vanya."

"What did he do?" Lizzie asked bluntly.

Henrietta waved her hand, as though pushing the subject away. "Oh, nothing in particular."

Lizzie had always been such a fun, easygoing big sister that Henrietta had forgotten how penetrating her gaze could be.

"Whopper," Lizzie pronounced. "At some point between leaving our drawing room on Monday evening and the day after, he did something. Did he…importune you at the front door? Should I have let Vanya escort him from the house?"

Oh God, I importuned him. And he ran straight to the arms of another woman. Did I disgust him? I wish he disgusted me…

Lizzie rose and came over to take her hand. "Henri, don't be hurt. Men are odd creatures. Did he kiss you?"

Many times. Henrietta nodded, closing her eyes to prevent the tears.

Lizzie smiled. "Didn't you like it?"

"Too much." Henrietta hugged her sister and pulled free. "But I find I don't like *him*. Don't worry about me, Lizzie. I'll be over him in no time. Have you been to the pump room already?"

When Aubrey returned to Black Hill, he was immediately introduced to his sister Lucy's betrothed. Which was somewhat startling, considering that she had always loathed the very idea of the man engaged to her at birth by a foolish set of parents. Aubrey did not excuse his own father from the idiocy.

Lord Eddleston, however, turned out to be the exact opposite of the staid, pompous middle-aged creature she had always imagined—and described so entertainingly since childhood. Not that any of them had ever met him before now. But Eddleston turned out to be the same age as Aubrey and something of a fellow spirit in the pursuit of fun. He was amusing and entertaining, but no fool. He could discuss the theater with Antonia in one breath, the plight of the rural poor with Cornelius in another, and in the next tell some funny story that had them all in stitches.

He was like quicksilver, and Lucy clearly adored him, a sentiment he seemed to reciprocate. More importantly to Aubrey, he seemed to understand her.

Lucy's happiness did not make Aubrey envious, any more than Julius's did. But it did make him think.

He had been so caught up in his hedonistic pleasures that he had almost forgotten his dependence on Julius, his lack of prospects, or a future standing on his own feet. While he had been raking around the town, Julius had involved himself in the town hospital and finding work for those wounded in the late war. Cornelius ran the estate. Roderick, though suffering terrifying nightmares, had begun a new business venture. Aubrey spent his meager allowance on too much wine and too many women.

He did not deserve Henrietta.

Not even if she had never seen him with Violet. Not even if he had never *been* with Violet. Only now did he understand it, when he fully realized his own shame.

That wonderful, amazing girl had *liked* him—loved him, even. She had chosen him out of all the myriad suitors who must have besieged her in the last year. And instead of appreciating the honor, of appreciating *her*, he had thought only of how to keep her dangling while he avoided commitment.

There would never be anyone like Henrietta, with all her quirks and sense of fun, all her kindness and sweet nature. The girl who wanted to be seen for more than mere physical beauty had seen and understood him. And still liked him. And he had hurt her beyond repair. She would rather face Maynard and his possessive eyes than spend a moment more with Aubrey.

And he had brought that upon both of them.

He needed to rethink his life. He needed to rethink *everything*. He needed to pay attention to the siblings who had always cared for him through the worst of times and the best. He should be helping Rod so that he didn't look so weary. He should make sure Felicia was safe—she had a reckless yet indescribably sad look about her. Something was going on with Cornelius, too.

I am not the center of the world. I need to stop behaving as if I am, blind and selfish...

He could do better. And he would.

Chapter Fourteen

MAKING A CONSCIOUS effort, Henrietta accompanied the children on Dog's first walk of the day and then joined the family for breakfast. She had to concentrate to keep up with the lively conversations she was used to, but she did so, and remembered to smile and laugh in the right places. Soon, she thought, it would be real again. She just needed a little while to practice while she forgot about Aubrey.

Vanya, yawning and drinking copious cups of coffee over his post, suddenly sat up and looked at her. "Lord Maynard says he will do himself the honor of calling upon me this morning."

"Calling on you?" Henrietta said, surprised but not displeased. "He did say something about calling today, but I'm glad it's you he wants to see. He needs more friends."

Vanya blinked. "Not sure I'm the kind of friend Maynard wants. He finds me much too ramshackle."

"That's why you are good for him," Henrietta said firmly. "Are we going to look at masks for Friday's ball, Lizzie?"

"I seem to have flung loads from Vienna into my trunk," Lizzie replied. "So we can try them all with the costumes."

"Can I see?" Georgiana demanded.

"Of course."

"I would go as a highwayman," Georgiana said.

Michael grinned. "I'd go as the soldier who captures you and hauls you off to gaol."

"Sadly, neither of you is invited," Lizzie said before war could break out. She frowned direly. "And none of your Vienna tricks! Old Lady Braithwaite will not see the joke."

Henrietta laughed, and she and Georgiana accompanied Lizzie upstairs to try on masks and costumes, leaving Vanya to entertain Lord Maynard.

In fact, only fifteen minutes later, Vanya joined them in the bedroom, looking perplexed.

Lizzie removed the black and gold mask in which she had been prancing around the room to make Georgiana giggle. "What is it?"

But Vanya was gazing at Henrietta. "Maynard says you and he have an understanding to marry."

Henrietta blinked. "No, we don't. That's silly. I barely know the man."

"He claims he proposed yesterday and you accepted, so he has called to ask for my consent."

"Of course he did not propose yest—" Henrietta broke off midword. She frowned. "That is," she said with less certainty, "I can't quite recall what he said. Or what I did. I wasn't paying attention."

For once in her life, Henrietta seemed to have achieved the impossible, reducing her sisters and her brother-in-law to stunned silence.

"Oh, Henri," Lizzie murmured at last, sinking down onto the bed.

Georgiana giggled. "Only you, Henri, could have so many suitors at your feet that you receive and accept a proposal of marriage without even noticing."

"Oh dear," Henrietta said, distressed. "It isn't funny, Georgi. How on earth do I tell him that I accepted only because I wasn't listening? The poor man will feel so humiliated." She rubbed the backs of her fingers against her cheek. "What on earth do I do?"

"Agree to marry him," Georgiana advised, "and then Michael and Dog and I will behave so appallingly that he will be glad to let you go."

"He isn't going to marry you and Michael and Dog," Lizzie pointed out.

"Invite us to live with you as a condition of accepting," Georgi said, refusing to give up.

Henrietta stared at her, plucking at her lower lip. There was the kernel of an idea in there, although it was still preposterous. "Preposterous to have done such a thing to him..."

"Quite," Vanya said. "I have said I will send you to him and abide by your answer. But you have to give him the truth, Henri."

"But how awful for him to be rejected in such a way when he thinks I accepted him!"

"You did accept him," Georgiana pointed out.

Lizzie scowled at her. "She didn't mean to."

"Which makes it worse," Henrietta said. "Oh, what on earth is the *matter* with me these days?"

Georgina laughed. "You must be in love!"

Which was so much the truth that Henrietta bolted for the door, grabbing Vanya by the hand. "Come with me."

Vanya dug in his heels. "I said I would give him five minutes alone with you."

Henrietta swallowed. "You're right, of course. I must deal with it myself, since I made the mess."

"We'll lurk outside the door," Georgiana promised.

"No, you won't," Lizzie said firmly, then ruined the effect by adding, "Vanya and I will."

Henrietta walked slowly down to the drawing room, planning what to do, what to say. She took a deep breath and walked into the room.

Lord Maynard turned quickly from the window and his face lit up with one of his rare smiles, intensifying her guilt.

"Miss Gaunt. Henrietta. I have spoken to Lord Launceton and he has agreed in principle, providing you are still of the same mind."

As he came toward her, Henrietta fought the urge to flee, though no longer because of his acquisitive eyes, but because of her own dislike of causing any creature pain.

In a flash of wisdom, she saw that they were both creatures in pain. She had misunderstood his loneliness before. Now, she empathized only too well. She wasn't sure he was capable of love beyond that for his collections, but he did *feel*. He did care. And she would never care for anyone but Aubrey.

She had been given a chance to do some good by her own mistake. She could look after this strange, obsessive man, look after his motherless children, make him comfortable as his late wife had done. It wouldn't be so hard.

She swallowed, letting him take both her hands. "I must be honest with you," she blurted. "I was upset yesterday and struggled to focus on our conversation. I didn't actually hear your proposal or my answer. *But*," she added hastily before the confusion and hurt in his eyes could make her weep, "when Vanya told me, I quickly realized what a fine solution it could be for both of us. I am honored by your offer, my lord, and would be very glad to accept."

DAZED BY THE speed of events, Henrietta received the slightly muted good wishes of her family. Lord Maynard did not appear to notice. He even agreed happily with Vanya's proposal that they keep the engagement between themselves for a few weeks, since Henrietta was so young.

It was clear he was giving Henrietta time to cry off without the world knowing. She didn't mind. She felt she was doing something good, and that pleased her.

Georgiana, almost beside herself with glee, barely waited for the door to close behind the successful suitor before she demanded,

"When do we begin?"

"Begin what?" Michael asked, bewildered.

"To give Lord Maynard a disgust of us."

"I'm sure he already has that," Michael said. "But it's Henri he's marrying."

"That's the point," Georgiana crowed. "He isn't!"

"He is," Henrietta said. "I thought about it and changed my mind. I shall marry Lord Maynard, and you're not to play any of your tricks on him. I like him."

"You do?" Lizzie peered at her closely.

Vanya threw up his hands and strode off to have a more reasonable discussion, no doubt, with his baby son, who had already been heard to say distinct words.

"Yes," Henrietta said. "I do like him."

"I must say I'm surprised." Georgiana looked disappointed. "He seems a bit of a dry old stick, to me."

"He is not," Henrietta said firmly.

"I still prefer Aubrey," Michael said with a shrug. "But I suppose it's up to you."

※

DIANE HAD JUST returned from the pump room with her father when a knock sounded at the door. She found Lord Maynard on the doorstep, looking extremely pleased with himself.

"I have news," he announced.

"I can see that you do," she said gravely, standing back to admit him.

She led him into the parlor, where her father greeted him with his usual charming manners while she went to make tea.

Only when she supplied them both with refreshment did she sit down and inquire, "So what is your news, my lord?"

"That I am betrothed to Henrietta Gaunt."

Diane blinked in surprise at such speedy work. Her father, who had closed his eyes as if falling asleep, opened them again and smiled.

"I have to thank you, Miss de Corentin, for your sound advice," Maynard said. "I did indeed listen to the young lady, which not only earned me her favor but taught me a deeper appreciation of her character."

"You mean you noticed she had one," Diane said cynically. "Everyone is more than a pretty—or ugly—face."

Maynard considered. "True. Though I would not care to look at an ugly one over breakfast each morning."

Was he making a joke? His eyes were certainly a shade lighter. Perhaps the Gaunt chit would be good for him after all. Besides leaving Aubrey free for Diane.

"My heartiest congratulations," she said. "I shall make a point to call and give her my best wishes."

"Thank you. I'm sure she will be glad of that."

Henrietta, however, did not look glad at all when Diane called the following day. She seemed, in fact, to have hardly slept in several days, and her smiles, while still there, lacked the usual sparkle that reduced men to gibbering fools.

"I came to wish you happiness," Diane said. "Though I understand you are keeping the engagement quiet for now."

"It was Vanya's condition," Lady Launceton said, an unusual frown on her face. "But I see his lordship is not keeping to it."

"Oh, he is," Diane said quickly. "I am afraid you must make allowances for me, since he confided his hopes of Henrietta to me some time ago. I don't believe he will boast to anyone else. It is not in his nature."

It was only later, as Henrietta rather listlessly showed her out, that Diane had the chance to say in private, "You are content with this engagement?"

"Oh yes, quite content."

Diane was still uneasy. She liked Henrietta, and the girl did not look like a happy bride. "I am glad," she said, watching her carefully. "I wondered, perhaps, if you retained your penchant for Aubrey Vale."

"Aubrey and I would not suit. I am too strait-laced. Lord Maynard will suit me much better, especially now that he has stopped regarding me as an item for his collection."

Has he? Diane wondered, though she kept her doubts to herself. It was hardly in her own interests to air them, and she was already looking forward to seeing Aubrey at the Braithwaites' masquerade ball.

She didn't mind receiving him on the rebound. The important thing was to secure him in marriage, for her own security and to calm her father, who was behaving with increasing oddity, writing long, incomprehensible letters for hours, and then vanishing without a word to her. So far, at least, he had always come home again, but in truth, he worried her sick.

ON THE DAY of the masked ball, the Vale twins were glad to run into Michael and Georgiana Gaunt. They had much in common, particularly in the spirit of adventure. But also, the twins, conscious of their own illegitimacy and newly curious about other people's reactions to it, were delighted to discover that Michael too bore that stigma and yet, like them, was treated as a full brother by his family.

But chiefly, there was also the matter of Aubrey, whom they discussed while sheltering in a cave from the rain, with the wet Dog lying across all four of them.

"Has Aubrey been to Graham Gardens since we dined with you?" Leona asked.

"He came a couple of times looking for Henrietta," said Michael, "but she wasn't in. I don't suppose he'll come back at all now."

"Why not?" Leona asked, frowning.

"Because of the big secret," Georgiana said gloomily. "We're not allowed to tell anyone, so keep it to yourself, but Henrietta has engaged herself to Lord Maynard."

"Who the devil is Lord Maynard?" Lawrence asked.

Michael sighed. "Good question. Ouch," he added as Dog shifted position and wagged his tail in Leona's face. "He's a bit of a dull old stick, a widower who collects art. Then Aubrey doesn't know about this?"

"He's never mentioned it," Lawrence said, "but he does seem to have lost some of his…"

"Joie de vivre," Leona supplied. "Did he quarrel with Henrietta?"

"Not in our hearing," Georgiana said. "Actually, it's quite hard to quarrel with Henrietta. She is always the one who keeps the peace. Besides, I'm sure they were kissing by the front door on Monday evening. While we were with you at the carriage. She was perfectly happy then."

"That's true. She was singing in her bedchamber," Michael recalled. "But the next day she was…different."

Lawrence looked at Leona, whose eyes widened in shock.

"He wouldn't," she said.

"Wouldn't what?" Georgiana asked, mystified.

"Nothing," Lawrence said hastily. "Aubrey didn't come home with us that night. He stayed in Blackhaven with other friends."

"Vanya does things like that, too," Michael said, meeting Lawrence's gaze. "It doesn't have to mean anything. He is faithful to Lizzie."

Lawrence nodded. "We'll speak to him. There's a masked ball at the castle, isn't there? Perhaps they will sort it out then. If not, we might have to give them another push."

Michael and Georgiana nodded sagely and told them about a

masked ball they had sneaked into in Vienna before being caught by the secret police.

By silent consent, the twins did not again discuss Aubrey until they were walking home.

Then Leona said, "How big a rake is Aubrey?"

"I only know what you do. Maybe he isn't ready to settle down yet. He is younger than the others."

"He's not younger than Lucy."

"Girls are different. The thing is, I don't know which is worse—to spend the night with some woman of ill repute, or to seduce Henrietta."

"Do you really think he might have?" Leona asked anxiously.

"He could easily have got back into the Gaunts' house that night, especially with her help."

"And then what? She regretted it? Or Aubrey abandoned her?"

"It would explain why she engaged herself to another man two days later," Lawrence said with a hint of adult grimness.

"Yes, but Aubrey is never unkind. I never imagined he would be dishonorable! I don't believe he is."

"No, it is unlikely," Lawrence agreed with just a little too much relief.

Yet as they trudged home, Leona couldn't quite shake the possibility from her mind. Could Aubrey, who had always been rather wonderful, brave, and cheerful in the face of illness and boredom, really have behaved so badly? Or was Leona just naïve? The twins' mother had been a noblewoman who thought nothing about passing them—another man's children—off as her husband's. Their real father, Sir George Vale, had been a shocking rake. He had been kind, too.

"The adult world is not simple, is it?" Leona said.

"No, it isn't. I think..."

"You think what?" she prompted him after several moments' silence.

"I think someone needs to give Aubrey a good kick."

Chapter Fifteen

Henrietta had once looked forward to the Countess of Braithwaite's masked ball. The whole idea reminded her of the family's days in Vienna. She, Michael, Georgiana, and Dog, sometimes with Lizzie, had stood in the street and gazed open-mouthed at the glittering nobility of Europe—sometimes costumed as unlikely peasants with jewels in their hair—sweeping into the grand palaces and lesser halls of the city.

She had ached to dance with Aubrey, perhaps even to confide her newfound love to her friend Alice.

Now, she went through the motions, trying to keep her smile pinned in place to prevent her spirits drooping further.

At least she was masked. Vanya was dressed as a cavalier from the civil war, with Lizzie and Henrietta as his ladies, in rather cumbersome dresses, odd hairstyles, and domino cloaks all of midnight blue. However, Henrietta abandoned the others early on to let them relive their days of courtship. If her chest tightened with the acknowledgement that she would never know such days, such emotion could surely not be seen behind her mask.

It was a merry party, hosts and guests entering into the fun of dressing up like children and behaving in a rather freer manner than they would as adults in their own clothes. One lady in a massively hooped gown wore a headdress with a puppy inside it. When the pup jumped out, she and several other laughing people chased it outside onto the terrace.

Once, Henrietta and her siblings would have delighted in such mischief. Now, she merely smiled at her partner and continued to dance. Neither of them recognized the other, and she tried to enjoy the anonymity. She tried not to gaze around her, searching for anyone who looked like Aubrey.

She thought she saw one of his brothers on the dance floor and hastily returned her attention to her partner. Over his shoulder, she saw a man by the darkening window, gazing fixedly in her direction. He was dressed as a pirate, complete with a gold earring and cutlass, beneath a black domino and a Venetian-style mask that covered most of his face. He was taller than the men around him.

Her heart thudded. *Aubrey.* She was sure of it. Why was he staring at her? Presumably, he had recognized her. Did he want to talk to her, to explain? The right time to do so was the morning she had seen him. When he hadn't followed her. Not that it would have made any difference. They both recognized that there was nothing to say.

He called later, asking for me, a pathetic voice whispered in her head.

It makes no difference. I cannot live with such a man. I cannot love him. It is over.

She wished the pain was over. She wanted everything to be as it was before she had met him. She wanted to go home to Launceton.

Instead, she replied to the conversation of her partner, smiling brightly, and refused to look again at the pirate.

≈

AUBREY ALMOST DID not recognize Henrietta. Which was odd, because he knew Vanya and Lizzie at once, and the lady with them was dressed very similarly to the latter. Something about her posture was wrong. And her smile. She cloaked herself in distance at large gatherings because such beauty could never avoid notice.

But now she could hide behind her mask. Almost as soon as she moved away from Lizzie, a Roman soldier asked her to dance. She snapped her head around in clear surprise. She had really thought, bless her, that, unable to see her face, no one would want to dance with her.

Was that the root of her *differentness* this evening? Or was she just sad?

He didn't want her to be sad. And yet he did, desperately, want to be missed.

"Are you trying to stare her into submission?" asked a light, faintly husky voice at his side. "Or to see beneath the mask?"

Aubrey turned to find a black-haired lady in domino cloak of such a dark green that it was almost black. Behind her mask, dark eyes observed him with detached interest. She gave him a mysterious smile that would once have alerted all his senses and inspired him to the challenge of pursuit and seduction.

"Am I so obvious?" he asked, trying to work out who the devil she was. One of the countess's smart London friends, perhaps? He was sure he had not met her before.

"If one is looking."

"And why would such a lovely and intriguing lady be looking in my direction?"

"I wasn't. I was observing Henrietta."

He acknowledged the hit with a quick smile, though he asked quickly, "How do you know Henrietta?"

"Oh, we are old acquaintances, Mr. Vale."

"You have the advantage, ma'am. And yet I believe we have never met."

"You wouldn't necessarily notice if we had. But, as it happens, you are right. Still, it appears we have mutual friends in the Launceton Gaunts."

"I have friends in the Gaunts. You, apparently, are merely an acquaintance."

A gleam of humor lit her dark eyes. "I do like a man who pays attention. In this matter, you may count them my friends."

"What matter?"

"The matter of Lord Launceton's danger."

Aubrey stared at her. She'd called them the Launceton Gaunts. As if distinguishing them from the other, more senior branch of the family headed by the Marquis of Tamar. "Are you Lord Tamar's sister?"

"Oh, well done, Mr. Vale. I did not even know you were aware of my existence."

"Henrietta told me. I saw a portrait of you once. Without the mask."

"Oh, I always wear a mask. Doesn't everyone?"

"I like to think I am an open book. Do you still believe Launceton is in danger?"

"I am sure of it. But it is a mere incidental part of something much larger and more dangerous."

"Not to Vanya, it isn't. Or his family."

She sighed. "It is all a question of numbers, my friend. Who do you think threatens Lord Launceton? Or Colonel Savarin?"

Aubrey searched her eyes, which were strangely serious. "I don't know. There is a seaman who may be French, and may be associated with a cargo vessel currently docked at Whalen but liable to sail up and down this bit of coast in between times. I saw him in the tavern with an elderly émigré called Corentin. Corentin's son fought in Bonaparte's army and was killed during the retreat from Moscow."

Her expression did not change.

He said, "Corentin is a gentle and courtly man who has lived in this country since the revolution began. I cannot imagine him as an assassin."

"Yet you imagine the seaman is?"

"It crossed my mind. But mostly I was clutching at straws."

"In order to spend time with the divine Henrietta?"

He closed his mouth. "Something like that. Do you know more?"

"Both more and less."

"How very cryptic. He doesn't take it seriously, you know. Launceton."

"Oh, he probably does," Tamar's mysterious sister said vaguely. "He just won't give in to it." She inclined her head, clearly about to move on.

Aubrey moved with her, saying urgently, "His family is not under threat, is it?"

"His family did not kill Corentin's son," she murmured, and slipped into the crowd now dispersing from the dance floor. Her words both relieved him and worried him further. Because she had seemed to take Corentin's part seriously.

With new anxiety, he went in search of Diane. But he had only spun around and taken one step before Henrietta passed him with her Roman partner. She neither met his gaze nor looked away. She did not even see him, and that seemed saddest of all.

"I see you are much taken by my betrothed."

Uncomprehending, Aubrey glanced at the speaker, a man in a blue domino cloak with very serious eyes. Maynard.

"Oh, no, my attention was quite elsewhere," Aubrey assured him, before the oddity of the man's words struck him. He frowned. "You are betrothed so soon? Who is the fortunate lady?"

"Miss Henrietta Gaunt, of course," Maynard said.

Blood sang in Aubrey's ears. For the first time in his life, he was conscious of an impulse toward savage murder.

"We are keeping it private for now," Maynard continued, blissfully unaware of his danger. "But I felt you should know."

The world came back into focus, too loud, too bright, too suffocating. Blindly, desperately, Aubrey followed a draft toward cool, fresh air.

THE PIRATE STEPPED from behind the large stone pillar. "Mademoiselle will grant me the honor of a dance?"

He even tried to disguise his voice, for all that would achieve. Henrietta already knew it was Aubrey.

"Perhaps later," she said coldly. "I am afraid I must sit and rest. Ex—"

"Allow me to find you a chair and refreshment."

For a moment, Henrietta gazed at his proffered arm without moving. So tempting—and so cowardly—to walk away. But, in fact, was this not the true temptation? To listen to his beguiling voice and be fooled all over again?

She *wanted* his explanation, however unpalatable. Although some smaller part of her wanted desperately to remain in ignorance. Most of her knew she needed the relationship to be over. And it wouldn't be until he spoke to her.

She took his arm, proud to see her fingers did not tremble on his sleeve. He did not lead her to a quiet corner of the ballroom, but through the half-open French window onto the terrace.

Well, there was more privacy there, and what they had to say to each other should most certainly remain between the two of them. And this was one encounter where she would be in control.

She walked to the end of the terrace and down the steps to the wooden bench, where she sat and spread her voluminous skirts so that he could not sit too close.

In fact, he did not sit at all. Which meant he loomed, but she refused to be intimidated.

"Who was that woman?" she asked bluntly.

Too late, she saw that she had chosen their privacy badly. While she and the bench were illuminated by low lanterns, she could hardly make out his face at all. No matter. It was nearly all mask anyway.

"What woman?" he asked. He sounded more amused than surprised. He certainly did not seem remotely ashamed.

Of course, ladies of breeding did not acknowledge their less upright sisters, let alone any improper relationship of their straying menfolk. Yet what truly annoyed Henrietta was that he tried to keep the silly French accent. Did he imagine he was somehow still fooling her?

"The woman wrapped around you like a scarf at six o'clock on Tuesday morning," she said dryly.

The pirate laughed softly, infuriating her beyond bearing. "Mademoiselle, walk with me and I will explain all."

He held out his hand to her.

Laugh at me, then. Tell me the lies I long to hear...

He never had the chance. A lady in a dark domino cloak appeared from nowhere and grasped his outstretched arm.

"There you are, my dear," she said affectionately, dragging him with her toward the terrace. "I have been looking for you everywhere."

Dazed, Henrietta watched them go. She felt a little as if she were watching a play while everyone around her watched another, quite different one.

Was this another of Aubrey's women? She wanted to laugh, but somehow it wasn't quite funny and she was afraid of sobbing instead. She should go back and find Lord Maynard, to whom she had not yet spoken this evening. He was not dancing—being still in mourning for his late wife, despite his new betrothal—and she had danced all the time.

One more moment...

She looked up at the sky, at the few stars managing to wink between clouds, and imagined herself flying up there among them, away from darkness and pain and guilt and…

The bench shifted as someone sat down beside her. She straightened in quick alarm to discover a man gazing down at her. She had been wrong. Though his face was still out of the direct light, she could see that he was masked. Enveloped in a dark domino, he seemed alarmingly large.

"Do not be alarmed, mademoiselle," he said in a low murmur. "I mean you no harm."

Again, she almost laughed. "What is wrong with the men at this party? Why do you all pretend to be French?"

"In fairness, some of us probably *are* French." He too kept the accent, and something about its intonation, its rhythm, chilled her blood.

"Monsieur de Corentin?"

He shrugged, spreading his arms. "Be reasonable, mademoiselle. It is a masquerade. I cannot introduce myself before the unmasking."

"Then I am right." And if she was, she should grasp this opportunity with both hands. Perhaps he did not recognize her in the dark. And perhaps he was not Corentin. His voice, though clearly disguised, did not sound very like an old man's. "I am sorry Diane could not come with you."

She thought that was rather clever, since Diane *was* at the ball. If this man was indeed Corentin, he would surely correct her.

His teeth gleamed in the darkness. "How unexpectedly devious of you. Forgive my intrusion. I only joined you because you look sad."

"Oh, no," she said, smiling brightly to prove it. "I was just woolgathering. I am very pleased to see you here. Diane was afraid you would not be well enough."

"What wool did you gather?" he inquired.

"I was just thinking about my family. I suppose you must think a great deal about yours, too."

"Not as much as I should, perhaps, but yes."

"Does the death of your son trouble you?" she asked boldly, trying for a balance of sympathy and casual inquiry. She wasn't sure it worked, for he regarded her in silence for several moments.

He drew in a breath—and a shot rent the air.

Before she could even register it as such, her companion flung an arm around her, whisking her back up the terrace steps so quickly that her feet truly did not touch the ground. At the other end of the terrace, a woman screamed someone's name, and all was light and confusion, but here, where her Frenchman halted, were only shadows and gloom.

Instead of releasing her, he drew her closer. For an instant, his mouth covered hers.

"Not everything is as it seems," he whispered, and spun her around, pushing her toward the French doors back inside, while he strode forward into the light.

Vanya!

Too late the possibility pierced her mind. Probably because Corentin had been with her. But the French seaman had not. *He* had shot Vanya…

Aubrey stared at the still body in Roderick's arms.

The man he had hoped would be his brother-in-law.

"He isn't dead," Roderick said, and strode away after Lord Braithwaite, carrying his burden as tenderly as a baby.

Good for Rod. Since Waterloo, loud noises were not good for his sanity, but he was certainly managing this crisis. Amidst his worry, Aubrey was proud. He went off in search of Lucy, and instead found Delilah.

"Lucy's taking Dr. Lampton up to him," Delilah said. "If he dies…"

"He won't die," Aubrey said confidently. "If you ask me, Eddleston's got out of worse scrapes than this." He gave his sister a quick hug and made sure the rest of his siblings knew.

※

DIANE, SEATED BESIDE Maynard, close to the half-open French doors, jumped at the sound of the shot. She always did—a legacy of the revolution when armed mobs had rampaged the streets. Now, she did not fear for herself.

In fact, the first thought that popped into her head was, *Papa... What have you done?*

But it was Maynard who took her most by surprise. Leaping to his feet with a speed she had never imagined him capable of, he strode off into the milling, agitated throng, then stopped dead when he saw Lord Launceton in front of him, looking surprised as he patted the clearly upset Henrietta's shoulder.

And then she saw her father emerging from the card room to see what was going on. She closed her eyes in relief.

It wasn't him.

She only realized she had said the words aloud when Maynard spoke beside her once more, his voice oddly authoritative and demanding. "Why should you imagine your father was responsible for the shot?"

Her eyes flew open, straight into his direct, steady gaze.

"I don't know," she whispered. "He thinks there is some connection between Lord Launceton and my brother's death."

"Even if there is, it was war," Maynard said.

"I know. He has forgotten, become influenced—" She broke off. Shock or relief was making her say too much.

"Influenced by whom?" Maynard asked.

His expression was not unkind, merely insistent. She realized suddenly he was a peer of the realm, a man of influence and power, used to running vast estates with innumerable dependents. And the urge to confide, to lay her burden on another pair of friendly shoulders, was too strong to resist.

"I don't know precisely. Somehow, he is in contact with malcontents in France and elsewhere—Bonapartists, I think, who will not accept that the war has to be over."

"It's probably harder to accept when you lose," Maynard allowed. "Only your father won, didn't he? The king is back."

"I think it was Gaspard's fault. We have letters from him—or purporting to be from him—praising Napoleon for making France great and glorious again. I suppose that much was true for a while... I don't think Papa cared much while Gaspard was still alive, but his death seemed to turn his mind. I don't know what to do."

"Don't worry. He has done no harm. Tomorrow, I'll speak to Launceton."

A~~~~~~~~~~~~~~~~~~~~~~~~~~~~~LTHOUGH THE BALL carried on, and Lord Eddleston was expected to make a full and speedy recovery, Lizzie was so obviously tired that Vanya decreed they should leave early.

Henrietta did not argue. Her heart and head felt full enough to burst, and she very much wanted to be alone. Lizzie, her head resting on Vanya's shoulder, looked contented enough during the short carriage ride home, but Vanya insisted she go straight to bed.

"I will see to it," he said sternly.

"But I need to be sure Jack—"

"I will look in on Jack," Henrietta said. "And on Michael and Georgi, though Misha is stricter than you are, and they are bound to be in bed by now."

Lizzie allowed that to be true and let Vanya take her up to the front door with his arm around her waist.

A lamp had been left lit in the hall for their return, but the rest of the house was in darkness. The servants must all have gone to bed—apart from Misha, presumably. Lizzie had told her maid not to wait up.

They walked upstairs slowly in silence, Vanya bearing the lamp from the hall. Henrietta barely noticed for the thoughts racing through her head, mostly to do with the pirate and the woman who had dragged him back to the ballroom, and with the other Frenchman who had assuredly *not* been Corentin.

As Lizzie and Vanya crossed the landing to their bedchamber, Vanya set the lamp on the table outside it. Henrietta veered away to Jack's room, where a night light always burned. She turned to say goodnight, but her words died as Lizzie and Vanya's door flew open and a complete stranger was revealed in his candle's glow.

Chapter Sixteen

VANYA'S REACTIONS WERE lightning quick.
He thrust Lizzie behind him, and the stranger barged past. Henrietta threw herself against Jack's door, spreading her arms in instinctive, furious protection. Only then she feared for Michael and Georgiana.

"Misha!" she cried.

But the intruder clearly had no intention of lingering. He fled across the hall to the stairs but didn't get far before Vanya hurled himself at the man's legs and brought him crashing to the floor. The candle went out.

The intruder kicked viciously, causing Vanya to grunt, although he still held on to one of the man's legs while his free hand reached for a better grip.

"Misha!" Henrietta yelled again, which turned out to be a mistake, for Michael's bedchamber door flew open and Michael charged across the hall in his nightshirt, wielding his cricket bat, a bloodcurdling battle cry issuing from his lips.

"Don't hit Vanya!" Lizzie shouted, snatching up the lamp and advancing on the still-struggling males.

Vanya sprang up, hauling the intruder to his feet by the collar. But the man was too desperate to give in and took a swing at Vanya, who ducked and delivered a more accurate punch, just as Michael leapt onto the stranger's back.

The intruder staggered back into the wall.

"Oof," grunted Michael, caught between them. The intruder shook him off as if he were a dog in the rain and threw himself once more at the stairs, Vanya at his heels, followed gamely by Michael with his cricket bat and Lizzie with her lamp.

Henrietta, giving up on Misha, opened Jack's door and found the baby sleeping peacefully through the racket. She left him to it.

"Henri, what the devil's going on?" Georgiana demanded from her doorway. "Is Vanya bosky?"

"No, there's a burglar," Henrietta said shakily, hurrying to the stairs. "He's trying to get away."

Inevitably, Georgiana followed her with more curiosity than fear.

In the hall below, the intruder was cornered by Vanya with his sword and Michael with his cricket bat. From somewhere, Dog was barking furiously, adding to the din.

Then the reception room door was wrenched open to reveal Misha, bleary-eyed and astonished. And Dog flew past him, knocking Michael aside and leaping at the intruder.

"He's growling!" Georgiana said in awe.

In fact, he was snarling. The intruder, with a startled grunt, fell under his weight, and for an instant Henrietta feared Dog was going to bite his throat and kill him.

But Dog, clearly considering his work was done, stood up and launched himself at Michael and Lizzie in happy welcome.

In the flickering light from Lizzie's lamp, the burglar looked younger than Henrietta had expected. Something tiny glinted in his earlobe as, unable to believe his luck, he sprang back up and fled toward the kitchen, Vanya and Misha at his heels.

Dog decided to join in after all, and lolloped after them. A mighty crash came from the kitchen, and Michael, rubbing the back of his head, began to laugh.

The back door slammed hard enough to shake the whole house.

"He's got away!" Georgiana exclaimed.

"Vanya and Misha will go after him," Michael said, scowling at his nightshirt. "Why am I dressed like this in the midst of a battle?" he demanded in disgust.

At which point Vanya reappeared with a candle, lighting more as he went. Misha was at his back, looking sheepish.

"He's gone," Vanya said. "The back door is locked again, and bolted this time. We think that's how he got in—picked the lock and left it open for a speedy departure."

"And you let him go?" Michael demanded.

"I did," Vanya said grimly. "And now Misha and I will make sure the rest of the house is safe."

"You think there are more of them?" Lizzie said, setting down her lamp at last.

"Better safe than sorry," Vanya said vaguely, opening the dining room door.

"Jack!" Lizzie uttered, and fled upstairs.

"He's fine," Henrietta assured her, snatching up a candle and hurrying after, for it had suddenly struck her that this was no ordinary burglary, but the threat to Vanya they had been warned about. In which case, could there be more of them hiding still in Lizzie's bedchamber?

While Lizzie went straight to Jack's room, Henrietta reassured the house servants, woken by the noise and excitement.

"We surprised an intruder," she said calmly, "but Lord Launceton chased him off and the back door is securely bolted now. From now on, you must make sure the bolts are shot. Go back to bed."

She walked into Lizzie's room, her heart drumming, her neck prickling. She held her candle high and shined it all around the room. She even looked in the wardrobe before dropping to her knees and looking under the bed. She looked behind the curtains, then gazed down into the street below.

All was quiet.

And no shouts of discovery issued from elsewhere in the house.

Had the intruder been waiting here to murder Vanya in his bed? Would he have attacked Lizzie too?

She shivered, icy fear crawling up her back.

But surely he could have killed Vanya already? A pistol shot from the bedroom door. A knife in the heart, either immediately or during one of their struggles. Vanya hadn't drawn his sword until later, for the fighting had been too close. But a short blade, a dagger, could easily have done the deed.

What kind of assassin came without a weapon?

She frowned, gazing around the room once more. What had he been looking for in here? Was he a genuine burglar after all?

Moving to the dressing table, she opened Lizzie's jewel box. Lizzie would have to look, of course, but it seemed to Henrietta that it was all here, including the diamond necklace that had first brought Lizzie and Vanya together.

She closed the box and walked out into the hall where the others had gathered.

"We are safe," Vanya said to Lizzie. "And *now*, you may go to bed."

Beside him, Misha met Henrietta's gaze, looking guilty and ashamed.

"Sorry," he muttered in his heavily accented English. "I fell asleep and heard nothing."

"Were you drinking?" Henrietta asked severely.

Misha shook his head, looking so indignant that she believed him. "Just tired. For four nights I hardly slept at all."

Vanya scowled at him. "Why not? What were you doing downstairs, anyway? I told you not to wait up."

Misha shifted from foot to foot, clearly torn between instinctive obedience to Vanya and his instructions from Henrietta.

"I asked him to keep watch when he could," Henrietta admitted.

"Why?" Lizzie asked blankly.

"Because of that nonsense Tamar spouted?" Vanya demanded.

"It's not nonsense. Tamar's sister should be taken seriously, according to Captain Alban."

"Who is Tamar's sister?" Lizzie asked, clearly bewildered. "What did she say?"

"Madame de Delon," Henrietta said.

"Aha. I always thought she was a spy. Though I could never quite work out who she was spying for…"

"Anyway, when were you talking to Captain Alban?" Vanya asked, blatantly changing the subject before it could return to Tamar's warning.

"I wasn't," Henrietta said, her cheeks flaming. "Aubrey Vale spoke to him."

"How the devil does Aubrey know anything about it?"

Henrietta tilted her chin. "I told him. Someone had to take it seriously, since you did not."

"Take *what* seriously?" Lizzie demanded.

Vanya's scowl blackened further as he glared at Henrietta, who, however, knew him too well to be afraid.

"Tell her," she advised. "You have to tell them all now, for everyone's safety. I am going to warm Lizzie some milk. Anyone else want some?"

HALF AN HOUR later, Henrietta sat on the side of Lizzie's bed watching her sister sip the last of her milk. The children and servants were back in bed, Jack still slept, and Vanya was discussing tactics with Misha downstairs.

"You should have told me," Lizzie said. "About this threat to Vanya."

"Perhaps I should have," Henrietta agreed. "But I thought you had enough to worry about. Do you feel well?"

"I feel wide awake, so it's a pity we didn't stay at the ball."

"What, and miss all the fun?" Henrietta said lightly.

Lizzie laughed. "Almost like Vienna all over again."

Henrietta, who couldn't recall ever being truly anxious in Vienna, whatever the adventure, said nothing while she reflected on the nature of growing up.

Lizzie set her glass down on the bedside table and reached for her book. "Perhaps I shall read until I fall asleep. You're not worried, are you, Henri?"

Henrietta shook her head. "Not now. My only worry was that Vanya wouldn't take the threat seriously enough. Now he's forced to, I know he will take more care of himself."

Lizzie nodded. "I'll make sure that Misha always goes out with him—and that all the doors and windows are bolted. Goodnight, Henri."

Henrietta rose. "Goodnight, Lizzie." At the door, she paused and turned back. "Lizzie?"

"Yes?" Lizzie glanced up from the open book in her lap.

"Do you remember we asked you once how you finally realized who Vanya truly was?"

A hint of a rather endearing blush rose to Lizzie's cheeks. "Yes. I recognized him when he kissed me."

"Then it's true?"

Lizzie's eyes widened. "Who else has been kissing you, Henrietta?"

"No one," Henrietta muttered, and whisked herself out of the room.

A white lie for her sister, but she could no longer lie to herself. The pirate had not been Aubrey. She still had no idea who he was, unless he was their burglar, who also seemed to have a stud in his ear. But the other Frenchman at the ball, who had spoken with an equally authentic-sounding accent, was not Monsieur de Corentin, as she had so foolishly imagined. *He* had been Aubrey.

That brief touch of his lips had told her more clearly than a thousand lanterns or a shouted introduction.

"Not everything is as it seems," he had whispered.

And perhaps it was not. Although it had been daylight when he embraced the woman on the steps on Tuesday morning. That, at least, she had not imagined.

***

AFTER THE BALL, Aubrey returned to Black Hill with his siblings, more than a little dazed. He was unreasonably disappointed that Henrietta had not been at the unmasking. Not that it would have made any difference, and God knew that part of the evening had been exciting enough, with Roderick's cast-off mistress claiming to be engaged to him, and Roderick then claiming he was already betrothed to none other than the earl's sister!

Lady Helen had confirmed this, much to everyone's surprise and outward delight. Even more astonishing, Lord Braithwaite had not opposed it. If anything, he had looked relieved. And Aubrey had never seen a man look quite so happy and quite so worried at the same time as Roderick on their way home. This would have amused Aubrey more had Henrietta not occupied at least half of his mind.

He had not meant to eavesdrop. He had been in the garden trying to live with his own fierce jealousy and anger and sheer anxiety that Henrietta had engaged herself to Maynard. The droop of her mouth when she thought no one was looking and her uncertain posture both convinced Aubrey that her betrothal did not make her happy. She was grieving. For *him*.

Although that knowledge brought shame, it also brought hope. She did not love Maynard. They had not been near each other all evening.

If I were engaged to her... He snatched back the pointless thought, returning instead to the moment he had seen her walk into the garden with another man. Along with inevitable jealousy—the pirate was not Maynard—had come concern. He did not like the way the man had hurried her from the light and the people, and so had come closer to see if she was in need of help.

"Who was that woman?" she had asked. *"The woman wrapped around you like a scarf at six o'clock on Tuesday morning."*

She'd thought the pirate was him. Elation surged—she was prepared to talk to him at last. And then fear seized him, because the man was deliberately misleading her.

He had started toward her when a lady breezed past him, almost touching, and whisked the pirate away. He had recognized Tamar's sister again—a lady who appeared to know no fear and was clearly so much in command that the pirate was led back to the ballroom like a naughty child or an errant husband.

Who *was* the damned pirate?

Aubrey had taken his place beside Henrietta from sheer instinct, but she hadn't known him either. Another blow to his self-esteem, and there had been no time for truth before the shot had scared everyone out of their wits and his one concern had been to get her to safety.

Their moment had passed again in fear for Vanya, and then fear for poor Eddleston. But still Aubrey hung on to the fact that whatever her motives in engaging herself to Maynard, she did not love him.

Of course, she might never love Aubrey again either, but he could *try* to win her back, win her in truth. By finally being worthy of her. He needed to find a means to earn his living.

"Aubrey?" Julius broke into his thoughts. The carriage had stopped outside Black Hill House. "Are you planning to sleep there?"

Aubrey grunted and climbed down.

He wondered if he could assist Cornelius in the management of the land? Although the estate could not afford two stewards' salaries, he could learn from his brother and then work for others...

It would take too long. He was too impatient to take the years necessary to learn about land and farming. Besides, he wasn't actually very interested in the subject, not like Cornelius.

No, Aubrey would be better with his own business, like Roderick, who had begun a company of guards for the protection and delivery of both people and valuable items. Roderick, of course, had the instincts and the organization of the soldier. What the devil did Aubrey have? A smart mouth, a capacity for trouble, and a great deal of useless learning acquired in his sickbed.

I'm the best-educated wastrel in Blackhaven. He doubted there were many advertisements for such. He would need to be creative. After a good night's sleep.

※

AMAURY DE CORENTIN had almost given up and gone to bed when he heard the scratch at his window. Louis.

Rising, he went to the front door and let in his compatriot, who followed him silently into the little parlor.

"Well?" Corentin snapped, turning to face his visitor. "Good God, what happened to you?"

Louis was disheveled, his clothes torn, his face cut, his eye swollen.

"They came back early," he said. "You were meant to make sure they stayed at the ball."

"So where is the child?"

"I never found any damned child. I found a large man with a sword and another with a wooden club. And a massive, slavering beast. I had to flee."

Corentin threw himself into the chair by the fire. These days, he was always cold. "You did not take the girl with you, did you? I told you to take the girl. That way the dog would not touch you."

"I improvised. I almost had the girl, then some woman mistook me for her husband and dragged me back to the ballroom, where she promptly vanished. So I took advantage of the excitement over the shooting and went to the house. It was easy to get in, and the house was quiet. I crept upstairs in darkness, careful not to show a light, and listened outside all the doors. I went through one and shut it before I lit my candle. It was an adult's room, no baby, no cradle, no nurse. So I opened the door again and was confronted with a crowd of other people."

He waved an impatient hand, indicating that Corentin could infer the rest. "Waste of my time."

"Actually, I don't believe it was," Corentin said thoughtfully. "Now, he is afraid. His family is afraid. This, I like."

"They didn't seem very afraid to me. They all came after me like a bizarre army of—"

"They were afraid," Corentin insisted. "Why else would they come after you? No, you have done well. Did you manage to punch Launceton, at least?"

"Slippery as an eel and damnably quick. I kicked him."

"It will do." Corentin sighed. "I suppose you had better lie low for a little. Just in case the family sees your bruises and recognizes you. We don't want you taken up by the law at this stage."

Louis cast him a sardonic glance. It was almost scornful, as if he would remind Corentin who was actually in charge. Such trivia did not interest Corentin. He wanted only revenge for Gaspard, security for his daughter, France, and death. Most definitely in that order.

Chapter Seventeen

Aubrey woke surprisingly early the morning after the ball, his mind full of memories. He had been dreaming of his father and the various places they had lived around the world. Endlessly fascinating places, seen by Aubrey often only in tantalizing glimpses, yet always leaving him with an impression, a point to research. And all those clever, intriguing, charming people who drifted past his sickbed while about their important duties and ambitions.

He sprang out of bed, stark naked, and went to the bureau below the window. He threw the shutters wide, then rummaged among the lower drawers of the desk until he found what he was looking for. Three notebooks filled with his handwriting, which he threw onto the open flap of the bureau.

Shivering, he reached impatiently for his dressing gown. It was too small for him, but it was enough to stave off the morning chill.

His father had always taken as many of his children as possible with him wherever he went, even when his wives were reluctant to join him. As a result, Aubrey had seen a great deal of the world, whether from his bath chair, as he had once claimed to Henrietta, or from his sickbed, through the windows of a carriage, or on occasional walks.

Places, people, and events that were commonplace to his siblings had captivated the far more sheltered Aubrey. He had written all this down, often burnishing his impressions with knowledge gleaned from books brought for him by his father, tutors, siblings, servants, or anyone eager to please the old gentleman.

As Aubrey read the pieces he had written over the years, vivid pictures leapt into his mind. They made him smile and laugh. Some, tinged with tragedy, brought a lump to his throat. Even at fourteen, he had been observant and perceptive and, he thought, had an evocative way with words.

Seizing a sheet of paper, he sharpened the pen he had used so little since returning to Black Hill, dipped it in ink, and began to transcribe, tidying and editing as he went, adding maturity to the freshness of the youthful writing.

When he had four short but decent pieces whipped into better shape, he sat back and scowled at them. Were they any good? Would anyone want to publish them, let alone read them?

Cornelius, he recalled, had always enjoyed literature of all kinds.

Throwing down his pen, Aubrey shrugged out of his old dressing gown and stuck his head in the washbowl. Five minutes later, he banged on Cornelius's door. Getting no answer, he ran downstairs, clutching his papers, and all but ran into the twins charging across the hall.

"Where's Cornel?" he demanded.

"Out, of course," Lawrence said. "It's past midday."

"Is it?" Aubrey said. "Damn. That man works too hard."

"Oh, he isn't working," Leona said wryly. "Or at least not much."

"Oh?" Aubrey cocked an eyebrow.

In perfect time, the twins drew their forefingers across their mouths, indicating their lips were sealed.

Aubrey shrugged. "You two need tutors," he said. "Or school."

"It's summer," Lawrence pointed out, and they dashed off before he could pursue the subject.

Aubrey stuck his head around the empty drawing room door, then discovered Delilah writing letters in the morning room. She was wearing old clothes, her hair escaping from its pins while she wrote with her usual speed and focus. She looked pretty and so *Delilah* that he smiled, reflecting on his good fortune in siblings. Not that he would ever tell them so.

"Are you busy, Delly?"

"Not so busy that I wouldn't like to be distracted." She turned to him at once. "You missed breakfast. Is everything well?"

"I don't know," he said honestly, thrusting his bundle of paper at her. "Would you do me a favor? Read this and tell me if it's rubbish."

She took it from him, and he nodded his thanks before wandering off as if he didn't care.

He was munching bread and cheese in the kitchen, making Cook laugh, and distracting the other servants from their work, when Delilah came to find him.

"Aubrey, these are brilliant!" she said without preamble. "What are you going to do with them? Put them in a book?"

Aubrey's cheeks burned with pleasure. "You think they're good enough?"

"More than good enough, but you must write more."

"I have more. But it will be a dull travel book without illustrations. I don't suppose you still have your drawings, do you?"

"Come with me," she said, and led him up to her room.

Delilah was not a great artist, but she was accurate, and Aubrey rather thought the very prosaic nature of her drawings juxtaposed with his evocative prose might work very well.

"This," Aubrey said, grinning at her, "is a start. Shall we make a book?"

HENRIETTA WAS READING in the drawing room when Lord Maynard

was announced. She rose immediately and went to meet him, smiling, and reflecting with some surprise that his presence no longer dismayed her. He stared less, it was true. Or perhaps she had just got used to him, accepting him for the way he was.

"Good morning," she greeted him. "Did you enjoy the ball last night? I barely saw you."

"I was being mindful of Lord Launceton's stipulation of secrecy. Even so, I was hoping for the supper dance, but you left too early."

"I know. Lizzie tires so easily just now that a ball is really too much for her. Oh, and we had some excitement when we came home." She told him all about the intruder and could not doubt that he was listening.

"How very...worrying," he said at last. "Is Lord Launceton at home?"

"I think so." She hurried to the still-open door and called, "Vanya!"

Maynard winced, and she blushed.

"Sorry, a bad habit," she said. "But the house is so small it seems silly to send a servant for him..."

She was vindicated by the sound of Vanya's quick, unmistakable footsteps on the stairs, though she suspected this didn't carry much weight with Maynard. He liked order and decorum too much.

Which made her just a little uneasy about their future life together, to say nothing of her family visiting. She had a vision of Dog charging around Maynard's priceless porcelain collection like the proverbial bull in a china shop and didn't know whether to laugh or shudder.

Fortunately, before either could occur, Vanya strode in, nodded a casual greeting to Maynard, and demanded of Henrietta, "What is it?"

"It was I who requested a word, Launceton. Henrietta told me of your intruder last night."

Vanya touched the cut on his forehead where the burglar's boot had caught him. "Indeed. A bit of an adventure."

"I don't suppose you caught him?"

"He managed to get out the house, and I didn't pursue him. I wanted to be sure my family was safe."

"Of course. That's really the point of my call."

Henrietta smiled to herself. At least one would never be flattered by Maynard, who had not, it seemed, come with the prime intention of seeing his betrothed. She waved him to a chair and composed herself on the sofa to listen.

"You should know," he said carefully, "that when I first met Monsieur de Corentin in this house, I saw on his face an expression of what I can only describe as pure hatred."

Vanya blinked. "What has Corentin got against you?"

Maynard's eyebrows flew up. "Nothing. It was you he was looking at."

"Corentin," Vanya said quickly. "Well, it certainly wasn't Corentin I was wrestling with on the floor last night."

"No, and he stayed at the ball until the very end, but—"

"We think he has an ally, a henchman," Henrietta put in.

Both men stared at her in some surprise.

She blushed. "Aubrey Vale saw him in the tavern."

Vanya opened his mouth, then closed it again to leave the matter for a later discussion, for Maynard had something else to say.

"I spoke at some length to his daughter last night. She is concerned for him. Not only that he is ill, but that he has fallen into the company of fanatical Bonapartists and is obsessed with revenge on the man he believes killed his son." He met Vanya's gaze. "During the retreat from Moscow."

Vanya lowered himself onto the sofa beside Henrietta.

"I might have," he said bluntly. "There was a lot of death for one reason or another. I did my fair share of causing it. I'm not afraid of Corentin. I don't even blame him. He is old, ill, and grieving. The henchman, however, troubles me." He swung his gaze on Henrietta. "Aubrey saw him in the tavern?"

"Yes, but we think he lives on a ship docked at Whalen called *La Colombe*. When I went there with the children, no one would talk to me about it. I think they were put off by Dog."

"I'll go to the tavern first," Vanya decided.

"Not without Misha," Henrietta said anxiously.

"Not without Misha," he agreed. "And most certainly armed to the teeth."

AFTER LUNCHEON, HENRIETTA accompanied the still-tired Lizzie to the pump room.

"You seem much more weary with this baby than with Jack," Henrietta said anxiously.

"According to Dr. Lampton, my body would have liked longer to recover after Jack. But I am perfectly healthy."

Lizzie usually preferred to sit at the outside table overlooking the sea, but since it was raining, they went inside, where Henrietta was shocked to see Aubrey Vale.

She had almost forgotten his health problems. Although she knew he did so, it seemed somehow odd to see him taking the waters along with the old and the ill and those merely obsessed with their own health. He must attribute his current relief from illness to the Blackhaven waters…

He was with one of his sisters at a corner table, deep in discussion while the pair riffled through a pile of papers. Without warning, he glanced up and saw her. His gaze locked to hers, paralyzing her. And then he stood and bowed to Lizzie, who was walking straight toward him. Henrietta could only follow.

"Have you met my sister, Miss Vale?" he said civilly to Lizzie. "Delilah, Lady Launceton and Miss Gaunt."

Lizzie held out her hand, friendly as always. "I know you by sight,

Miss Vale, so I'm very pleased to meet you at last. May we join you?"

Wretch, thought Henrietta in panic. "May I fetch water for you, Miss Vale?"

"Oh, no thank you. I'm only here to force-feed it to Aubrey."

"I have been a good boy," Aubrey said wryly, upending his glass, "and drunk it all down."

Then perhaps he will leave directly. Annoyed to find that her hands shook as she fetched a glass for Lizzie, Henrietta ordered one for herself at the same time. By the time she returned to the table, Lizzie was telling the Vales about last night's intruder and Aubrey was scowling.

"I trust Lord Launceton is now taking the matter seriously?" he said with unusual sternness.

"Oh, quite," Lizzie said. "He and Misha—his servant who has been with him forever, even in his army days—are looking into it."

"I trust no one was hurt?" Delilah said.

"I suspect the burglar came off worst," Lizzie said with satisfaction, and Aubrey's lips twitched, as they did when he found unexpected humor in a situation.

Henrietta's heart ached.

"Have you heard how poor Lord Eddleston is?" Lizzie asked.

"I believe he had a good night," Delilah replied. "Lucy is at the castle now, and Julius will move him to Black Hill tomorrow."

"He is a most appealing young man," Lizzie remarked. "Who on earth would shoot him?"

"His brother-in-law, apparently," Aubrey said wryly. "The man was married to Eddleston's sister, and is now charged with her murder as well as the attempted murder of Eddleston."

"I never realized there were such awful people in Blackhaven," Lizzie said, distressed.

"There are awful people everywhere. But most of us are harmless."

Henrietta, who had almost finished her water, wrapped her sister's hand about her glass. "Drink, Lizzie."

"Oh, are you in a hurry?" Lizzie asked her.

"No," Henrietta said, trying to hide her desperation. "Just a promise to the children."

"I was going to call on Miss Talbot at the hotel," Lizzie remarked. It was the first Henrietta had heard of it. "And hopefully see Mrs. Macy too. She is to be your sister-in-law very soon, is she not? Perhaps you would care to accompany me, Miss Vale? And Aubrey may escort Henrietta home."

Henrietta stared at her. *Traitor.* "I am quite capable of remembering the way home. I would not inconvenience Mr. Vale, who is clearly busy."

"I am not busy in the slightest," Aubrey assured her, rising to his feet. The papers he and Delilah had been looking at were now nowhere to be seen. "I would enjoy the walk, and I can meet you and Antonia at the hotel, Delly."

Henrietta could not fight it further without making a scene. She accepted with what grace she could, bidding a polite goodbye to Aubrey's sister before sailing out of the pump room ahead of Aubrey.

For the first few seconds, they walked in awkward silence. He did not offer his arm, for which she was grateful. And yet it seemed so sad that they should have been reduced from easy friendship to this.

He said abruptly, "Are you really going to marry Maynard?"

"Yes," she replied. "I am really going to marry Maynard."

His gaze burned into her averted face. "Why? You loathe him."

"No, I don't." She swallowed. "I'll admit I did not care for him. But that was before I realized I was judging him by appearance, as I hate to be judged. He stared at me all the time, just because of how I look. But now that he is used to me, he no longer gazes in the same disconcerting manner. In fact, he is a most interesting and clever person."

"Shallow reasons to marry a man. And damning, if I may say so, with faint praise."

"You may not say so, for it is none of your business. In fact, I have come to realize that Lord Maynard is the only kind of man I could be happy with—a man who is honest and upright and faithful. Someone whom *I* can make happy."

She risked a quick glance at him and away. She thought his face had whitened, though his next words were light and bantering.

"Then it is not just because you saw me wrapped around Violet—er…like a scarf, at six of the clock on Tuesday morning?"

She swung on him. "It *was* you!"

"I overheard," he said calmly. "I was not your pirate."

"I know *that*," she said witheringly. "You were the other man, who dared to kiss me while pretending to be French!"

"I thought it was *de rigeur*," he said. "Pretending to be French, I mean. The kissing was all my own idea." He drew in a breath, suddenly serious. "Don't marry him just because I am not a good man, Henrietta. I am becoming one. You will see."

"I won't," she said shakily. "Oh, I know you believe it now, and I am flattered, in a way, by your intended sacrifice. But you'll never keep to it, Aubrey, unless it's for *you*, not for me. And there's the rub. I never wanted to be the rope that binds you, restricts you from what you really desire to be doing. I wished to *be* what you truly desire. As I am to Maynard. As Lizzie is to Vanya."

Oh God, why couldn't she keep quiet? She turned her face away, determined at least to keep the tears from him. But she felt him shake his head.

"Oh no," he said harshly. "That is all other people's desires. What do *you* actually want, Henri?"

The use of her family's pet name almost undid her. "I want to be needed," she whispered. "I want to be loved. I want to love *you*, and now I can't. Oh, please go away, Aubrey, just leave me alone…"

Through her tears, she saw they were almost at her front door, so she fled and didn't look back.

Chapter Eighteen

On his daily promenade with his daughter from the pump room to the harbor, Corentin acknowledged with some complacence that his plans were well laid. Savarin-Launceton must be increasingly rattled. He believed his wife to be unfaithful—surely the fact that he had whisked her home from the ball so early proved that—and everything was in place for his final fall.

On top of which, Aubrey Vale was freed for Diane by Henrietta's engagement to Lord Maynard. The betrothal was not yet being announced, but the parties concerned all knew about it, which was good enough for Corentin. Provided Diane played her part properly. After all, she was a sensible girl.

"We have not seen much of Aubrey Vale in the last few days," he remarked.

Diane sighed. "Give him time, Papa, to get over his previous hopes. I shall be a most sympathetic ear. He danced with me at the ball, remember."

Corentin nodded. "Perhaps now would be a good time to draw back from your friendship with Henrietta."

"Papa!" She glared at him with genuine temper. "Will you please stop trying to organize every aspect of my life? I am five and twenty and quite capable of choosing my own friends, husband, and pastimes."

"You will have to, my dear, for I shall not always be here."

"You are here now," she said, taking his arm.

"I shall be gone more quickly than you think."

"Stop it, Papa. We shall not be morbid. In fact, you are looking better today."

If only she knew he was not yet talking about death, but about France. He would miss her, but she had made it clear her life was in England, and with the Vales she would be safe.

At that moment he caught sight of his enemy walking up the steps from the beach. His wife was with him. In fact, he was holding her hand, and she was laughing up at him. While rage gathered in Corentin's heart, Lord Launceton hugged his wife in public. For an instant she rested her head against his shoulder in a touching gesture of trust and affection, and then she took his arm and they walked on more decorously, but still talking animatedly, enjoying each other's company as though they hadn't a care in the world.

They didn't even see Corentin and Diane approach, for they had strolled off toward the market.

Seething, Corentin wondered why the seed of his wife's affair with Aubrey had not quickened into distrust. Perhaps he had simply picked the wrong man. Aubrey had been too obviously besotted with Henrietta, perhaps, for it to be believable that he merely used her as a means to get closer to her sister.

By that one glimpse, his enemy was not suffering nearly enough.

And then he saw his salvation.

Young Lord Tranmere and his friends, looking utterly dissolute, were lurching toward the harbor, probably from the tavern. Apparently, Tranmere was in the area upon a supposed repairing lease, but he couldn't have been saving much expense.

Smiling, Corentin patted Diane's hand and extracted it from his arm. "Go on home, my dear. I shall be back directly, after a quick word with my young friend…"

It wasn't difficult to separate Tranmere from his friends, since some remnant of courtesy still clung to him.

"I hear you are a wagering man, my lord," Corentin purred.

"I'm afraid so. If I wasn't, I wouldn't be stuck up here in this backwater. My grandfather found the most isolated inn in the world and sent me there." Tranmere grinned. "Didn't say I couldn't take my friends. And then, I'm not sure he knows about Blackhaven."

"Won't he notice your repairing lease isn't repairing as much as he hoped?"

"Truth to tell, I'm running short," Tranmere confided. "Which is a pity with Muir's card party coming up on Saturday." He sighed. "Should be some high-stakes games, too."

Corentin blinked. He thought the card party was being run by the vicar and his wife, in which case the stakes were likely to be tediously low. However, since it was hardly in his interests to point this out to Tranmere, he merely smiled.

"I'll make a side wager with you, then," Corentin offered. "If you win, you'll have all the money you need for Saturday."

Tranmere cast him an assessing look. And it was true that Corentin, though indubitably a gentleman, hardly looked like a wealthy one. He let his eyes gleam.

"I am not so old that I cannot keep a little by for my own amusement. And even if you lose, you will enjoy the trying."

"I will?" Tranmere was intrigued.

"You must be acquainted with the delightful Lady Launceton."

Tranmere grinned. "Charming," he agreed. Then he growled deep in his throat and kissed the tips of his fingers. "Acquainted with her sister, too, though not as well as I'd like to be."

"She casts most females in the shade," Corentin allowed, "though I think if you look closely, you'll see that her sister Lady Launceton has the advantage in liveliness and passion."

Tranmere stared at him. "That so? Don't fancy getting on the husband's wrong side, though."

"Nonsense, it'll do him good. He is far too arrogant. However, that is my wager with you, my lord. That you cannot seduce Lady Launceton."

"Damn well can," Tranmere responded.

TRANMERE, IN FACT, was ripe for mischief. The novelty of being banished to the wilderness and defying his grandfather, merely by taking his party with him and continuing his debauchery, was wearing thin. As was his allowance.

He'd won a fortune the night he hosted a wild card party at his inn, and then lost it again over the next three nights, most of it on cards and dice, the rest on a woman whose face he could no longer remember but who had robbed him blind in the middle of the night.

Yes, there was a sameness to country depravity, so old Corentin's wager came at just the right time. Accordingly, abandoning his friends at the inn taproom—they were becoming tedious in any case—he sauntered around to Graham Gardens, where, according to Corentin, resided the Launcetons.

He was lucky enough to find the ladies at home, although with other guests, including some moonling who gazed constantly at Henrietta with a fatuous smile on his face. Not that Tranmere blamed the moonling for that. He was damned if he'd ever seen a lovelier girl anywhere. But it was the sister he had come to inspect.

And he could see immediately what Corentin meant. The curve of her elegant neck, the slender, capable hands that were most alluring as she poured cups of tea, her every movement unconsciously graceful. Her face, while lacking Henrietta's perfect beauty, was pretty and full of character and laughter. More than that, she possessed a delightful figure that Tranmere was eager to undress. A knowing, married body, full of passion…

He smiled dazzlingly at her as he accepted his cup of tea from her fair hands. *Damn me, I'm glad I took this wager.*

He knew how to tantalize. As soon as the moonling was forced by his mother to depart, Tranmere took his place beside Henrietta and paid court to her. She smiled tolerantly. If he hadn't known better, he might have imagined he bored her, but since his main object was her sister, he didn't much care.

Although he didn't have much time to complete his seduction before the card party on Saturday, he was careful not to overstay his first morning call. However, he did invite Henrietta to walk with him along the seafront and perhaps enjoy an ice at the parlor.

"Perhaps you are free to accompany us tomorrow, my lady?" he asked her sister, carefully casual.

"Perhaps I am," she agreed, and he included her in his charming smile as he took his leave.

He felt like rubbing his hands together. What an enjoyable wager this was going to be, and from this promising beginning, he was sure of success.

***

AUBREY SPENT THE days following the ball working hard on his writing, which Delilah described as his "travel vignettes." Several of them matched up with her drawings.

"Why don't we ask Lady Helen to color one of them, and we can use it as a frontispiece for the book?" he suggested.

Delilah looked doubtful. "She is an artist. Her talent is of a quite different caliber. Did you see her paintings at the garden party? I would be embarrassed to ask her such a thing."

"I'll do it, then. She is very good natured. Roderick is one lucky man."

For not only did Rod's claim of betrothal to Lady Helen stand, the marriage was to be this Friday by common license. The Vales were stunned by the speed. In fact, if it had been anyone but Helen, Aubrey would have suspected his brother of excessive dalliance, but Roderick would never deflower so young and innocent a lady.

The twins appeared to be happy with the arrangement, and so was Lucy, so Aubrey merely shrugged and got on with his work.

Since his last devastating conversation with Henrietta, he knew he could not afford to fall apart. She needed to be saved from Maynard. And if he was to do it, he needed some kind of security and ambition to offer her, to convince her that his promises were not mere lip service or intentions that would fail at the first temptation.

Beside Henrietta, there *were* no temptations. No other women interested him anymore, and not merely because she was his latest obsession. Because she was Henrietta.

And so, he worked.

Then, on Wednesday, a totally unexpected new opportunity opened up for him.

Roderick, who had been away for most of the week because of his new business, went into Blackhaven to sign legal papers with Braithwaite, concerning marriage settlements and the lease of a house Braithwaite was giving the couple as a wedding present. Aubrey, keeping to his routine of water drinking, abandoned his vignettes and accompanied him in the carriage.

Because it needed to be said, Aubrey tried to convey how impressed he was by Rod's new guarding venture and blurted something about his own ambition to be self-sufficient.

Roderick's rather hard gaze bored into his face. "I never thought to ask you, but you are very welcome to join Skelton and me in this venture. You would be an asset."

Aubrey grimaced. "Hardly. Not really guard material, Rod. You couldn't rely on me." Anything could still trigger one of his attacks.

What if he had to go into a smoky tavern, for example?

"There's more to it than hard riding and looking threatening," Roderick told him. "There's observation, administration, being charming. And besides, you were the one who captured the stolen horse."

"My one heroic gesture to prove I could," Aubrey said. He was ridiculously touched by his brother's offer, even suspecting it was made in pity, but he owed him honesty. "No, I wouldn't be reliable. And to be frank, Rod, it doesn't interest me."

"Pity. You're an observant sort of fellow."

"Not much else to do when you're lying on a couch."

"Or sitting in drawing rooms, ballrooms, pump rooms…"

"Other people's lives are fascinating."

"You make them so," Roderick said unexpectedly. "I always enjoyed your letters. And I learned more about what was going on at home from your amusing epistles than I ever did from the girls' chatty ramblings or Cornelius's concise reports."

Aubrey flushed under the praise, and almost told him about the travel vignettes. But inevitably, they slipped into easier banter and the moment was lost. Still, Aubrey was left with a feeling of warmth and hope that he wasn't so useless after all, not to Roderick, and maybe not to Henrietta or anyone else.

When they parted so that Roderick could keep his appointment at the solicitor's office, Rod said abruptly, "Do you know the print shop on Candle Row?"

"No, but I can find it. Why?"

"I'll meet you there in a couple of hours."

AFTER DRINKING A second glass of water, Aubrey wondered what to do with himself for the best part of two hours. He wished had hadn't agreed to wait for Roderick, for he would far rather be home, working.

Or calling on Henrietta.

The anguish on her face at their last meeting tore him apart. He longed to comfort and reassure her—except that his presence would do the opposite. He had made such a mess of this...

For now, all he could do for her was to stay out of her way while he endeavored to be a better man.

And so he walked round to the Corentins' cottage to see if there was at least anything he could do for Launceton's situation.

Corentin, however, was not at home, so he could not remain alone for very long with Diane or tongues would wag.

She regarded him with a long, perceptive look. "You're looking a trifle worn, my friend. Burning the candle at both ends?"

"A little," Aubrey admitted with some truth, although not in the way Diane was clearly imagining.

"I expect she was your first love. That always hurts the most."

Aubrey did not wish to talk about love or Henrietta. So he said bluntly, "Someone broke into the Launcetons' house on Friday night. Is it possible your father had anything to do with that?"

"Of course not," she said coldly. "He was at the ball. You saw him there."

He held her gaze in silence until she looked away.

"Someone was here that night. At least, before dawn. I woke and heard voices. More than just my father's. I don't know who he was." She swallowed, adding with some difficulty, "He is beginning to frighten me, Aubrey. His obsession with Launceton, justified or not, is threatening everything. I'm afraid...he thinks he is about to die and he has to somehow arrange everything to his satisfaction before he does."

"Including Launceton's death?"

She nodded. "That is what I am most afraid of. More worryingly, Lord Maynard is afraid of it, too."

"Maynard?" he repeated, startled.

Diane smiled sardonically. "I know he is your rival in love, but you must allow him some skills in observation and interpretation. I think he and the incident of the intruder have convinced Launceton to take more care. I saw him yesterday with his wife, and that scary Russian servant was following closely enough to protect them if necessary."

Aubrey nodded. After a moment, he said, "What do you think of Henrietta's engagement to Maynard?"

"I think it is in reaction to you and your rakish ways. You must have been very indiscreet."

"I was. And for the first time, innocent at the same time. A delicious irony, if one cares for such things."

"She is not for you, Aubrey," Diane said gently.

"Perhaps not. But does she have to marry a dry old stick like Maynard to prove it?"

"He is not a dry old stick," Diane retorted. "I doubt he is more than ten years older than you. He may be a little strange, but he is actually a very interesting and honorable man."

"So I hear," Aubrey said bleakly. Pulling himself together, he said, "I must go. But let me know if I can help with your father in any way. Or with any other trouble—I find I am much better with other people's than my own."

"Aren't we all?" Diane said ruefully. "Thank you, Aubrey. You are a good friend."

With nothing else to do, Aubrey went looking for Roderick's print shop, which turned out to be a trifle run-down and located in a street in no better condition. Two shop fronts had been boarded up further along.

The printer, a Mr. Nimmo, clearly had time on his hands to chat, and Aubrey, being naturally curious, was soon in the back of the shop, fascinated by the workings of the printing press and the movable type.

Which was where Roderick found him when he eventually turned up. Being Roderick, he came straight to the point, ordering more business cards and leaflets.

"Tell me, Mr. Nimmo," Roderick said, "do you have the capacity here to print a newspaper? Say, every fortnight to begin with?"

Nimmo sighed. "I have the capacity but not the orders."

"Could we sit down and discuss the possibilities of partnership?" Roderick said briskly. "I have some money set aside which I can put into such a venture."

Aubrey stared at his brother in disbelief. "You want to produce a *newspaper* now? When the devil are you going to have time to do that?"

"I'm not," Roderick said. "You are."

Aubrey's jaw dropped. For once, he truly was speechless.

"If you want to," Roderick continued. "You are the ideal writer, editor, the reporter of news. You know more than anyone else about what goes on in this town—with the possible exception of the twins—and you have an excellent yet concise turn of phrase. I can organize the business and Mr. Nimmo can print it. If we can come to an agreement."

Aubrey's head reeled. Rod was serious. And this… This was exactly what Aubrey needed, a congenial occupation, a regular income. If he could make a success of it. And with the possibility of a book to supplement it, surely lots of possibilities were opening for him. Excitement soared, along with a deluge of ideas and terror of failure.

"I'll make tea," said Mr. Nimmo.

Aubrey swallowed. "Got any brandy?"

WHEN HE AND Roderick got home, they were still full of plans and ideas, which quickly infected their siblings with excitement.

"We'll help you," the twins offered with glee.

"I'm counting on it," Aubrey replied. "In fact… Come with me. I have an assignment for you."

But his assignment had nothing to do with the upcoming newspaper. "I'm going to be a bit tied up with organizing this over the next week, so I want you to keep an eye on someone for me."

"Who?" Leona demanded. "We're not spying on Henrietta."

"I should think not!" Aubrey exclaimed, and she blushed.

"Sorry," she muttered, "but you are both being so *stupid*—Ouch." She glared at her twin, who had kicked her in the ankle, then turned her ire on Aubrey. "*Did* you seduce Henrietta Gaunt?"

It seemed to be a day for speechlessness.

"No," he exploded at last. "And you do more harm to her than to me by even suggesting such a thing."

Leona breathed out in a rush. "We knew you hadn't. We just needed to be sure. Who do you want us to watch?"

"Amaury de Corentin. Do you know him? Elegant old émigré, lives in a cottage near the harbor with his daughter Diane."

"We know who he is," Lawrence said. "What has he done?"

"That's the trouble," Aubrey admitted. "I'm not sure that he's done anything, but I'm very afraid he means to cause harm to Lord Launceton. I'd like to know where he goes and who he talks to. But twins?"

They were already halfway out the door, though they did pause as if they were paying attention.

"You're not to get in his way. Nor the way of any of his associates," Aubrey said severely. "Just observe and report without being noticed."

Having thus delegated one of his worries, he bent his mind and his considerable energy to the establishment of the *Blackhaven Chronicle*.

Chapter Nineteen

On Friday, Roderick wed Lady Helen Conway. They were married in Blackhaven's St. Andrew's Church by the vicar, Mr. Tristram Grant, who was both amiable and amusing.

Aubrey's feelings were unexpectedly strong and very mixed. Mostly, he was glad for Rod, for his deserved happiness, and Helen, though young, was sweet-natured and loyal. But at the same time, Roderick was the first to break up the band of siblings who had all lived at Black Hill together for the first time. Aubrey realized how much he had valued the steadiness of life with them over these few months, and how much he would miss it. Miss *them*.

Roderick had moved into a house in town. Lucy would soon marry and move away with Eddleston. Before that, Julius would marry Antonia, and she, however sisterly and accommodating she was trying to be, might well resent sharing her home with the zoo that clung to Julius's coattails.

And then Aubrey imagined himself in Roderick's place, only marrying Henrietta. And he ached all over again.

Henrietta was somewhere in the crowded church with her family. Giving in, he removed his gaze from his brother making his vows and looked for her.

He couldn't see her. She must have sat too far behind. But he did notice a face he doubted should have been there. Meg Maven,

Roderick's former mistress, who, Aubrey suspected, had deliberately tried to cause trouble at the masked ball. Now she looked stunned, as if she had not believed Roderick would actually go through with his wedding to another woman.

With growing unease, Aubrey watched her, and when Mr. Grant pronounced the couple man and wife, her face crumpled into a mask of misery so intense that she looked mad.

Uh-oh…

"Change of plan," he murmured to the twins as they left the church. "After the wedding breakfast, ignore Corentin, at least for today. Instead, keep watch on that woman. I'll take over before dark, if she doesn't leave Blackhaven."

Leona, following his gaze, narrowed her eyes. "That's—"

"We know who she is," Aubrey interrupted. "And she's not to cause trouble for Helen or Rod."

"Absolutely not," the twins agreed.

"Where would I be without you?" Aubrey said.

Some problems, however, could not be delegated. Cornelius, his hardest-working and most reliable brother, cornered him as they left the wedding breakfast at the castle, and asked him to be his second in a duel.

And I'm the rakehell of the family? he thought indignantly.

"LORD MAYNARD IS not a very devoted suitor, is he?" Georgiana remarked the day after Major Roderick Vale married Lady Helen Conway.

Along with Lizzie and Vanya, Henrietta had been at church to see it and afterward attended the magnificent wedding breakfast at the castle. Prepared to avoid Aubrey as much as she could, she was slightly piqued to discover she didn't need to. He seemed preoccupied with other matters and other people.

Which, of course, was just as it should be. She had said everything necessary and more, and sent him away. And yet if their parting had caused him any unhappiness, she could see none in his face. He looked a little tired, perhaps, but there was a certain vital energy about him that she had never noticed before. He laughed at jokes, entertained, bantered with his brothers, and was perfectly charming to Helen and Alice. He had even made the dowager countess smile, which was quite an achievement.

Henrietta gazed at Georgiana, who was squashed onto the window seat beside Dog, until her words made sense.

Lord Maynard is not a very devoted suitor...

"Why do you say that?" Henrietta asked.

"Well, he hardly ever calls now. Before you agreed to marry him, we were forever falling over him. Have you quarreled with him, too?"

Ignoring the *too*, Henrietta said, "Of course not."

Though now she came to think of it, she had only seen her betrothed once since he had called the day after the ball to speak to Vanya. Perhaps, now that he was used to her appearance, he found the rest of her wanting.

Lowering as this was to her self-esteem, she felt a twinge of relief at the idea of breaking the engagement to please him. After all, she had hardly missed him. Georgiana had noticed his absence more than Henrietta had.

"Well, here is Tranmere," Georgi said brightly. "He is attentive, at least. I don't think he's bosky, either."

"Georgi!" Henrietta exclaimed, trying not to laugh. And then Lord Tranmere was swaggering into the room and bowing over her hand, while Georgiana hung on to Dog. She thought for an instant that Tranmere was going to kiss her fingers, then he met Georgiana's highly interested gaze and straightened.

"Tell Lizzie his lordship has called," Henrietta said to her little sister.

Georgiana stood and released Dog. "Stay," she commanded him without much hope.

Dog actually obeyed, probably because it coincided with his current desires. Though he wagged his tail off, he remained on the window seat and made no effort to leap on the wary Tranmere.

Georgiana trailed out of the room with clear reluctance, leaving the door open, rather to Henrietta's amusement. Aware of Tranmere's reputation, she didn't take him remotely seriously as a suitor, but she had grown familiar with him over the last few days and found him an amusing distraction from her misery over Aubrey.

"I hope I'll see you at the card party this evening," he said, smiling down at her as he continued to hold her hand.

She tried to withdraw it, but found it held fast. She pretended not to notice and awaited her moment. "Oh yes, I believe all of Blackhaven is going. It should be fun, and for such a good cause."

Tranmere looked baffled.

"For the hospital," she reminded him. "And other local charities run by the vicar."

"Oh yes, of course. You know, you really are the loveliest creature I have ever seen."

Henrietta sighed, and, since his grip of her hand relaxed, slipped her hand free, only to discover his arms around her instead.

"Just one kiss," he said huskily. "You owe me that much."

"How do you work that out?" she demanded furiously, shoving him hard in the chest. "Of all the—" The rest was lost in a blast of sour wine breath as his mouth mashed hers.

Henrietta had long been subject to the lunges of men, and was much more angry than frightened. Once, she would have laughed, for apart from the genuine ridiculousness of the lunges, she had found that being laughed at cooled young men's ardor with remarkable efficiency. But Tranmere was abusing his position as a guest in her home, and besides, she no longer found kissing funny.

In this case, she found it repellent to the point of nausea.

She wished she was wearing boots rather than slippers as she stamped hard on his instep and aimed an energetic buffet at his head.

Tranmere began to laugh. "Oh, sweetheart, hardly ladylike," he mocked, sweeping his hands down over her hips. Which was when Dog joined in, throwing himself joyfully into the fray and sending both Henrietta and Tranmere flying apart.

Since Dog had already made friends with Tranmere, he was unlikely to attack him as he had the intruder after the ball, but his playfulness was equally disruptive. Henrietta, used to his boisterous ways, regained her footing faster than Tranmere, who was sent sprawling onto the sofa with a ludicrous expression of surprise on his face.

Henrietta pointed at the door, shaking with anger. "Out!"

Tranmere got slowly to his feet. For a moment, his mouth turned ugly, and then, without warning, he laughed again. He even bowed on the way out, closing the drawing room door behind him.

Henrietta sank onto the sofa. "Oh, Dog," she whispered, throwing her arms around him and burying her face in his fur.

She didn't know why she was crying, but somehow it had more to do with Aubrey than with Tranmere. It was some time before it came to her that she hadn't heard the front door close.

AUBREY WAS IN Nimmo's printing shop when the twins almost burst through the door.

He had had a busy few days, even visiting the offices of Carlisle's local newspaper to see how things were done. That had been before Roderick's wedding. Now, the day after, he had already prevented Roderick's former mistress from setting fire to his woodshed, if not his home, and hauled her off to the hospital, for she was clearly barking mad.

Buoyed up with having been able to help Rod and Helen, he quickly lost himself in the technicalities of the printing press and the relative costs involved in various sizes and frequency of the proposed *Chronicle*.

The sudden appearance of the twins took him by surprise. He had set them onto watching Corentin once more. What on earth had the old devil been up to get them in such a lather? His stomach twinged with alarm, even as he straightened and went to meet them.

"Where's the fire?" he asked lightly.

"Graham Gardens," Lawrence said curtly. "We followed Corentin there, but he didn't go in. Instead he walked past, and nodded to your bosky friend. Tranmere. Tranmere *did* go in."

Aubrey reached for his coat. "You think Tranmere's doing his dirty work? I can't really see it somehow. I doubt he could hurt Launceton if he tried."

"Launceton isn't there," Leona said, tugging him by the hand toward the door. Lawrence gave him his hat. "He's gone fishing with Michael."

"How do you know that?" Aubrey barely had time to raise a hand in farewell to Nimmo before the twins were dragging him at a fast pace along the street.

"Tranmere asked the maid," Lawrence said grimly. "We heard him. He's up to something, Aubrey."

And knowing Tranmere, Aubrey could guess what. Now it was he striding along the street, the twins trotting to keep up with him.

"Is Lizzie there, too?" he barked.

"And Georgiana. And Dog," Leona replied.

"Then everything is probably fine," he said, wondering whether he was trying to convince them or himself. But of course it would be fine. Only it nagged at him that Vanya, and therefore Misha, were out of the house, and that Corentin knew Tranmere was there.

Something was going on…

It was not far to Graham Gardens, and they made it in next to no time.

Aubrey rattled the knocker hard.

"Wait here," he instructed the twins. "And if Tranmere comes out, trip him down the stairs."

As soon as the door opened a crack, Aubrey was inside. "Miss Henrietta," he demanded of the maid. Although he should have asked for Lizzie…

"In the drawing room, sir," said the maid, which was when Aubrey saw that the door was shut.

He barged straight in and almost collided with Henrietta and Dog. He stared at her, taking in her tear-stained face, the pin falling from her hair, and the wild anxiety of her eyes.

"He didn't leave," she blurted. "Tranmere. It's Lizzie he really wants."

"Show me," Aubrey commanded.

LIZZIE HAD BEEN inspecting her available evening gowns for the charity card party, and wondering if the very small tear in her favorite blue silk would be noticeable, when Georgiana stuck her head around the door.

"Tranmere's here again."

"Drat, I suppose I'd better go and chaperone."

"Dog's there," Georgiana said with some satisfaction. "I told him to stay, and he did, even though I left the door open."

"Goodness," Lizzie said, suitably impressed. "Perhaps his training is finally working."

"I think the burglar gave him a fright and taught him he had to protect us."

"That might be a *little* optimistic, but you never know."

"I'm going to paint," Georgiana announced, and departed.

Lizzie began to follow her out but, on the way, caught sight of her reflection in the glass. A lock of hair had escaped its pins. In fact, not expecting callers today, she had dismissed the maid early for her half-day off and bundled her hair up rather than dressed it.

She was just replacing the final pin and deciding it would have to do when the door swung open. She turned toward it and was astonished to see Lord Tranmere.

Her hands fell to her sides.

He smiled. "Making yourself beautiful for me?" he asked, and closed the door. Before her bemused eyes, he turned the key in the lock.

"What the devil do you think you're doing?" she demanded, angered into unladylike language. She marched toward him and reached for the key. "Get out of my bedchamber this instant, and—"

His hand closed over hers on the key, gently but inexorably drawing her away. There was a light of lust and excitement in his eyes, his face worryingly free of any kind of doubt or anxiety.

"I think I'm seducing you," he said softly. "And I think you want that almost as much as I do."

"You are deluded," she said coldly. "And that will be the end of you. My husband will kill you." She stated it as fact—which it would be, should Vanya ever come to hear of this.

But Tranmere only smiled again. "But you're not going to tell him, are you? What wife would? He is not here and unlikely to be for some time. Let us make the most of it. You are utterly irresistible." His hands closed around her waist, slid lower over her hips, drawing her against him. "Especially when your eyes flash with such passion," he said hoarsely. "Let us begin…"

One hand slid up over her breast while he lowered his mouth unhurriedly toward hers.

Outraged, more furious than frightened, Lizzie snatched out the hairpin she had just replaced. Tranmere, misunderstanding, laughed softly—before she jabbed the pin into his neck, just above the line of his cravat.

He yelled and dropped her, clapping his hand to his neck, staring at her with an astonishment that turned into something much uglier.

"Oh, no, my lady. For that, you pay!"

He seized her, his hands much rougher now as he clamped her to his body, bending her backward and tugging at her bodice. She brought up her knee, but somehow he had got his leg between hers and she missed her target. Panic surged as she fought him—and quite suddenly something thudded against the door, making them both start.

Dog barked dementedly.

Lizzie tore herself free, backing several steps away from him.

"You nasty, repellent little commoner," she spat at him.

Something else was battering at the bedroom door, something sharper than Dog's body. A boot. The wood splintered and Dog charged through, closely followed by Aubrey Vale.

"Dear God," Henrietta whispered, barging past them to get at Lizzie, which was when she realized that there was blood on her hands and her gown.

For an instant, Lizzie clutched her sister. "It isn't mine," she said shakily. "I stabbed him in the neck with a hairpin."

A hysterical laugh broke from Henrietta, quickly cut off. "Oh, Lizzie, you are wonderful."

They broke apart, turning to face the empty room. Below them, the front door slammed. Then came a cry and a series of thuds as the front door was opened and slammed again.

As one, Lizzie and Henrietta ran to the window. The Vale twins, grinning, were walking innocently along the street. In the other direction, Aubrey appeared to be supporting Tranmere, who was unaccountably limping.

AUBREY HAD NEVER hit anyone before, except his brothers in play fights on the odd occasions he had been well enough. Even then, he was sure they had let him. But there was a fierce, perverse pleasure in striking Tranmere so hard that his knuckles hurt.

Tranmere staggered under the blow. For an instant, he looked genuinely outraged, and then, no doubt seeing the fury in Aubrey's face, he turned and bolted, Aubrey at his heels. Dog, bounding ahead of Aubrey, slowed him up.

Damn it all, he'll get away before I shut his damned mouth…

The door slammed behind Tranmere, but even before Aubrey wrenched it open again, he heard the cry and the unmistakable thuds of a man falling down the stone steps.

God bless the twins. Aubrey spared them a grin as he leapt down and hauled the groaning Tranmere to his feet.

"There, there, poor you," he said cheerfully. "Let me help you to a quiet place I know."

"Aubrey, it's not what you think. Give a fellow a—"

"Shut up," Aubrey said fiercely. "First, I will speak, and not until we're in private."

He probably looked most solicitous of his friend as he supported him down the road and onto the beach. Rain spat down on them, but so halfheartedly that neither paid it much attention.

At this end of town, away from the sandy shore and the harbor, there was a pebbly bit of beach neglected by all but local children, none of whom were about.

Aubrey dumped Tranmere unceremoniously on the pebbles and stood over him. "What sort of despicable animal are you? Assaulting an innocent girl and then immediately trying to rape her pregnant sister?"

"Not rape, Aubrey!" Tranmere said feebly. "And damn it, I didn't know she was pregnant."

"Would it have made any difference?" Aubrey demanded.

"I wouldn't have raped her," Tranmere said sullenly. "Pregnant or not. She was willing enough to begin with, but I wouldn't have pushed it too far."

"*Willing to begin with?*" Aubrey repeated. "You mean she invited you into her bedchamber while her little sisters were in the same house? I suppose she locked the door? I suppose you stabbed your own neck, while she tore her own clothes to entice you?"

Tranmere whitened. His hands shook as he pushed them both through his hair and swore. "Got a bit too carried away," he mumbled. "Not entirely sober, Aubrey. You know what it's like. Haven't been sober in a while, to be honest."

"Is that meant to be an excuse?" Aubrey spat.

"No. Just the way it is. I was in the wrong. I'll apologize to them both. But you needn't be so damned self-righteous about it. You're no saint yourself."

Aubrey sat down, his own shame mingling with Tranmere's. "No, I'm no saint," he agreed. "But you've got to have boundaries, Tranmere. Limits. I found mine, found I didn't much like myself. I like you even less."

"Prig," Tranmere said, aiming for humor.

Aubrey didn't smile. "Hardly. I'm glad I hit you. If you'd hurt Henrietta, I'd probably kill you."

Tranmere cocked his eyebrow. "That still the lie of the land? I heard she was engaged to Maynard. Didn't think you'd care."

"Oh, I care. So much so that I'd happily leave you to Launceton's less-than-tender mercies."

Tranmere nodded ruefully. "I suppose I deserve it."

"Oh, you do. What the hell happened to you?"

Tranmere looked confused. "Been on a bit of a bender. A spree. You know what it's like."

"No. Assault and rape have never been on my list of pleasures. Why the hell are they on yours?"

Tranmere shrugged. "Got any brandy?"

"No."

"Ran out of money," Tranmere said. "Bored. Didn't mean to touch Henrietta at all, to be honest. Not part of the deal. But she's so damned beautiful, I couldn't resist a kiss. She kicked me, so I took the hint and left her alone."

Aubrey stared at him. "What deal? Tranmere, did someone *send* you there?"

"French fellow. Corentin. But of course he didn't send me. Wagered me I couldn't seduce Launceton's wife. Just the sort of dangerous challenge I like, given Launceton's reputation. Only, she was harder than I expected, wasn't giving in fast enough, and I needed the money for tonight." He looked morose. "Can't play now. Didn't win."

"Look on the bright side," Aubrey said sarcastically. "You're not yet dead or in the custody of the magistrate."

Tranmere clutched his head again, then raised his bloodshot eyes to Aubrey's. "Gone too far?"

"Much too far. Can't you see it?"

Tranmere swallowed. "Suppose I'll have to. When I'm sober. The party's over."

"Not much of a party, Tranmere. More of a rampage. You've become an addled commoner with no self-control. Your only friends are the ones who live off your allowance."

Tranmere closed his eyes tight, perhaps hoping this was all a nightmare. "What should I do, Aubrey? Go to Launceton?"

Aubrey regarded him thoughtfully. "Not sure I want Launceton hanged for murder."

"Look on the bright side—the Lords would probably let him off."

"Or your grandfather might have enough influence to see him to the gallows. Actually… It's possible Lizzie or Henrietta will tell Vanya, of course, but since you came off worst out of both encounters, I imagine they will reason, like me, that Vanya is really better not committing murder. Also, I might make use of you. Come to the card party, preen before Corentin… You didn't tell anyone else about this despicable wager, did you?"

"No, of course not."

"So you knew it was beyond the pale," Aubrey pointed out.

"Perhaps," Tranmere said bleakly. "You're right. I don't like me much either."

"Then send your hangers-on away. Come to the card party and face Launceton if you have to. Most definitely apologize to her ladyship and Henrietta—from a safe distance, with myself present, in fact. And we'll lull Corentin into believing it's time to act. But Tranmere? You stay stone-cold sober. If I get a whiff of brandy or even ale tonight, I'll call you out myself. I still want to kill you."

Tranmere stumbled unsteadily to his feet. "Part of me wishes you would."

"Too easy. Christ, man, you were born with every privilege, the kind of life other men would die for. You'll be an earl one day. Look to your lands, your people, your family, the state of the damned country, and *do* something."

Aubrey rose and walked away from him.

"What are *you* going to do?" Tranmere's voice followed him, still with a trace of defiance.

"I'm going back to learn about printing presses."

Chapter Twenty

It was Lizzie who insisted on going to the card party. Vanya, who was nothing if not observant, sensed something was not right, even before he saw the splintered door and listened to the tale of Lizzie fainting in her room and Michael kicking in the door. He would have decreed they all stay at home, had not Lizzie claimed to be quite recovered and eager for company.

"Besides, I promised Mrs. Maitland," she said, Mrs. Maitland being Aubrey's widowed sister.

"Mrs. Maitland?" Vanya repeated. "I thought it was Mrs. Grant's party?"

"Oh, the vicar and his wife are host and hostess," Lizzie said airily. "But, in fact, the organization was all Bernard Muir's and Felicia Maitland's."

Henrietta understood that attending the party was Lizzie's way of regaining her equilibrium while Vanya's attention was at least partially distracted. She also wanted to speak to Aubrey. So did Henrietta, though not because she doubted his discretion.

Michael and Georgiana sulked about not being able to come too.

"The twins will be there," Georgiana said moodily.

"Only to run errands for Felicia," said Lizzie without knowing anything about it. "Besides, we need you to guard the house with Dog, for Misha needs to be with Vanya."

"What if Tranmere is there?" Henrietta murmured when Lizzie came to collect her from her bedchamber, where she had been staring at herself at the mirror and seeing Aubrey's face instead. "Do we give him the cut direct?"

"People will wonder why. No, if he has the gall to be there, we nod distantly and otherwise ignore him. It's my belief he'll co-operate."

However, it seemed Lizzie misjudged, for after being shown into the inn by the twins, and entering the gaming hall—normally in the inn's large common room—the first person Henrietta saw was Tranmere.

He was with a group of other men, but he saw them enter right away. His lips moved, and the man nearest him turned.

Aubrey.

Henrietta was flabbergasted. "Look!"

Lizzie squeezed her arm.

"What?" asked Vanya.

"Nothing," Henrietta said, and hastily latched on to the unexpected presence of the newlyweds. "Just Lady Helen and Major Vale are here."

"Shall we join them?" Lizzie smiled at Vanya, who was clearly itching to play some higher-stakes games with the Earl of Braithwaite and his friend Lord Wickenden. So she and Henrietta made their way across the room to Helen without him.

Before they got there, they were suddenly confronted by Lord Tranmere. Aubrey, the traitor, was still by his side. Wildly, Henrietta began to speculate that Aubrey had set the whole thing up to punish her for sending him away...

Her head barely moved as she acknowledged Tranmere's bow. Lizzie, her expression icy, waited for them to stand aside.

"Though there is no excuse possible, I offer my apologies," Tranmere said, his voice low and oddly hollow. In fact, he looked terrible.

His eyes looked bruised. His chin was cut, and his collar rose almost ridiculously high to hide where Lizzie's pin had pierced his neck. "And my promise never to trouble you again."

He bowed once more and walked swiftly away.

Aubrey's gaze flickered from Henrietta to Lizzie. "Are you both well?" he asked, the significance of his question clear.

"Quite," said Lizzie, the ice in her manner vanishing. "Was that apology at your instigation?"

"I may have suggested it."

"And stayed with him to see that he obeyed?" Lizzie asked shrewdly.

"No. To be sure you did not feel threatened. I'm sorry." He bowed and walked away in the opposite direction.

Henrietta, ashamed now of her first, angry suspicion, started after him. Lizzie did not stop her.

"How did you make him do it?" she blurted.

He paused and glanced down at her in surprise. A faint smile flickered across his face and vanished. "I lectured him to within an inch of his life."

"Is that why he limps?"

"No. The twins tripped him down your front steps."

A breath of laughter took her by surprise. "He had a bad day."

"He deserved it all and more." He glanced around him to be sure they were not overheard. "For what it's worth, Corentin seems to have put him up to it."

Her eyes widened. "Corentin? But why?"

"To hurt Vanya through Lizzie. For once in your life, you were incidental. Corentin wagered Tranmere, so he couldn't resist. And actually, I think it frightened him to realize how far he had fallen to behave so."

"It must have been quite a lecture."

"Oh, it was. I've had practice."

She dropped her gaze, afraid of the rueful not-quite-humor in his eyes. "He wants Vanya to suffer before he—"

"Well, let's pretend he is suffering," Aubrey interrupted. "Perhaps Lizzie could try to look a little cowed and submissive before him."

"She could try," Henrietta said doubtfully.

"You all need this to be over," Aubrey said. "I hate that he used Lizzie in this way. We just have to be ready to stop him from taking his final step."

Killing Vanya. Her blood ran cold.

"The twins are watching and reporting." He hesitated, then added, "They tell me Lord Maynard is a frequent visitor."

"I think he is watching too. It was he who first saw the hatred for Vanya in his face."

Aubrey did not dispute it. "Things are being moved out of his house. Usually when Diane is not at home."

Her breath caught. "He is preparing to leave! Where are his things being taken?"

"To Whalen."

"Where the Frenchman's ship is… But Aubrey, if he's ready to go, he has to kill Vanya very soon! We have to stop him. Can't we have him arrested?"

"For what? Making a silly wager with a drunken young man? Taking a dislike to the man he believes responsible for his son's death?"

"He's not quite sane, is he?"

"It could be part of his illness, but no, he does not seem terribly stable or rational." He glanced around the room. "I was hoping to see Lord Tamar's sister here, She might be able to help, but I don't see her. Perhaps Tamar knows where she is. I'll speak to him."

"Why are you doing all this for us?" she blurted.

His eyes were intense, but not smiling. "Because I love you," he said.

"Etta," exclaimed Lady Alice, distracting her. "Come and play with

Helen and me!"

And when, dazed, Henrietta glanced back at Aubrey, he had gone.

It was a strange evening. Henrietta was conscious of a tension in the air, a sort of suppressed excitement—or perhaps those feelings were just hers, because Aubrey was here. Because he had said those amazing words. *Because I love you.*

As she drifted through games, smiling and distracted and steadily losing what was left of her allowance, happiness seemed to have settled about her, along with the excitement that something was bound to happen now, though she didn't know what.

It didn't really make any difference, she told herself. She had no reason to disbelieve Aubrey, but the fact remained that they were still incompatible, and she was still engaged to Lord Maynard. Nor would she have it any other way, she told herself. But still Aubrey's words were a balm to her soul, soothing and unbearably sweet.

She did not expect to see Maynard at such a gathering, and was actually glad, for it left her free to bask in the moment without guilt.

Except that Maynard did arrive, albeit slightly late, gazing about him in his stately way before walking immediately toward her table. The game was breaking up, so she was able to stand and stroll about the room with him as though debating which table to join next.

In fact, Maynard said, "Something is happening. Corentin has moved a trunk out of the house and has told Diane nothing about it. She is beside herself with worry over him."

Henrietta immediately felt guilty for being too lost in her own misery and worries about Vanya to have called on her friend.

"Will she come tonight?" she asked quickly.

Maynard looked shocked. "Not without her father. That would hardly be appropriate."

"Of course not. How foolish…"

"You have had no more break-ins, no further threats to Lord Launceton?"

"No…" Apart from sending the dissolute Tranmere after Lizzie. "But I think it is coming to a head. If Corentin is about to leave… That is another thing. If he has not told Diane, does he even mean to take her with him?"

"I don't believe she wants to go. She has a small but close circle of friends in London, and the prospect of marriage in England. Her life is here."

"The prospect of marriage to whom?" she asked, but of course she knew the answer.

"Aubrey Vale. She believes they are compatible."

How can they be compatible if he loves me? she wondered, unreasonably indignant, and an instant later, *How can Lord Maynard and I be compatible if I love Aubrey?*

He peered at her a little more closely. "Shall we join a table for whist? Or loo, perhaps?"

He was not interested in cards. Neither was Henrietta unless it was for fun, usually with her family. Playing for money spoiled it for her, but here at least her inattention here would benefit a charity.

While she played, she wondered for the first time if she was being quite fair to Lord Maynard in marrying him. She still believed they could make each other comfortable, each obtaining what they needed from the union. But she did not love him. It hadn't seemed to matter before she knew that Aubrey loved her…

Should she break it off now?

Her heart sank. She could not hurt him so. He might not love her as she understood the emotion, but he was undoubtedly lonely and in need of a companion to care for him, his children, and his homes.

Aubrey was not ready for marriage. But one day, perhaps, he would be. How would she feel then, tied to Maynard while Aubrey married someone else? Diane, for example?

Confused, she didn't notice at first that another late arrival had strolled into the room.

Corentin.

Her gaze flew to Vanya, who lounged at one of the high-stakes games, a glass at his elbow, so relaxed that she almost expected him to put his feet up on the table. With him were Lord Wickenden, Bernard Muir, Lord Daxton, and Lady Braithwaite. Surely he was safe, as he could be in a public place.

She turned her attention back to Corentin, who was his smiling, urbane self. Only his extreme thinness and the pallor of his drawn face betrayed his illness.

After bowing over Mrs. Grant's hand as she welcomed him, he smiled and paid his entrance fee before strolling around the tables. He did not appear to notice Vanya. Then Tranmere walked up to him, looking smug. Had he been at the brandy again?

Henrietta could only guess their conversation, but she saw the direction of Corentin's gaze. He was looking straight at Lizzie. Casually, he passed something to Tranmere, who pocketed it and walked jauntily off to play *vingt-et-un*.

Her blood froze. Had Tranmere just lied about Lizzie to win his wager? What if Corentin told Vanya the same story?

She could hardly wait for her own game to end before she jumped up, claiming to be going in search of Lizzie. Instead, she walked straight up to Aubrey and actually took his arm to detach him from the group surrounding his sister Felicia Maitland's game of piquet.

"Corentin is here," she hissed. "He paid Tranmere!"

"I know. I told him to pretend to have won his wager."

She dropped his arm as though scalded.

"How else is Corentin to believe he has won? We are already agreed that Lizzie should look frightened and submissive."

"Yes, but what if he tells Vanya?"

"That it was a wager? Apart from the fact that Vanya would no doubt kill him before he is ready, he doesn't *want* Vanya to know about the wager. He wants him to believe his wife merely had an affair because she chose to."

"This is horrible," she said intensely.

"It is," he agreed. "I'm sorry for it, but we'll have the last laugh. In the meantime, come and watch my sister fleece this fellow…"

He sounded so inordinately proud of his sister that Henrietta found herself watching the game, seeing the banknotes and vowels on Felicia's side of the table mount higher. And they were playing for eye-watering stakes. Had Henrietta not heard somewhere that Felicia's husband had left her destitute and indebted?

Churned up as she was, she could not cope with another mystery, so slipped away, only to find herself facing Delilah Vale.

"Bored with cards or with Aubrey?" Delilah asked.

"Cards," Henrietta admitted.

"Me too," Delilah confided. "Although in this case, it might be a pleasure to watch Felicia win."

"She might not."

"Clearly, you have never played cards with Felicia." Delilah moved a little further away from the crowds. A large part of the room had cleared to watch Felicia's game, so for once there was space.

Henrietta did not even see Delilah signal, but the innkeeper's wife brought them each a glass of wine and they sat down at the side.

Delilah sipped delicately. "Did Aubrey behave very badly?"

Here was directness! Heat surged into Henrietta's face, but she could think of nothing to say.

Delilah sighed. "I'll take your silence for affirmation. I knew he was ashamed of something."

"It doesn't matter," Henrietta said hastily.

"It matters to Aubrey. I have never seen him so cast down, not even when his illness was at its worst."

"He does not seem cast down to me," Henrietta said. "In fact, he looks..."

"Refreshed? Revitalized?"

Henrietta stared at her, hoping she didn't look as insulted as she felt. How dare he be revitalized by her dismissing him?

Delilah smiled. "He is, in a way. Your quarrel, whatever it was, gave him the kick he needed."

"For what?" Henrietta asked.

"To be worthy. To make something of his life beyond merely celebrating not being dead."

Shocked, Henrietta lowered her glass without drinking.

"Oh yes, his life truly was that bad. He was so weak as a child he could hardly run without having an attack—some of them almost killed him. I swear I felt his heart stop once. Can you imagine a childhood without running? Of only watching out of the window as your siblings played? Mere *loneliness* doesn't even begin to describe it. I know he longed to join in. I know it pained him beyond what you or I can understand, but he bore it, made the best of it. I think sometimes he fought so hard to live because of how devasted the rest of us would be without him."

Delilah sipped her wine thoughtfully. "When the attacks began to lessen—he was about eighteen at the time, I think—he was afraid to hope. We all were. But he continued to improve, to grow in strength, until we began to believe." She smiled. "Can you imagine what it was like for him? Suddenly released into the joys of the world he had only ever seen from afar?"

"From his bath chair," Henrietta whispered.

"Exactly. Only he was a man by then, with a man's tastes and pleasures and a lifetime of them to catch up on. We never discouraged him. His joy was ours."

And mine...

"He has had a ball raking around Blackhaven, drinking, womanizing, getting into trouble. It is something he had to do."

"I know."

Delilah held her gaze. "It isn't who he is, you know. It was just a delayed chapter of his life that most youths get over at university. He is already over it."

"Of course he is."

Delilah raised one eyebrow. "You don't believe me? Why else would be devoting so much effort to his newspaper? His book? His new writing?"

"His what?" Henrietta asked, confused.

"At the same time as saving Roderick's neck from a threat the rest of us did not even guess, managing some business for Cornelius that I'm not even supposed to know about, and keeping the twins busy over some business that I suspect has to do with you."

Henrietta frowned, trying to find her way through all of this. "Are you...scolding me?" she asked cautiously.

Delilah smiled. She had a delightful smile that softened her rather severe countenance and made her eyes twinkle with fun. "No. I'm asking you to give him a second chance. Because if anyone deserves such a thing, it is Aubrey."

Delicately, she clinked her glass against Henrietta's and then rose and moved toward Miss Talbot, leaving Henrietta in turmoil.

"Not everything is as it seems."

THE EVENING BELONGED to Felicia Maitland and Bernard Muir. Not only did Felicia fleece the man who had apparently beggared her husband, but Mr. Muir caught him cheating. And while the cheat tried to turn the tables, or bolt, the rest of the Vales, including Aubrey, blocked his escape.

Something else to which Aubrey was central.

By then, Corentin had gone again, and it was too late for the twins to be following him about the darkened streets of the town. However, before Henrietta could panic, Aubrey brushed past her.

"Don't worry," he murmured. "One of Roderick's men is watching the house."

He did not stay beside her, although all of her ached for his presence along with his reassurance. He was looking after her family because he loved her… But like her, he clearly knew they could not be together.

There were men who loved but who could not remain faithful to that love. Yet Delilah had seemed to be saying that Aubrey was not such a man.

Restlessly, Henrietta prowled the tables without appreciating or even seeing the games, while her heart and her head wrestled with the right thing to do. She was almost glad when Vanya swept her and Lizzie homeward. Except that it took her away from Aubrey.

She was walking through the front door at Graham Gardens before she realized she had not even said goodnight to her betrothed.

Chapter Twenty-One

By the following Tuesday, when Julius married Antonia Macy, a great deal seemed to have happened to Aubrey's family.

Felicia had engaged herself to Bernard Muir, whom Aubrey counted a friend, and Cornelius surprised everyone but Aubrey by announcing his betrothal to Lady Alice Conway. The only reason Aubrey was not as amazed as everyone else was because, after acting as Cornelius's second in the not-quite duel over another woman, he had accompanied him on a mad chase, and been privileged to witness his brother's besottedness with Alice. And her subsequent, defiant announcement to her family.

What with all of that, closely followed by Julius's wedding, Aubrey had found little time to move forward with his newspaper project.

However, waiting with his brothers for Antonia to arrive at the church, he said to Roderick, "I can invest in the newspaper too, now. Felicia is repaying the legacy money we used to bail her out of debt, now that she is in funds once more."

"Then we can start sooner," Roderick said, nodding with approval. "And as a partner, of course, you'll get a larger salary."

"If we succeed," Aubrey said, just so nothing was hexed. He had every intention of succeeding. He had to, although he also had to think of a way of ending Henrietta's betrothal to Maynard.

He liked to think that if she was happy, he would bow to her wishes. But she was not happy. They were entirely unsuited to each other. And surely he had read love in her eyes when she had looked at him… She was too loyal for that to have changed so soon, no matter how much she disapproved of him.

A rustling at the back of the church and Julius's accompanying intake of breath made him turn to watch Antonia walk up the aisle on her father's arm. He felt stupidly emotional. He could not even look at Henrietta as he longed to, for he would never look away. And this was Antonia's day. Hers and Julius's.

After the ceremony, Julius, looking particularly handsome and dashing in his dress uniform, handed his lovely bride into the waiting carriage.

"Never seen him smile so much," Aubrey remarked, grinning as he and his family followed the carriage on foot to the hotel, where the wedding breakfast would be served.

"It's obligatory," Lawrence said. "Even Rod smiled at his wedding."

"No he didn't," Helen said. "At least, not enough."

"Well, he's making up for it now," said Aubrey, and ducked to avoid Roderick's inevitable buffet.

It was a day of happiness, filled with hope and friendship. It struck Aubrey, contentedly munching his way through several courses, that the numbers filling the church and congratulating the happy couple in the hotel showed just how far the Vales had embedded themselves into Blackhaven. Mostly in the six weeks since the twins had held their family meeting and insisted they needed to take Julius to the assembly room ball in order to make him part of the community and bring him true happiness.

The twins, he thought, regarding them with some amusement across the table, were very wise little creatures. And he was fairly sure they had been machinating behind the scenes on behalf of the others, too. Probably even him. After all, he had involved them in the drama of Henrietta's family, but they were already friends with her siblings. And Dog.

Sensing his scrutiny, they both looked back at him. He lifted his glass, and they grinned their almost exactly alike grins. With a sudden, sharp ache, he saw their father's clever subtlety behind their smile, and wished the old gentleman had been here to see Julius finally married. In many ways Aubrey, so reliant on his father, had been closest to the man, but Julius had always held the place of pride as his firstborn son.

For no reason, Aubrey thought of Corentin losing his first and only son, first to the revolution, and then to death in the folly of Napoleon Bonaparte's invasion of Russia. It was not, perhaps, so surprising that the man's mind had turned in grief to revenge. A parent should never outlive his child, although God knew it happened frequently enough.

Revenge.

Something clicked into place in his mind, like the gear of some complicated machine. His gaze flew to Henrietta, further down the table, to Vanya and Lizzie beside her, and Michael and Georgiana opposite the twins. They were all here.

Except Vanya's firstborn son.

Recently, Corentin had become aware of being followed on some occasions. Other times, he was possibly over-suspicious, but a couple of times he had definitely seen that fool Maynard dogging his steps. If it wasn't for the man's connection to Launceton through Henrietta, he would have ignored him utterly. As it was, he found it easy enough to shake him off when he wanted to.

As far as he knew, Maynard was not invited to the Vale wedding breakfast, so Corentin was wary and watchful as he made his meandering way around the streets toward Launceton's house. However, he heard no footfalls, and whenever he made a pretext to stop, however suddenly, he saw no one anywhere near.

Only as he walked briskly along the back lane did he come across the soldierly man he had seen here once before. Corentin couldn't help smiling to himself because he had rattled Savarin—Launceton—to the degree that he had actually hired someone to guard his house.

Today, of course, he needed to be rid of the watcher. And he had planned for that.

Turning into the street, he was pleased to see his partner Louis strolling toward him. Louis halted at Launceton's front steps, gazing up at the windows.

Passing without looking at him, Corentin murmured, "If you would be so good."

He had not taken many steps more before the soldier's footsteps could be heard, then the sound of Louis's sudden bolt across the street. Trying not to smile, Corentin turned back as though alarmed by the sudden activity. The soldier was haring after Louis, just as Corentin had known he would.

Corentin waited until they were out of sight, then walked smartly back to Launceton's house and knocked on the door, still trying not to laugh at the sight of the man's pathetic guard deserting his post to chase after his decoy.

Since Launceton was out at the wedding, Corentin did not expect the door to be opened by the dangerous-looking Russian manservant. In fact, it was a tiny maidservant.

Corentin removed his hat. "Good day. Is Lord or Lady Launceton at home?"

"I'm afraid not, sir."

"Ah, what a pity. Miss Henrietta, perhaps?"

"No, she's out too, sir. The whole family is at Sir Julius's wedding."

Aware she had said more than she should, the maid blushed furiously and bit her lip as though that would destroy her mistake.

Corentin smiled reassuringly. "Of course. I had forgotten it was today. Perhaps you would pass on a message for me?"

"Of course, sir."

"Tell his lordship—Ah, it's complicated. Perhaps I should leave him a note."

The maid had clearly seen him before, for she at once opened the door wide and invited him to step into the reception room.

"Here you are, sir," she said, indicating the desk with writing paraphernalia already set out. "When you're finished, just ring the bell and I'll come and take your letter and show you out."

"Excellent," Corentin said, beaming. It was indeed excellent. He needed none of his excuses to get rid of her. "Thank you."

He moved toward the desk as the maid hurried off, then he immediately returned to the door until the coast was clear. He had already established that this was the usual time for the baby's nap, so he was not surprised to hear no crying, none of the silly voices women used to address and entertain infants.

He knew from Louis that there was no separate nursery as such. The baby's room was next to the Launcetons', at the far side of the landing. Corentin walked swiftly upstairs, making as little noise as possible and yet refusing to look furtive. It would never do to be caught *creeping*, or no one would believe he had a right to be up here.

But as it turned out, the whole task was ridiculously easy. The baby was sound asleep in his cot. Corentin simply picked him up, walked across the landing to the stairs, descended, and left the house, closing the door behind him.

In perfect time, too. The carriage he had ordered to be here at exactly this hour was already waiting. He gave the jarvey his instruction, climbed into the carriage, and sat with the child in his arms.

Colonel Savarin's child. His firstborn son and heir.

Oh yes, Savarin would know Corentin's pain.

The first part of the journey took no time at all. In fact, he had originally planned to leave Blackhaven as soon as he had the child. But he had his daughter to think about. He was slightly ashamed that he had given to Tranmere the money he had saved for her dowry, just to make Launceton suffer a little more.

It was true Launceton wasn't suffering very obviously from his wife's adultery, but Corentin drew comfort from the fact that he never seemed to let her out of his sight. Inside, he would be dying. Which was nothing to what he would suffer in just a few hours.

At the cottage, Corentin alighted, told the driver to wait, and let himself in through the front door.

"Papa?" came Diane's voice from behind the kitchen door. An instant later, she appeared in the hall, drying her hands on her old apron. He hated to see her dressed as a servant, doing a servant's work. And yet he had given away her only means of escape—her dowry.

"Would you like a cup of... What on earth is that?"

Her eyes had widened in astonishment, darting around in search of someone else. Or an explanation.

"It's a baby," he said calmly. "It's time to go home. I will die in France. I had wanted to see you settled before I left. But—"

"Whose baby is it?" she interrupted, dread and suspicion whitening her face.

"It doesn't matter," he said. Probably, she already knew. She was not slow, his beautiful daughter. The baby stirred and squawked in his arms. "Come with me or stay. But if you come, it must be now."

It seemed she couldn't take her eyes off the child, who, finding himself with a stranger, began to cry. "What are you going to do with him?" she asked hoarsely.

He turned away. "You have been my all, my daughter. Know that I love you. I believe Aubrey Vale is a good man who—"

"Papa!" she interrupted again, her voice shrill over the yells of the wriggling baby.

"Goodbye," he whispered, and opened the door again. She must have seen the carriage waiting by the gate, for a sound of terror issued from her throat. For an instant, he closed his eyes, stumbling along the path to the waiting carriage, where he climbed back in and stared with dislike at the angry, bawling, writhing little creature glaring up at him. It would be easy, after all...

Just as he was about to pull the door shut, Diane hurtled in and threw herself down beside him, taking the baby from him.

For a moment, he was afraid she would bolt back out again, and he reached out to snatch the child back. But the carriage jerked forward while she was soothing him, crooning at him, and the moment had gone.

He wanted to weep, because he would have the comfort of his daughter after all, even with her knowing what he would do.

HENRIETTA, MORE AWARE of Aubrey than of anyone else at the wedding breakfast, including the bride and groom and those nearest her at the large, informal table, saw him rise quite suddenly and stride toward the dining room door.

She set down her fork and excused herself. She had been waiting for a moment to speak to him in private, ostensibly to thank him for all he had done to help Vanya. Though in reality, she thought she just needed to hear his voice. And his advice. She could not see her way clear to doing the right thing, although why talking to Aubrey should help when he was the cause of the dilemma, she did not know.

She did not hurry too much in case she drew unwelcome attention. Everyone should presume she was going to the cloakroom. But in the foyer, there was no sign of him—except a closing front door.

If he was not in the street, then he must be in the gentlemen's cloakroom. And, in fact, she could think of no reason for him to go out during his brother's wedding breakfast, yet instinct propelled her in that direction. The liveried porter opened the door for her, touching his hat at the same time. She thanked him distractedly.

Aubrey was outside, without his hat, his hand on the door of a waiting carriage for hire.

Curiosity drowned any hesitancy as she rushed over to him. "Aubrey? Where are you going?"

His foot already on the step, he glanced around. "Your house," he said with a quick, apologetic smile. "I'll only be a few minutes."

His urgency frightened her. She pulled his arm out of the way. "Then I'll come too."

He didn't argue, merely stood aside for her, then leapt in after her and closed the door.

"What is it?" she demanded, without even waiting for him to land the seat opposite.

"I just need to be sure of something. Because you are all out of the house, and Misha is at the hotel guarding Vanya. Roderick's man is watching the house, so I'm certain everything is fine."

"No, you're not, or you wouldn't leave your brother's wedding breakfast. How could anyone harm Vanya from the house? He—" She broke off, staring at him. Little Jack was at the house. "Jack is with Lottie, his nursemaid, and the other servants. No one would hurt a *baby!*"

"Of course not," he agreed.

And yet he was here. Jack was Vanya's firstborn son. As the late Gaspard, perhaps killed by Vanya, was Corentin's.

"Oh, God," she whispered. "He wouldn't, would he?"

"I don't know," Aubrey said, switching suddenly to the honesty that came naturally to him. "I need to find out, because it seems I can't think of anything else until I do."

He opened the door before the carriage was properly stopped and leapt out, almost carrying Henrietta with him.

And there, on the doorstep, arguing with James the footman, was

Lord Maynard.

All sorts of bizarre suspicions raced around her reeling head—and vanished as Maynard caught sight of them and looked so relieved that he almost smiled.

"Henrietta, thank goodness," he said. "Your man here won't let me in or tell me who has been here—"

"Why do you want to know?" Aubrey demanded, already striding into the house. James let him, since Henrietta was there too.

"Because I've just come from Corentin's cottage. It's empty. The front door wasn't even closed. Their neighbor told me they left in a hired carriage."

With a cry of fear, Henrietta ran upstairs, shouting, "Lottie!"

The men thundered after her, while below, a door banged and Lottie said, "Miss?"

Henrietta burst into Jack's room. His crib was empty, though she could still see the indent of his little body. A moan escaped her lips.

"Lottie, where is he?" she demanded. There was a plea in her voice as she prayed for Lottie to say, *Oh, I brought him down to the kitchen with me—he's with Cook.* Or something, anything other than the terrible thing she feared.

"He's having his nap, miss," Lottie said, clearly bewildered as she panted to the top of the stairs. "And begging your pardon, but I don't think these gentlemen ought to be disturbing…"

"Oh, dear God," Henrietta whispered. "Was someone here, James? After we left?"

"Not a soul," James replied.

"Except that kind old French gentleman," Lottie said. "He wrote a note for his lordship." She frowned suddenly. "I hope he didn't forget to leave it."

"When did he call?" Aubrey demanded, brushing past Henrietta to the crib and laying his hand on the indented part of the sheet.

"Not long…maybe ten or fifteen minutes ago," Lottie said. Her eyes, suddenly frightened, were fixed on the empty cot. "He said he would ring for me when he'd written his note, but he never did…"

She turned and bolted back down the stairs, all but flying into the reception room, which Henrietta already knew would be empty.

"Oh God, miss, oh God!" Lottie whispered in despair. "He was such a gentle—I never thought…"

"He's only fifteen minutes ahead of us at most," Aubrey said, striding for the door.

"But you don't know where he's gone," James protested. "You need—"

"Whalen," Henrietta uttered. "The ship in Whalen. *La Colombe.*"

Chapter Twenty-Two

Vanya enjoyed weddings. These days, they always reminded him of his own, which was the happiest day of his life. There had been very few nights apart from Lizzie since then. Just to know she was in the same room added intensity to any pleasure.

Never quite sure what he had done to deserve such happiness in his life as Lizzie and Jack, he let gladness for the newly married pair enfold him.

His eye was caught by Sir Julius's brother, Major Roderick Vale, who was married only days himself. The major leaned back in his chair, listening to something urgent being muttered into his ear by a panting, rather agitated-looking man.

Abruptly, Roderick's gaze flew to Vanya's.

The familiar prickle in his neck that had always kept him alive now almost floored Vanya. He surged to his feet, almost at the same time as Roderick. They met several feet from the table.

"What is it?" Vanya demanded.

"My man watching your house followed someone suspicious. When he returned, a carriage hurtled past him. Henrietta was inside. So was my brother Aubrey, and someone else he couldn't see."

Rage and anxiety swept over Vanya. "If he's hurt a hair on her head—" he said savagely.

"Aubrey wouldn't hurt her," Roderick protested. "Look, I'm just going to go to Corentin's—"

"Go where you like," Vanya snapped. "I'm going after them."

"Don't be silly—you don't know where they've gone!"

Vanya was already striding out of the room. "Yes, I bloody do. The border. The bastard has snatched her from Maynard and means to marry her out of hand. I won't have it!"

Leaving Roderick perplexed and inclined to take umbrage at the insult to his brother, Vanya strode furiously out of the hotel, shoving aside some servant who tried to speak to him.

Behind his rage, he wondered why Aubrey had gone via the house. Perhaps he had allowed her to take some things with her. But the thought of sweet, innocent little Henrietta at the mercy of such a rake—such a rake as Vanya had once been, only worse—made him ill.

At least he had never resorted to eloping with young girls.

"The Scottish border!" he yelled at the coachman who was first in line, then threw himself into the carriage.

Only then did he realize it was already occupied by an amused and rather beautiful lady with raven-black hair. She looked oddly familiar.

The carriage lurched into motion at a brisk clip.

"Good day, my lord," the lady drawled. "I hope you remember me. My name is Anna de Delon. We met in Vienna."

Vanya closed his mouth. "I'm sorry. I seem to have commandeered your carriage." He reached up and thumped the roof. "Let me drop you—"

"Oh, we're going the same way," she assured him.

He scowled and glanced out of the window. "No, we're not. And the idiot has taken the wrong road—"

"He has taken the correct road for Whalen," she said mildly.

"I'm going north," he snapped. "I'm sorry to be rude, but this is an emergency."

"It is indeed. Your answers, like mine, are in Whalen."

Vanya paused, his anger peeling back to allow him to think. Vienna had been a hotbed of spying and information peddling, sharing, dealing, and hiding, and this young woman, elusive and eternally mysterious, had, he was sure, been at the heart of much of it. And yet he had never disliked her.

Had she not been in the room when the secret policeman Schmidt had denounced…?

There was no time for reminiscences.

"My emergency is personal."

She nodded. "Yes, but it is not quite what you think. My emergency concerns Bonapartists who would free the former emperor and cause yet more carnage to restore him to the throne. We are ready to nip it in the bud, and need to arrest the men aboard the inaptly named *La Colombe* before it sails."

"I don't give a damn about Bonapartists," Vanya retorted. "Not right now."

"I know. You only care about your sister-in-law."

That deprived him of breath. But he had never been slow. Or so he thought. "Henrietta is in Whalen? Why? Why would Aubrey take her there?"

"Because…" Anna said slowly. "Um, you're not going to like this bit. She and Aubrey Vale are not eloping. They're following the man who stole your son. I sent a man to bring your wife to me, but you will do just as well."

"WHAT IF THE ship has sailed?" Henrietta burst out as they swept into the large but slightly dingy town of Whalen. "What if Corentin has already *murdered*—"

"No," Aubrey said quickly, reaching for her hand, and then stopping himself, no doubt because her betrothed sat beside him.

Who cared about such nonsense at a time like this?

"Diane is with them," Maynard pronounced. "No harm will come to the child."

"Then why is she there?" Henrietta demanded.

"I don't know," Maynard admitted, "but I *do* know she is not a monster."

"None of us thought Corentin was," Henrietta said darkly. "At least not *this* evil. Killing Vanya is one thing—a lot of people might think he deserved it, though Lizzie would disagree—but an innocent child? That is *wicked*. How—"

"We're at the docks," Aubrey interrupted, though with surprising gentleness. "Where exactly is this ship, Henri?"

Even then, in the midst of such fear, she noticed his use of her pet name. It steadied her, warmed her iced blood just a fraction. "Around the middle…here." She jumped up, thumping the roof, and the carriage halted.

Thank God. The gangway was still down, although there were sailors on the deck who were working purposefully.

Henrietta flew out of the carriage without waiting for the men and ran toward the gangway. The men's footfalls pounded after her.

"Oi!" yelled the coachman in outrage, as though he could see his fare vanishing aboard a ship and across the world.

"I'll pay you double if you wait!" Aubrey shouted over his shoulder. He caught up with her at the gangway. "We'll need transport back to the wedding, after all."

He sounded confident, unconcerned, even as a large sailor confronted them, blocking their path. He didn't look like the "burglar" Vanya had fought with.

"*Non*," he said.

"*Oui*," Aubrey corrected him. "This is Lord Maynard, a very important man, and if you ever want to set sail, you will take us immediately to Monsieur de Corentin."

The huge sailor tugged his lip in indecision, but presumably concluded he could always throw them off later if required, for he called an order to another sailor before leading them through a hatch to a ladder. He climbed down, while the other sailor waited behind them. Aubrey followed the first sailor, and Henrietta hurried after him.

Below, she could hear a low yet intense murmur of voices. They sounded like Diane and her father, arguing.

Under normal circumstances, Henrietta hated to hear Jack cry and would do anything to comfort him. Today, she would have given everything she had to hear him make a sound of any kind, however distressed, just to know he lived.

His silence filled her with dread. He could be in a different part of the ship entirely, she told herself, though he would be cold and hungry and frightened…

"…my mind is made up," Corentin was saying irritably in French. "Now, give me—Ah!" He switched to English. "The moment we have been waiting for. Mr. Vale, I presume you have come for my daughter. Miss Gaunt."

Saying her name, he sounded unpleasantly surprised. Henrietta stumbled down the last two steps of the ladder and was steadied by Aubrey. She swung around, sweeping her gaze about the room in dread.

It was a large sleeping cabin, with a round table in the middle covered with charts, and a large, sloping window at one end. Corentin stood in front of it, looking as frail and urbane as ever. And beside him stood Diane, an apron over her gown and a baby at her hip. She was dandling him up and down, which explained his silence.

"Oh, thank God," Henrietta whispered, her relief so profound that it temporarily paralyzed her.

Not so Lord Maynard, who brushed past her and stalked straight to Diane, presumably to take Jack from her. Henrietta started forward, too, though Aubrey caught her hand warningly, for Corentin was scowling, rage in his eyes as he glared at some point beyond their heads.

"Are you hurt?" Maynard asked low, staring down not at Jack but at Diane.

Understanding swept over Henrietta. Maynard had not come for her sake, but for Diane's. And Diane, very briefly, brushed her cheek against his arm.

He loves Diane. That meant something important, something good, surely, if only Diane was not complicit in this mess. But at the moment it did not matter. Only Jack mattered.

"Where is Savarin?" Corentin screamed, making Henrietta jump.

Jack began to cry. He hated angry voices.

"Launceton?" Aubrey drawled. "At Sir Julius's wedding breakfast, I imagine. For which you should be grateful, for if he was here, you would already be dead."

"I think not," Corentin said, snatching up a long, wicked-looking pistol from the ledge beside him. He waved it menacingly at Maynard. "Go and stand over there with the others."

The aim of the pistol shifted. Diane pushed the baby into Maynard's arms. Jack was so surprised he stopped crying, and Maynard, holding the child with surprising familiarity, brought him to Henrietta.

Jack, clearly delighted to see her, grinned and gurgled. "Eni," he enunciated so cleverly that even now her heart ached with love and pride. He squeaked because she hugged him so hard.

Corentin addressed the large sailor in French. "Louis is not aboard?"

"Noy yet."

Corentin was irritated. "He'll arrive with the Russian. Go back on deck and bring me the Russian as soon as he gets here."

While the sailor obeyed, Henrietta stared at Corentin over Jack's head. "You stole Jack just to bring Vanya here?"

"Not *just*, no," Corentin replied. "Though it certainly does no harm to cause him a bit more fear and anxiety on the way."

"Well, now that you have undoubtedly done so," Aubrey said, "to say nothing of the rest of us, why does Henrietta not take the child ashore and feed him? It can make no difference to you. Vanya will come anyway, now."

"No!" Corentin snapped. "The child remains here. You may go, Miss Gaunt, as may Mr. Vale and Lord Maynard—one of my sailors will escort you. Diane, you may choose to stay or go as you please."

"I'm not going without Jack," Henrietta said.

Corentin shrugged as if it didn't matter. "And the rest of you will no doubt stay with Miss Gaunt. No matter. Probably best if Savarin has no warning."

"Neither will you when he kills you," Henrietta promised, clearly taking Aubrey and Maynard by surprise. They both blinked at her, though only Aubrey's lips stretched into a reluctant, admiring smile.

Corentin shrugged. "I am already dead. I live only to avenge my son."

"And you have decided Launceton is responsible for that?" Diane demanded. It was clearly an old argument, but it seemed she would not give up trying. "Not some other, lesser Russian soldier? Not someone greater, like General Kutuzov or the tsar himself? Nor Bonaparte, who invaded Russia in the first place *and* ordered the retreat? Not some other Frenchman who could have died in Gaspard's place if only he'd had the courtesy and the forethought?"

"You understand nothing," Corentin said dismissively.

"Being merely a woman?" Diane retorted. "And merely your daughter who has lived with you throughout every day since we left France? Unlike Gaspard, who had the misfortune not to escape, and then chose to fight for the revolution that dispossessed and exiled us, who lauded Bonaparte and had the glory of dying for him as he would have chosen."

Something in the bitterness of her reproach must have caught her father's attention. For an instant the pistol wavered in his hand, and Henrietta felt Aubrey tense beside her.

Oh, no, no heroics, she pleaded silently.

"Papa, Gaspard was a *soldier,*" Diane said intensely. "*This* is an innocent child. Do you really not see the difference? Or are you mad indeed?"

The pistol straightened. "Perhaps," Corentin admitted. "But it is something I have to do, to make it right that I go home to France."

"I won't come with you," Diane threatened. "I shall stay in England."

"I always meant you to. You belong here now."

"Not after you shoot my friends and murder their children. Do you really think anyone will speak to me, let alone marry me, now? Do you wish us both to be so shamed? I am destitute. Which is still better than morally bankrupt."

But she had lost him. He no longer paid attention to her. His head was cocked, listening. A smile flitted across his lips.

Henrietta heard it too, with dread. Surely that was Vanya's voice among the footsteps sounding overhead?

And then came another, not entirely unfamiliar voice: "Down there."

Shouting a warning to Vanya would make no difference. He would keep coming through a hail of gunfire to save his son.

Vanya descended the ladder front-wise like a sailor, which let him take in the cabin and its occupants at the same time. He might have been entering a ballroom, his expression untroubled, his poise confident. And yet Henrietta, who had lived with him for almost two years, knew she had never seen this side of him before. This was neither the reckless, fun-loving Vanya nor the eccentric, provoking Lord Launceton. This was Colonel Savarin, preparing to be ambushed.

And there was nothing any of them could do.

For behind Vanya came another man with a drawn pistol. A man well enough dressed to have been a ship's officer, yet no one of great account, despite the nagging familiarity of his face. In a blink of sunshine from the cabin window, something glinted at his ear. A small gold stud.

The pirate from the masked ball. The burglar who had fought with Vanya. A pistol dangled casually from his hand, yet he was undoubtedly prepared to use it.

Corentin's pistol followed Vanya unwaveringly to the foot of the stairs, and his eyes flashed with excitement. Aubrey had taken advantage of the old man's focus and moved closer, which gave Henrietta yet more to worry about.

There was a recklessness in Aubrey. She didn't know if it had always been there or was the result of his sudden release from ill health, and right now it didn't matter, for if he got in Corentin's way, the Frenchman would simply shoot him. There was the armed pirate and a shipload of sailors to make sure Vanya stayed to die by some other means.

But not until Vanya had witnessed the death of his son.

With a gasp, Henrietta swung around, turning her back on both pistols, putting her own body between Jack and the weapons. It was the best protection she could give them.

"Colonel Savarin," Corentin said, his voice almost shaking with excitement. "I have waited a long time to meet you."

Vanya shifted away from Henrietta and Jack. "I go by Launceton in England," he drawled. "And we have met several times before."

"No," Corentin said. "For you were hiding. And so was I."

Jack, hearing his father's voice, stopped plucking the lace on Henrietta's best day gown to peer over her shoulder, looking for him.

"I never hide," Vanya said, spreading his arms. "This is me, whatever you call me, whatever you think I have done. So let me be honest. I don't remember your son, but I might have killed him."

"You didn't even look him in the eye," Corentin said with contempt.

"It's easier that way. Then the nightmares don't have faces."

That got Henrietta's attention. Somehow, she had imagined Vanya was one of those natural soldiers who, while honorable, did their duty and simply swaggered off to the next fight. But he was not untouched by battle. He too was in pain that no one saw, except perhaps Lizzie.

Whatever, it made no difference to Corentin, who snapped, "Oh, please, spare us the whining of a killer."

At which point, Jack finally located his father.

"Pa-pa!" he cried, and threw himself to the side, stretching out both arms.

It took Henrietta completely by surprise, for in that instant, Jack was vulnerable.

And Corentin was ready for his perfect moment. The shot exploded around the cabin.

Chapter Twenty-Three

Aubrey, who had been moving so casually, so gradually, closer to Corentin, knew Henrietta was protecting the child. Jack clearly took her by surprise, hurling himself away from her body's shelter. *This* was Corentin's moment.

And Aubrey's.

With an impossible mix of determination and resignation, he leapt at Corentin, knocking up his arm just as the pistol fired.

Around the cabin, all hell broke loose. Under Aubrey's weight, the frail Corentin fell back against the cupboards with a cry of rage. Aubrey snatched his pistol and hauled him upright by the cravat, desperately seeking Henrietta and the baby at the same time. Where in God's name had the pistol ball gone?

Jack was now in his father's arms. Apparently unconcerned by the firing pistol, he had hold of Vanya's ears and was chuckling happily. Henrietta…

Henrietta, her eyes huge, her face deathly pale, stared back at him, the echo of her terror still clear. But dear God, so was the love.

She loved him.

And there was no time to think of that yet, for though no blood had yet been spilled, the crisis was far from over.

"Louis!" Corentin screamed. "Shoot! Kill them both!"

Aubrey had almost forgotten the second armed man, Louis—who

looked very like that other, shadowy Frenchman from the tavern, the same man he had followed through Blackhaven and watched sweep mud from a path in Graham Gardens.

In Aubrey's desperate calculations, Vanya should have somehow dealt with Louis already, while Aubrey was tackling Corentin. But Vanya, grinning fatuously at having his ears pulled like a dog, seemed more concerned with his son.

"One shot!" Corentin cried. "Take it!"

He was an old man, but Aubrey shook him anyway.

"I'll break his neck," he warned Louis. "If you or anyone else moves."

Louis shrugged. "I am moving," he pointed out, advancing into the center of the room. All eyes turned on him. His pistol remained by his side.

Henrietta, Maynard, and even Diane, clutching Maynard by the hand, moved instinctively to protect Vanya and the baby from him.

"Quickly!" yelled Corentin.

"I thought you wanted to do it yourself," Louis said. Though he didn't sound remotely respectful, he was raising his pistol arm in obedience.

"Don't," Aubrey said impulsively. "Please, not the child…"

"Not the child," Louis agreed unexpectedly, and pointed his pistol at Corentin's head. "You can release him now. Anna, where are you?"

"I'm here," said a woman, clattering down the ladder. "I was dealing with a very angry coachman who wants his money. I sent him to the inn."

Only when Aubrey's stunned brain registered that this woman was addressing him did he recognize her voice—surely the masked lady from the castle ball, Tamar's sister, who had first sent the warning to Vanya.

Slowly, still suspecting some trick, Aubrey released his grip on Corentin's cravat and stood back.

"Traitor," Corentin whispered to Louis, his fury evaporating into the disappointment of failure. "Traitor."

"It's over," Louis said. There was no trace of a French accent. He might have been English. "We have all your Bonapartist friends. It's possible the British and the King of France will both be grateful to you for leading us to the plotters. Whether Lord Launceton forgives you is another matter."

"What about forgiving *you*?" Henrietta burst out, glaring at Louis. "You broke into our house!"

"I did," Louis said ruefully. "Hardly my finest hour. I was only familiarizing myself with the place, preparing for all eventualities in case we used Launceton as bait. You were all supposed to be still at the ball and your household asleep. I did not expect to be attacked by mad Russians, cricket bats, swords, lamps, and dogs. Though actually, it was quite funny." He glanced over at Vanya. "Sorry."

Vanya began to laugh.

Aubrey had a hysterical urge to join in. "Who the devil *are* you?" he demanded.

"He drove us here," Vanya said. "But I don't think he is a coachman."

"He is my husband," said the ever-surprising Lady Anna.

Diane appeared at Corentin's side, fearful and yet still determined. "What will happen to my father? Can he still go to France, away from everyone he has tried to hurt?"

"France was rather among those," Louis pointed out. "My country has been at war for a quarter of a century. Enough have died and been ruined without any more plots and revolts."

"He is dying," Diane whispered.

And quite suddenly, Aubrey came up with a brilliant and not entirely selfless solution.

"Perhaps," he said, "Monsieur de Corentin might be released into the care of a peer of the realm? He is in poor health and doesn't have long. Call it house arrest, if you like."

"Not my house," Vanya said flatly.

"Of course not," Aubrey said. "I was thinking of Lord Maynard here."

"Why on earth would Maynard do such a bizarre thing?" Vanya demanded.

"Because Diane will be there," Henrietta said, and Aubrey smiled because she always understood him, was probably even ahead of him. She held Maynard's startled gaze. "You *are* going to marry Diane, are you not?"

Maynard swallowed. "I have given my promise elsewhere. As you know."

"I release you," Henrietta said kindly.

"Don't be silly," Diane protested. Her voice shook slightly. "His lordship has no interest in me."

"Actually, I have," Maynard said, with a hint of desperation. "I never even noticed your beauty until this moment. I was too absorbed in *you*."

"What the devil are you talking about?" Vanya demanded, clearly perceiving only the insult to his sister-in-law. "You're not making any sense. You are eng—"

"He's making perfect sense," Aubrey interrupted. "Anyone got any brandy? Or shall we just repair to the inn for a quick one before we return to Julius's wedding?"

THEY LEFT MAYNARD and Diane with Lady Anna and her mysterious husband, to decide the interim fate of Corentin. But Henrietta's secret hope of time alone with Aubrey at the inn seemed doomed to be foiled. She only wanted to tell him how brave he had been to run straight into Corentin's pistol, and how glad she was he had survived.

Words that didn't come close to what she was feeling, which might have been what tied in her tongue on the short walk.

And then they were in the busy coffee room at the inn.

Vanya, as soon as he sat, leaned across Jack, who was bouncing on his lap, and clinked his brandy glass against Aubrey's. "My debt to you is one I can never repay. My thanks and Lizzie's. And while I'm at it, my apologies for imagining you were eloping with Henrietta."

Henrietta blushed, unsure whether to be embarrassed or indignant.

"Even I am not so ramshackle," Aubrey said, then, with a hint of a challenge, "What would you have done if I *was* eloping with her?"

Vanya favored him with a ferocious smile. "Killed you."

"Vanya!" Henrietta exclaimed.

"Don't worry," Vanya replied. "I'm sure he runs very fast."

"Who says I would run?" Aubrey countered. "What were you saying about debt? Not that I acknowledge there is one. What I did was for Henrietta and Lady Launceton, and your small son. I like them. I'm not sure about you."

"I'm not sure about *you*." Vanya drained his glass in one sip and set down his glass with a deliberate thump. "But I will say you're a good man to have around in a crisis. Drink up. I'll go and dig up your wretched hackney. I'm sure our household is in uproar."

It was a rarity to see a man lugging a small child around on his hip, but Vanya didn't appear to notice as he swung between the tables and out the door. Henrietta liked that about him.

She hung on to the thought, willing it to drown the suddenly profound awareness of Aubrey, so close to her, so large and agile and wonderful… And Vanya, contrary to his words, clearly did trust Aubrey, or he would never have left them alone.

He was right to trust Aubrey, yet some wicked part of her wished he was not, longed for Aubrey to treat her as he had that woman on her doorstep…

"Shall we walk?" he said, and she realized his gaze had never left her face.

Her heart began to beat faster. She didn't speak, rising to her feet by way of answer. She didn't know this inn, but clearly Aubrey did, for as they left the coffee room, he turned left rather than right to the front door.

She followed him into a quiet garden with an awning. The clouds were threatening rain, which was presumably why there was no one else around.

While she had the chance, she blurted, "You were wonderful. Thank you for what you did."

"Don't," he said, his voice unexpectedly harsh. Hurt, she dropped her gaze, wondering miserably if she should just go and find Vanya.

Aubrey drew a deep breath and added more moderately, "I'm not. We both know that. I'm not a good man and I have behaved badly. Like a starving child at a banquet, wolfing everything he can before he is thrown back out on the street, I pursued every pleasure that came my way."

"I know. I don't blame you. Perhaps I did before, because I was hurt, but I do understand, a little."

His eyes returned to hers, intense and yet vulnerable. "I don't want to be that man. That...*Tranmere*. Can you ever believe that?"

"It was only ever part of who you are," she said.

His lips twisted. "The other part was pure idiot. From the moment I met you, I stopped wanting other women. I just didn't know why. I was enjoying myself so much, I wasn't ready to change. I wanted to carry on raking about, drifting from pleasure to pleasure, but I couldn't, because you had become my only pleasure. I tried to go back to old lovers, to convince myself you changed nothing. But I couldn't bring myself to stay with them. I always left and went home without...intimacy."

He drew in his breath. "It was the same with Violet, the woman you saw me with that morning, only I was so drunk I fell asleep on her sofa the night before. She went to bed, and I tried to make a discreet exit the following morning. She caught me on the doorstep, but for what it's worth, we both knew it was goodbye. I tell you this not to be congratulated on my self-restraint—in truth, there was none, for I was still following my own desires—but because I know it hurt you, and it needn't have."

He halted by a beech tree and peered down at her. "I don't know if you believe me. If you can *ever* believe me. I thought you were one of many, but I already knew you weren't. I think it took your refusing to speak to me to make me realize that I love you. That I always had and always would."

He took her hand, far more tentatively than he ever had before. "I'm not asking for declarations. Just friendship, and a little time. I'll understand if you refuse, but I won't ever stop trying to win you. I have so much to tell you—" He broke off, biting his lip. "Later. If you let me."

"Later," she agreed, her voice trembling more than she liked. "I want to hear all about your writing and your newspaper. But since we don't have long, you could always kiss me."

His serious face lightened at once. He bent his head toward hers, then paused, his eyes darkening in the way that melted her innards. His hand came up and cupped her cheek, and she closed her eyes with the bliss of his touch.

Only then did he kiss her mouth.

It began as soft, tender, respectful, and that was lovely, but she needed *more*. With a little gasp, she opened wider to him, touching her tongue to his, and he wrapped her hard in his arms, his mouth plundering and demanding with a desperate passion than fed her own.

Lost in him, in the sensation of his devastating mouth and tender hands, she pushed back against the growing hardness pressing into her abdomen. Her whole world was sensual delight and love and—

"So much for trust," Vanya raged behind them.

Henrietta jumped, trying to pull free. But Aubrey raised his head unhurriedly and only loosened his hold a little.

"Unhand her," Vanya snarled, "so I can thrash you into next week."

"You can try," Aubrey said, his voice only slightly hoarse. "But I thought we were in a hurry to return to Blackhaven. You can thrash me later if you're up to it."

"If you imagine you are accompanying us after that display—"

"I was thinking more of your accompanying me," Aubrey said. "After all, I hired the carriage. If it makes you feel better, I believe you interrupted Miss Gaunt's reply to my proposal of marriage."

Henrietta smiled and laid her head on his shoulder.

"Fustian," Vanya stated. "An hour ago, she wanted to marry Lord Maynard—whom, incidentally, I still prefer to you."

"You marry him, then," Henrietta said. "I shall marry Aubrey."

"I withhold my consent," Vanya said grandly.

"On what grounds?" Aubrey asked, drawing Henrietta's hand into the crook of his arm and strolling beyond the hedge toward the waiting carriage.

"The grounds that she is merely seventeen years old, while you are a scoundrel and a lying rake."

"Like you, Vanya?" Henrietta said innocently. "When you met Lizzie?"

Vanya closed his mouth, swallowing his retort with clear difficulty in order to prevent the coachman overhearing. But he made sure it was he who handed Henrietta into the carriage. Aubrey held the door, presumably to prevent them leaving without him.

He sat on the back-facing bench, opposite Henrietta and Vanya, who continued to glare at him. He had an unnerving glare and knew it. Aubrey bore it with studied indifference.

Henrietta said quietly, "You haven't answered me, Vanya. Is Aubrey not a little like you were when you first met Lizzie?"

Vanya fumed silently and transferred his stare to the window. She thought he wouldn't answer.

Then he said, "Lizzie is my life. My one and only. Can you say the same, Aubrey Vale? Can you be faithful, body and soul, to my little sister-in-law? Because—"

"Yes," Aubrey interrupted.

"—because if you cannot, I will never allow it," Vanya continued as if Aubrey had never spoken. "I love Lizzie's sisters like my own, and I will never allow a man to make Henrietta unhappy. And live."

"You don't need to keep threatening me, you know," Aubrey said mildly. "I agree with everything you're saying."

Vanya peered at him. "You do?"

"I do."

"Aubrey," said Henrietta, "tell Vanya and me all about your newspaper and your other writing…"

ONLY SIX WEEKS later, Henrietta and Aubrey were married in Blackhaven's St. Andrew's Church. The nuptials were announced in the second issue of the *Blackhaven Chronicle*, which accounted, Henrietta thought, for the church being unexpectedly full of unknown townspeople as well as family and friends. Their kindness delighted her.

As Vanya walked her down the aisle, he seemed very proud. He still sparred with Aubrey, of course, but he liked him and had come to trust him, too. *How odd*, Henrietta thought irrelevantly, *that I, who was once meant to save the family fortunes by making a brilliant marriage to a rich man, should marry a poor one…*

Not that she cared. The *Chronicle* was off to a good start, and they would have enough to live.

Then she saw Aubrey waiting for her, and everything else flew out of her mind. Happiness surged up and her face broke into smiles that would not stop. Her heart began an excited little tattoo that became the backdrop of the whole day.

Aubrey, looking smart and handsome but slightly dazed, smiled back. She managed to drag her gaze away from him for a moment to find Lizzie, Georgiana, and Michael in the front pew, and on the other side, the crowd of Aubrey's siblings and spouses spilling over two rows.

And then she stood beside Aubrey, and life was even more wonderful. Mr. Grant, the vicar, was smiling too, as if he couldn't help it.

She made her vows, still smiling, her voice clear and sincere, her eyes locked with Aubrey's. His fingers curled around her hand, gripping, and she thought with awe, *This is the rest of my life now. With Aubrey.*

It should have been just a little frightening. Sometimes, during the past few weeks, it had been, as she contemplated living in a house that didn't contain her siblings or Vanya, who had become so much part of their family. Or Dog. They would all return to Launceton, soon without her, but that was fine too, because she would be with Aubrey, and in any case, she would see them all again in a few months…

She almost wept with happiness, with sheer emotion, when they were pronounced man and wife. She had never been so proud as when she walked out of the church on Aubrey's arm to find more people smiling and blessing her.

Dog blasted through them, dragging Misha in his wake. The watchers all laughed, including Henrietta, who hugged the dog before he jumped. Michael and Georgiana, highly delighted, took charge of the lead.

For once that summer, there was no sign of rain, so Henrietta got her wish to walk from the church to the hotel for the wedding breakfast. It turned into a happy, laughing procession that included the vicar and his wife, several local people like the Muirs and the Lamonts, and some of the castle family too.

There was little chance for the bride and groom to be alone, but that didn't seem to matter. Henrietta felt surrounded by shared goodwill and happiness. With Aubrey, there was a more silent communication, a meeting of eyes, a quirk of the lips in humor or understanding.

Sitting beside him at the wedding breakfast, when they finally had the opportunity to talk to each other, she decided to get the serious news out of the way first.

"I had a letter from Diane yesterday," she murmured.

Diane had married Maynard by special license more than a month ago, and taken her father to live with them.

"Her father is dead," Henrietta said. "She wrote that he was peaceful at the end, and she was glad he died surrounded by the beauty of Maynard's home. He seemed to repent, but that may be Diane's wishful thinking."

"Perhaps."

"Maynard's physician agrees with Dr. Lampton that his brain was affected by his illness, so even Vanya has forgiven him."

"And is Diane happy?" Aubrey asked. "Do you think Maynard is?"

It was a concern, considering Aubrey had contrived the match so that he and Henrietta could be together. They didn't want to begin their own marriage in guilt, but in truth, she felt none.

"I believe they both are, despite her father's passing, which cannot have been easy. She has security and he has comfort. But more than that, I think they understand each other."

"And love?" he asked.

She smiled. "That, too."

There was a promise, a hunger in his eyes, that caught at her breath.

Soon, they would be alone…

They would spend the next couple of nights here at the hotel, and after that, they would remove back to Graham Gardens, since the Gaunts were returning to Launceton. Aubrey was taking on the lease of the house, since that had seemed simplest, and they both rather liked the place. Though if Henrietta was honest, she would have been happy to live with him in a hovel or a cave.

Later, when the breakfast had turned into a milling throng, Henrietta sought out Lord Tamar. She could see now the resemblance between him and his sister. They had the same black eyebrows and regular good looks, although in Anna they were both less dramatic and more refined.

"I was sorry not to find Lady Anna in Blackhaven," Henrietta said.

"Ah yes, I understand you had quite the adventure. Don't tell me the details. Anna never does."

"Then why are you smiling?"

"Because I like to see her happy. She leads a rather odd life, but somehow or other, it suits her."

Some people thought that Tamar, the painting marquis, also led rather an odd life.

"Do you know where she is?" Henrietta asked.

"No idea."

"Doesn't it bother you?"

He shrugged. "Anna can take care of herself. When she can't, she has Louis. As you have Aubrey. Serena and I wish you very happy. We know you will be."

Since neither Henrietta nor Aubrey could bear a grand exit, they slipped away, separately, to their large rooms on the first floor.

Arriving first, Henrietta found herself alone for the first time that day. They had a comfortable sitting room decorated in tasteful, warm colors, and two bedchambers. Henrietta's personal things had been placed in the larger, more ornate bedchamber, Aubrey's in the other.

Was that how it was meant to be, she wondered? Lizzie and Vanya had always shared a room, but when she thought about it, her parents had not. Lizzie had talked to her about her wedding night, so she was aware of the odd physicality of what was to come, softened by Lizzie's assurances of delight. *"Don't worry. Just trust and listen to your body."*

Henrietta, who had delighted in all Aubrey's kisses and caresses, was more than happy to do so, though she had the vague idea she already knew all the physical pleasure there was. The rest was merely in being with him.

The door opened, and she spun around to face Aubrey.

"Look, it's almost like having our own house," she said, running over to take his hand and lead him around the accommodations.

Opening his own wardrobe, he eyed his evening dress and second-best morning clothes. "What do you think? Should we go for a walk? We can slip out the back way, if you like, and no one will see us."

"Oh yes, that would be lovely," she enthused. "I'll fetch a pelisse and bonnet..."

After extracting them from their respective cupboards in the larger bedchamber, she felt Aubrey's presence in the doorway and turned to smile at him. His eyes lit with instant response, though behind that was a deep, gnawing hunger that excited her.

She had seen it before, that look, and was aware that in their brief times alone together he was exercising some kind of restraint.

"Don't look at me like that," he said softly, "or I will have to kiss you."

She dropped her pelisse on the bed, walked into his arms, and raised her face to his. He took her mouth with aching tenderness, and she sighed against his lips, melting into his arms. She rejoiced as the kiss turned more possessive, more demanding, at once fiercer and more worshiping.

As she held him, his fingers slid through her hair, scattering pins everywhere. He kissed not only her lips and cheeks and eyes, but her throat and shoulders. It was so blissful that Henrietta didn't notice he was undressing her until her gown slid down to her elbows.

It seemed there would no walk just yet.

Not with his hands on her naked skin, her breast, her hip; not with her own trembling fingers tugging off his cravat and coat. She didn't really know why, except that she needed to be closer to him, and her whole being hummed with a fiery arousal she had never known.

Trust, Lizzie had said, and she did. But more than that, she *wanted,* her hunger surely as powerful as his. She understood now that he had been waiting for her, and this, now, was his reward. She would make it so, with such delight…

And yet the delight was hers as he showed her the ecstasy of her body, previously glimpsed only in dreams. This was so much more overwhelming. And still not all there was. As she kissed him with passionate gratitude, he began to enter her body, and she cried out.

"Hush," he whispered. "I'll be gentle. I'll make it sweet…"

As he moved, the pleasure of her body caught fire again. *Sweet* was not the word she would have used, but dear heaven, it was wonderful. She loved the sensual undulating of his body beneath her stroking fingers, the slow loss of his trembling restraint as she tumbled into deeper, wilder bliss and was held there by the awesome ferocity of his own.

This was joy.

TAKING HENRIETTA WAS both the hardest and easiest pleasure of Aubrey's life. Her trust almost undid him; her beauty inspired; her passion delighted. To have pleasured her was his pride and joy, and yet he had not expected the sheer intensity of his own climax.

Afterward, contrary to his previous encounters, it was she who fell asleep in his arms, while he lay and enjoyed her softness, her breath, her beauty, while the sun sank slowly into darkness and the world grew quiet. Only then did he sleep.

And sprang into wakefulness when she stirred at first light. There was more joy to be had, and he took it with care and delight, giving and teaching as he went.

Later, lying in the bathtub while he took his time sponging her splendid body, she said suddenly, "I have been rather an idiot about beauty, haven't I?"

"In what way?" he murmured, still happily appreciating hers.

"In resenting people for liking the way I look. After all, I like the way you look."

"Do you?" he said, smiling. In truth, he felt like preening.

"I always did. It was what first drew me to you, though I could not admit it to myself. It isn't why I love you, but it is *part* of the feeling, and there is no shame in that for you or me. It is all you."

He kissed her, sweeping his hand into the bathwater to stroke the full length of her. "And all of you belongs to me. How did I get to be so lucky?"

"By being you."

After such mutual appreciation, they dressed and ordered breakfast in their room before sallying forth into the drizzle for their long-postponed walk.

On impulse, they stopped off at Roderick and Helen's house, to find most of Aubrey's siblings were there already.

They all cheered as the newlyweds walked in, which made Henrietta blush adorably and gave him an excuse to insult his brothers. It was a laughing, fun gathering, as spontaneous meetings often were, and he was pleased to see Henrietta so contented in the midst of it. No longer shy of them, she was joining in the nonsense, even encouraging the twins.

"Good Lord," Julius said suddenly. "I've just realized there are only the twins left to marry off."

"And Delilah," Aubrey said—and was intrigued when Delilah, who had been pronouncing herself happily on the shelf for years, only smiled and walked out of the room.

Epilogue

Three years later

AUBREY AND HENRIETTA were hosting a Venetian breakfast in their rather beautiful Blackhaven garden when Dog bounded through the back door.

Catastrophe beckoned, for among their attendees were the great and the good and the rich of Blackhaven. Even the old, run-down businesses of the town had revived in recent years, thanks largely to the *Chronicle*'s advertising reminding people of their existence and attracting more custom from the surrounding area, including Whalen. The *Chronicle* itself was selling well as far afield as Carlisle and even the Scottish border regions, as well as in the south. Those visitors who came to Blackhaven for the waters often left with a subscription to the *Chronicle*, which kept them up to date with local events and generally attracted them back to the town.

This success had made Aubrey, Roderick, and Mr. Nimmo a very decent living—Henrietta wore a new silk gown of cerulean blue, and the food and wine served that morning were of the best. But this was the first time they had dared to mix the well-to-do tradesmen with their aristocratic neighbors.

Henrietta was enjoying the novelty, happily introducing the Countess of Braithwaite to the awed Mrs. Nimmo and looking forward eagerly to her family's upcoming visit. They were expected tomorrow.

On the lawn, the Vale twins were playing with *her* twins—well, hers and Aubrey's—who were bouncing on a blanket and rolling around to be tickled, a pastime that appeared to cause the Vale twins equal amusement.

The guests were sitting on garden chairs and blankets, glasses of wine and fruit punch on the scattering of tables, breakfasting in a casual but civilized manner, when the advent of Dog threatened everything.

A cry of "Don't let him go!"—heard from the kitchen—was clearly too late.

Dog, the smell of food and favorite people in his nostrils, was unstoppable. Snatching a smoked salmon pastry from the plate of Mrs. Grant, he hurtled straight at Henrietta, grinning around his pastry with untold delight.

"Dog!" cried Lawrence, which was a mixed blessing. Instead of leaping at Henrietta and knocking her over—clearly his prime intention—he was distracted and veered toward the remembered voice. Once he smelled the small twins, God knew what damage he would cause.

There was nothing more dangerous than Dog's friendly nature.

Henrietta bolted after him, closely followed by a stream of Michael, Vanya, Georgiana, and Lizzie with her little Eleanor.

Lawrence poised himself to catch Dog but was too low down. Dog would simply jump over him and land among the babies.

Everyone had stopped talking to stare, open-mouthed—whether with outrage or entertainment probably depended on their character.

"Dog!" Henrietta cried in a last-ditch attempt to reverse his attention. But it was too fixed—until Aubrey stepped out of nowhere into his path.

In a bizarre repeat of the long-ago incident on the beach, he and Dog embraced each other.

This time, Aubrey didn't allow himself to fall beneath those huge, shaggy paws. He just held the dog until Michael clipped on his lead. And this time, there was no terrifying asthma attack. Those had almost entirely stopped, and even when the odd one did occur, it was relatively minor.

"Oh well done," Vanya said to Aubrey. "Very stylish. I hereby award you the title of chief Dog catcher. How are you, Aubrey? Not interrupting, are we?"

"Not in the slightest," Aubrey drawled, reaching over Dog to shake hands.

By then, Henrietta was laughing—with as much relief as pleasure—and hugging Lizzie and little Eleanor before flinging her arms around Michael and Georgiana and accompanying them and Dog back to the house to find somewhere to make him safe.

"We've been reading some of Aubrey's travel vignettes in the newspapers," Lizzie told her proudly. "The newer ones are very good, too."

"There's a new collection being published at the end of the month," Henrietta told her with equal pride. "And he does a few for the *Chronicle*, as you know. In the autumn, we're going traveling, and he can write some more. The newspaper will manage without him for a month or two."

"How wonderful! Will you take the twins?"

"Yes, but also a nursemaid!"

"Then everything is still going well for you? That is a fine array of guests I glimpsed in the garden."

"It's all going wonderfully," Henrietta said with perfect truth.

In fact, her life was all she had ever dreamed of—and more, because it was *real*. Content with a husband she loved beyond life, and who loved her in return, she took pride in his success and commiserated on his few bad days. They rejoiced and worried about the children together, entertained friends in the town, spent time with Aubrey's family, which was now hers. She spent her days caring for her children, giving her time to various charities, and keeping the house a comfortable place for her family.

She met Lizzie's gaze. "Did you—*do* you—ever fear it can't last? Such happiness?"

A shadow passed over Lizzie's face. "At Waterloo, I did. It was like a premonition. But he came home from that, too. And now, I never fear such things. It doesn't stop them happening, after all, only interferes with the joy of *now*."

Henrietta linked arms and, leaving Dog to be fed and calmed by Misha, led Lizzie back out to the garden. There, Michael and Georgi had already joined all the twins, chattering away with delight at being together again. Vanya was laughing with a wool merchant and the Earl of Braithwaite.

Aubrey was strolling toward them, smiling. Henrietta's heart still skipped when she saw him suddenly.

"Oh, you are right," she said softly. "I do so enjoy the *now*."

Author's Note

I hope you enjoyed the tale of Aubrey Vale and Henrietta Gaunt.

For readers who don't know, Henrietta first appeared in ***Vienna Waltz***, my first ever book with Dragonblade Publishing, along with Lizzie and Vanya, Michael, Georgiana, and, of course, Dog. I always had a soft spot for those characters, and when a reader asked me about a story featuring a grown-up Henrietta, the idea lingered at the back of my mind.

Even at the age of fifteen, when most of us are fighting spots, puppy fat, and cringing awkwardness, Henrietta's beauty turned heads. I began to wonder how such stunning looks might affect a possessor who was of a particular sweet and modest disposition, the opposite of the stereotypical spoiled beauty. ***The Rake's Mistake*** is the result.

If you are interested, you can read Lizzie and Vanya's fun romance in ***Vienna Waltz*** (The Imperial Season, Book 1).

About the Author

Mary Lancaster lives in Scotland with her husband, three mostly grown-up kids and a small, crazy dog.

Her first literary love was historical fiction, a genre which she relishes mixing up with romance and adventure in her own writing. Her most recent books are light, fun Regency romances written for Dragonblade Publishing: *The Imperial Season* series set at the Congress of Vienna; and the popular *Blackhaven Brides* series, which is set in a fashionable English spa town frequented by the great and the bad of Regency society.

Connect with Mary on-line – she loves to hear from readers:

Email Mary:
Mary@MaryLancaster.com

Website:
www.MaryLancaster.com

Newsletter sign-up:
http://eepurl.com/b4Xoif

Facebook:
facebook.com/mary.lancaster.1656

Facebook Author Page:
facebook.com/MaryLancasterNovelist

Twitter:
@MaryLancNovels

Amazon Author Page:
amazon.com/Mary-Lancaster/e/B00DJ5IACI

Bookbub:
bookbub.com/profile/mary-lancaster

Printed by Amazon Italia Logistica S.r.l.
Torrazza Piemonte (TO), Italy